▽   ▽   ▽   ▽   ▽

CHARLOTTE VALE ALLEN

D1491379

PERFECT
FOOLS

**Island
Nation
Press LLC**

♦ 144 ROWAYTON WOODS DRIVE ♦ NORWALK, CT ♦ 06854 ♦

Perfect Fools

ISBN 0-9657437-7-2

First Published in the USA
by New American Library 1978
Published in the UK
by Magnum Books 1980

This edition published by
Island Nation Press LLC 1998

Cover & book design by deLancey Funsten.

Island Nation Books LLC
144 Rowayton Woods Drive
Norwalk, CT 06854 USA

Printed in the United States

Visit the author's website at:
http://www.charlottevaleallen.com

PROLOGUE
London—1944

IN THE FEW SECONDS AFTER THE BOMB HIT AND BEFORE SHE DIED, SHE gave no thought whatsoever to Sarah. Nor did she think of Stephen. The walls around them burst inwards, sending up great gusts of plaster dust, and she attempted to sit up, thinking, Damn, damn! It's not fair, not bloody fair! And then the upper stories of the house descended through the ceiling, taking her and Nigel, the bed, the room, the entire floor, down, down.

The whole street was razed and it took two days for the patrols and workmen to dig their way through the rubble to the bodies. Digging further, they turned up a woman's handbag and quite a number of files of papers and letters. Since all the residents of that particular building had been accounted for with the exception of Nigel Ramsdale, it was generally agreed upon that the male body had, therefore, to be his. And the woman, according to the identification contained in the handbag, was one Olivia Breswick. An address in Mayfair. Two nude bodies, white with plaster dust, purple with internal bleeding, their limbs and heads battered, bloody. An officer was dispatched to the Mayfair address.

She'd said she'd be back in two hours, Sarah thought again and again, trying the door repeatedly, hoping to find it somehow unlocked. A long long time, she knew. It'd been ever such a long time, lots longer than two hours. And she needed to go to the toilet so badly. She couldn't hold it in any longer and, feeling dreadful, knowing Mummy would be frightfully angry with her, she used the teapot. Then she sat on her bed in the dark crying, knowing, almost hearing, how angry Mummy would be.

Sitting in the dark, she dared to peek out past the heavy blackout curtains hoping to see Mummy coming back up the mews. But the street was empty, black. The sky went bright, then dark; there was the dulled, distant crashing of bombs, and, later on, the all-clear sirens. She switched on the small lamp and looked at the clock, trying to decide what time it was, further upset because she couldn't remember if the big hand gave the hour or the little one. Was it three past ten or ten to three? She started crying again because no matter which time was the right one, Mummy had been gone a long, long while. Finally, exhausted, she curled up on the floor by the door and fell asleep, telling herself that when she awoke Mummy would be back and the door would again be open.

When she did wake up, feeling stiff and achey-cold from having slept on the floor, she sat up on her knees to try the door, withdrew her hand from the knob with a cry at discovering the door still locked, and got to her feet to pound on the door with her fists, crying out loudly for Mummy to come. Then, going quiet, she listened to the silence of the house. She's not there, she thought, turning to look about the room. She went over to switch off the lamp, then picked up the clock and looked at it again, this time trying to decide if it was nine to five or five past nine. It must have been five past nine because beyond the blackout curtains it was very light outside. She put down the clock and went to tug open the curtains and gaze down the length of the mews to see the lady who lived over the way coming out of her door with her shopping bag. Mummy will be back soon, she told herself, moving away from the window to look at the tray on the table. The teapot. She'd peed in the teapot. Mummy would be livid. Thinking now about the teapot, she suddenly had to go again. Badly. And she was hungry, too. There was nothing left of yesterday's tea; she'd eaten it all. And now she had to go again and she was so hungry her stomach hurt. She ran to the door to pull at the knob with both hands. Enraged, she kicked as hard as she could at the door, succeeding only in hurting her foot which made her start crying afresh.

When she couldn't wait any longer, she used the teacup and the plate, then covered them with the traycloth, backing away knowing she'd be punished horribly for doing this. She felt awful—wet and sticky, because she hadn't had anything with which to wipe herself, and angry, so angry. It seemed to be filling her up inside, making her want to start screaming. When Mummy did come back, Sarah would scream at her. It was all your fault I had to, you stayed longer than you promised. But she'd never stayed out so long before. Never.

The anger gave way to a new, different kind of fear; she returned to the window to watch the street. She wrapped her hands around the two bars running across the lower half of the window, the bars Mummy said were there to keep her from falling out in summer when the window was allowed to be kept open only if Sarah promised not to go near it. Holding on to the bars, she stared out, positive at any moment she'd see Mummy appear at the entrance to the mews and come clicking over the cobblestones in her high-heeled shoes. She felt a spurt of elation imagining it. She could almost see her, she wanted it so much. Come *on*, Mummy! Come home now! I'm ever so hungry and where have you been? The elation dissolved; the anger returned. She kicked the wall under the window. Where *are* you?

In the late afternoon, when it began to get dark, she got up and went yet again to the window, to look once more down the length of the mews, then at the houses on the far side, the ones she could see. They all had their curtains drawn. I *won't* draw them! she thought defiantly. And she'd keep the light on as well. But then, thinking about it, imagining all sorts of things—her mother's anger, or one of those airplanes with the bombs seeing the light from her window and dropping its bombs right there in the mews—she thought she'd best draw the curtains after all and dragged over the chair to stand on it, pulling the weighty curtains into place. The dust tickled her nose, making her sneeze as she jumped down from the chair and stopped to gaze at the covered tray with its bad-smelling plate and cup and teapot. If she had to go again she didn't know what she'd do; there was nothing left to go in.

Sitting on the floor with her back against the bed, feeling the cold air pushing in from under the door, she looked very slowly around the room. She was dizzy with hunger and anger, and fear now, too, because perhaps Mummy had decided to go away forever and wasn't ever coming back. All the times she'd yelled so loudly, or muttered as if Sarah couldn't hear or understand. *Why the bloody hell did it have to happen to me? What did I ever do to deserve this?* She'd looked at Sarah with her mouth all tight and her eyes hard like green glass so that Sarah knew she'd done something terrible, some awful thing in getting born, and because of that, Mummy was always angry with her.

Reaching over to pull the blankets off the bed, she wrapped them around herself, remembering way way back to when Mummy had taken the blackboard and had printed out the ABCs to teach them to her. Then, becoming impatient, she'd knocked down the blackboard and the chalk, left the crayons and the pieces of paper, and had stalked out, enraged, to go slamming things about in the kitchen getting the tea. So, thinking to surprise and please her, Sarah had carefully, slowly copied all the letters on to the pages with the orange crayon, her favorite color. But later on when Mummy had come up with the tea, she hadn't even wanted to look at what Sarah had done.

Then, some other time—Sarah couldn't remember when it had been—Mummy had tried again, with some little books. She'd sounded out words, explaining how the letters fitted together, again becoming furious. Always so angry. She'd thrown the little books on the floor. Her anger had made Sarah feel sleepy and thick. But she'd left the books and Sarah sat with them for hours on end. Now, she knew them all by heart, every single last one of them. She could even print the words; but Mummy never wanted to look, didn't ever again bring out the blackboard or come with any new books. She'd brought in an old wireless and shouted at Sarah never to touch where the wire went into the holes in the wall. It was the last thing she'd ever brought.

She doesn't love me, Sarah concluded, not for the first time. Love was something she recalled from the time she was very very small, a long time ago when there were two of them. Daddy. He was fighting in the war. The war was why the bombs came at night. Maybe he'll come back and open the door, I've got to go so badly.

She pulled the blankets over her head and slept on the floor beside the bed. If she wet the floor it wouldn't matter so much as it would if she wet the bed.

▽

She heard the banging at the door and threw off the blankets, jumped up to run to the door of her room, crying out to let whoever was out there know she was inside. She waited, listening. The banging came again, then stopped. Her heart pounding, she ran to the window and yanked back the curtains, but even pressing right up against the bars she was unable to see who was down there. No more banging. They were going away. She struggled to raise the window but it wouldn't budge and she wasn't strong enough, could hardly reach up to the sill. She began pounding her fists on the glass, trying to make enough noise to let them know she was in there. Her fists shattered the glass. The glass made blood. She pulled back her hands, gaping at them, for a moment forgetting what she'd been doing, in awe at the sight of her own blood.

Outside, hearing the glass breaking, the officer stepped into the middle of the mews to look up but saw only the broken window. Someone was in there, right enough though, and had smashed that window. He hurried back to the front door, half-expecting it to open, trying to make some sense of what was happening. He debated for several moments then braced himself and applied his foot to the door. It took four good kicks before the wood around the lock splintered and the door burst inwards with a tremendous crash.

He wondered if there'd be a to-do about the broken door as his eyes took in the entrance hall. Wealthy people lived here. *Had* lived here. The woman was dead. But obviously there was at least one other. He moved towards the stairs hearing an odd, muted wailing coming from above, almost an animal sound. His eyes took in the pictures on the landing wall and the closed doors which confronted him as he followed the noise down the hall. He came to a stop and tried the door from behind which the sounds were coming. Locked. What the bloody hell? he wondered, asking aloud, "Who's in there, then?" and heard the garbled sounds take on renewed strength and volume.

In for a penny, he thought, loudly saying, "Stand well back from the door!" He applied his foot to this second door which gave at once and swung open. He stood staring at the tiny, wild-haired child with a dirt and tear-streaked face, a cruelly twisted upper lip, holding out her bloodied hands. His nostrils were assaulted by the foul odor in the room.

"Here now," he said, approaching the child who looked no more than three or four. "You've cut yourself, haven't you? Let's have a look, luv."

She lifted her head to look at him with large, very deep blue, very frightened eyes and began making strangled, indecipherable noises.

"No need to be afraid," he said quietly, squinting slightly as if that might better enable him to understand the stream of guttural, choked-sounding noises issuing from the child's misshapen mouth. He reached into his pocket for his handkerchief, thinking to wrap her hands and stop the blood; but realizing that wouldn't be of much use, he placed his hand gingerly on her narrow little shoulder to direct her out of the stench in search of the bathroom where there was bound to be something more appropriate to use on her hands.

She seemed to be trying to say something and plainly growing frustrated with the effort, her small but somehow very mature features screwing up as she persisted in trying to make herself understood.

"Everything's all right now, luv," he said, automatically opening the doors on the landing one by one until he located the bathroom. "You come along in here with me now and we'll see about cleaning up those cuts."

She shook her head violently, sniffing impatiently at the tears and mucus running down her face, pushing out yet more nonsensical sounds at him. Poor tot, he thought, directing her hands under the cold-water tap and telling her, "Stand here while I have a look, see if I can't find some plasters or bandage, something to put on those cuts."

She did as she was told, he was relieved to see. Her chest was heaving as she obediently stood with her hands under the cold water— on her very tiptoes in order to do it—her round blue eyes following his movements about the bathroom, her mouth not quite so awful-looking now that she'd calmed down a bit. The plasters and medicines were in the chest on the wall, she knew, but couldn't get him to understand so she went silent and waited for him to find out for himself. She imagined how Mummy would react to this man's being in the house, looking through their things this way. But where *was* she? And it jolly well served her right for not being here all this time. It made her angry and scared all over again, thinking this, and she shivered, feeling frozen as the water turned her hands numb, even made her teeth feel cold. Her teeth and her hair, all of her cold. Then, remembering, she said, "I'm hungry," hoping he'd understand.

"Nh ngr," he heard and turned, wishing he knew what she was trying to say. He'd found a bottle of iodine and some sticking plasters and went to turn off the water, then dried her hands carefully, saying, "Afraid I can't make out what you're trying to tell me, luv. This'll sting a wee bit now," he said, opening the iodine bottle. He glanced up to see her nod. She seemed very trusting, her eyes following his every movement with interest rather than suspicion.

"Cut yourself up nicely, didn't you?" He smiled, dabbing at the numerous cuts with the iodine. She flinched but didn't make a sound and he admired her for it. His own two would've brought the roof down with their screams. But this child didn't give way. She sniffed once or twice, her eyes never leaving his face as he ascertained to his satisfaction that there were no fragments of glass lodged in any of the wounds. "Good girl," he said with another smile, giving her a pat on the shoulder when he'd finished bandaging her hands as best he could. "We'll give your face a wash now. And later on, get a doctor to have a look at you."

Was this Daddy? she wondered, then thought he couldn't possibly be. She said something and he strained to understand her.

"I'm sorry, luv," he said gently. "Afraid I just can't make sense of what it is you're trying to tell me." He studied her small face feeling an odd, welling affection for her. She seemed to be making such a valiant effort to communicate. "How old're you then, luv? Do you know?"

She nodded and held up five fingers of the one hand and two of the other.

"Seven? You're never seven!" he exclaimed.

She nodded again. Then, her features drawing closed, she thought for a moment before holding out her hands and making writing motions, watching his face intently as she did, willing him to comprehend.

"What?" he asked, bending down closer to her. She made more noises in her throat and he watched her hands, all at once understanding, and reached into his uniform pocket for his notepad and pencil, handing them over to her with mounting curiosity. He watched as she positioned the notepad on the rim of the sink and began slowly, carefully printing out neat little letters.

"Where is Mummy?" the printing read. He looked at it feeling a sudden heaviness in his limbs.

"Mummy's had an accident," he explained, moving to take her hand. He'd bring her to the station where they'd see to a doctor and from there perhaps she'd go to one of the children's shelters. She pulled back her hand, reaching once more for the notepad. He gave it to her and she printed, "Eat," then showed it to him.

He smiled, thinking she wasn't half clever. "Hungry, are you? We'll set that right straight away."

Taking a careful hold of her impossibly small hand, trying to make himself accept that a child this size could possibly be seven, he led her down the stairs asking, "Where's your coat, then, luv?"

She shook her head, looking at him blankly.

"It's all right," he said reassuringly. "I'm going to take you where you'll be looked after."

She shook her head again and pointed to his uniform pocket, her eyes no longer blank.

Beginning to feel wearied by all this, he again gave her the notepad.

She printed, "no cote."

"No coat? You haven't got a coat?"

She shook her head.

"That's daft!" he argued. "Of course you've got a coat."

Her head went from side to side. She opened her mouth and got out a decipherable, "No!"

"Well, there's bound to be something," he said, throwing open the cloakroom door to lift a jacket down from the hook. "This'll have to do," he said, fitting her thin little arms into the sleeves. They hung a good foot past her hands and the bottom reached to the floor. Imagine a child not having a bloody coat! he thought. No bloody coat and living in a house like this! There must be one and she's just being stubborn or afraid. He buttoned the jacket, once again took hold of her damaged hand, and moved with her towards the front door. On the threshold, she hung back, pulling against his hand.

"It's all right," he repeated, wondering what was bothering her now.

She tried to tell him but he simply didn't understand what she was saying. *I've never been out, never been out into the street. Mummy never took me. I'm afraid.* Yet she was curious, too. Very curious.

"Come along, luv," he coaxed. "No harm'll come to you. I'm a police officer. You understand?"

A police officer. She didn't understand. She'd thought perhaps he was one of the soldiers in some kind of uniform. What's a police officer? she wondered. Sometimes they'd spoken of police people on the wireless, but Mummy hadn't ever explained who they were or what it was they did.

A cluster of neighbors had collected just outside the front door, wondering what was going on. Sarah looked through the open doorway at them.

"Does any of you know the child," he asked the neighbors, noting the puzzlement creasing their faces. "Or the parents? Any of you?"

One woman, her eyes on Sarah, whispered to the woman beside

her, "Poor child looks frightened half to death. What d'you suppose is wrong with her mouth?"

"Do you know her?" the policeman asked.

"It's one of them harelips," the other woman whispered back as the first woman gave Sarah a sad little smile and said, "She must be 'ers. But it don't make no sense, does it?"

"Sorry?"

"What I mean, see, is I been char next door 'ere nine years now and I never did know the one 'ad a kid."

"The one? You mean Mrs. Breswick?"

"That's right. I remember years ago seein' 'er, askin' when was the baby comin' and then there never was no baby, was there? And you don't like to ask, do you? I thought she must've lost it, poor thing. I was that sorry for her, I was."

Nothing was making sense, he thought. He'd get the child to the station and let the others figure out what to do with her.

"Someone will be coming round shortly to see to the door," he addressed the small knot of people. Selecting one man who looked to be a responsible sort, he said, "You might keep an eye on the place, if you would, sir. We'll have someone round within the hour."

"I say," the man said awkwardly, "has something happened to Mrs. Breswick?"

"Caught in the raid two nights back, I'm afraid," the officer said somberly, adjusting the chin strap on his helmet.

"I expect you'll be wanting to notify Captain Breswick won't you?"

"Army, is it?"

"That's right."

"Do you know the child, sir?"

"Afraid not," he answered, staring at Sarah so that she averted her eyes, looking down at the ground and moving slightly closer to the policeman. "Had no idea actually there was a child in the house. Extraordinary!" he said, looking mystified. "Quite extraordinary! One's usually well aware of children."

"Come along, luv," the officer said quietly, sensing the child's fear. "We'll get you something to eat on the way." He looked down at her. She was quite a pretty child, really, except for her mouth. Lovely large eyes of a wonderful violet blue. Scrubbed up, with some decent clothes and her hair brushed, she wouldn't be half bad. As they walked along, he wondered what sort of people lived in a house like that and kept a child of seven locked away in an upstairs room.

She looked around as they walked, her legs feeling funny. She'd never walked on pavement before. And she didn't have proper shoes, she didn't think. The pavement was hard, made her legs jar into their sockets. And these, she thought, must be the shops where Mummy goes. *These are shops and I'm walking on pavement and this is a policeman and we're Outside. I'm being let Outside. Mummy will be frightfully angry.*

THE MIDLANDS

1969–1972

▽　　　▽　　　▽　　　▽　　　▽

One

THE CAR WOULDN'T START; NOTHING HAPPENED WHEN SHE TURNED
the ignition key. She got out and looked at the front door of the
house for several moments, debating whether or not to ring the
garage and have them send someone round. But she hated the telephone and wouldn't have had one at all if Uncle Arthur hadn't
insisted upon it. And near the end, it had come in useful.
Nevertheless, every time she was obliged to use it, she seemed to
become more garble-mouthed than ever and had to struggle to make
herself understood. So, no. She'd walk to Crossroads and, on the
way, pop into the garage and have a word with them about the car.
Mr. Beaconstead might be there and he was always so helpful when
there was a problem.

He wasn't there. In his place was a young man she hadn't seen
before, a young man who, despite the dirt on his overalls, seemed to
give an impression of exceptional cleanliness, his face aglow with
good health and something else she couldn't begin to attempt to ana-
lyze. He was very polite, for which she was grateful, and listened to
her describe her problem with the car as if unaware of how awful she
looked and sounded.

"Sounds like the battery's in need of recharging," he said. "We're a
bit backed up just at the moment, but I'll make sure someone gets to
it before tea time."

He wrote down her address, smiled again at her and she left the
oily-smelling interior of the small garage office to continue on her
way to Crossroads, wondering when Mr. Beaconstead had taken on
this new young man. She felt the small gratification she experienced
whenever someone new displayed kindness, friendliness. She held
herself always at the ready for the fixed stare, the hastily averted
eyes, the faintly squeamish narrowing of the eyes and mouths of
strangers. But every so often there was someone who met her eyes
and smiled. The smiles themselves fell into a number of categories:
there were those who smiled because they had about themselves
some perhaps less obvious defect and readily understood her visible

one. The people who fell into this category and offered their unstated empathy made the days worthwhile. Then, there were the ones who smiled from a sense of superiority. They were in no way flawed and could therefore make a display of their indulgence by magnanimously allowing her passage through their viewing range. There were some who smiled out of profound embarrassment at having been caught in the act of staring at her. And, finally; a very rare few smiled simply because their eyes and hers had made contact and that was a nice thing. The smile stated: we're both simply people and, given the proper time and circumstances, we might like one another, might even become friends. She cherished those rare few.

As she hurried across the High Street, she decided that the young man in the garage fell into this last, special category. And it sent her through the front entrance of Crossroads in heightened spirits. She usually felt anticipatory, quietly glad upon arriving here; each morning was an opportunity to throw off her heavier self and be real and alive as she never was anywhere else. These people, these elderly souls, didn't judge her or find her defective in any way; they loved her just as she loved all of them, even the most difficult ones—the chronic bedwetters and the hopelessly senile. She loved the dozen or so whose old, defeated bodies contained strong, young minds and whose thoughts and sometime whimsical inspirations came like gifts.

She hung away her coat in the small staff room, tucked her handbag and string carrier-bag down into the space between the two oversized armchairs that nearly filled the room, then went into the big, spotless kitchen to pour herself a cup of tea from the pot which Doreen, the head cook, made each morning for the kitchen staff of three and the half-dozen who ran the residence. She carried the cup back to the staff room and drank it while enjoying the one cigarette she'd have time for before midday.

She stood looking out of the window at the quiet street, breathing deeply, savoring the cigarette, her hand warmed by the cup, feeling safe within these walls, and secure the way she felt nowhere else, not even at home. Thinking about home, she decided yet again she'd have to do something about decorating, have the painters in. Uncle Arthur had been dead close on two years and she still hadn't done anything about getting rid of some of the old, clumsy furniture, or about having the dark, dreary wallpaper stripped and replaced with brighter, happier patterns. The upstairs loo hadn't been functional

in months and she'd been intending to call in the plumber, writing
it down day after day in her diary but never getting round to it. Now
that the cold had set in, it was awful, first thing in the morning, to
open the kitchen door and hurry into that freezing outside loo. It
hadn't been at all unpleasant in the summer. With the window ajar
she'd been able to breathe in the scent of flowering honeysuckle and
admire the sight of the greenery crowding in against the window
glass. But it really was miserably cold in there now first thing in the
morning and she was, she admitted, procrastinating terribly.

If she was going to go ahead and have the plumber in, she told herself, why not have the bathroom redone while she was about it and
have the old bath and basin torn out, have a shower installed and a
new basin, and one of those super heated towel rails?

What was she waiting for? she asked herself, finishing the tea. She
picked a stray tea leaf from the tip of her tongue before taking a last
puff on her cigarette. There was enough money for it. She'd have to
go easy, but there'd certainly be no hardship.

The thing was she really couldn't believe Uncle Arthur was gone;
two years and she still couldn't completely accept it. They'd had
such good times together, such fine, close times. And even when
she'd seen him dead in his bed she'd been unable to grasp the full
implications of his death. For twenty-three years he'd grumbled and
grinned at her, had fumbled his way through his never-expected role
as parent. But he'd loved her and had sought to comfort her before,
during, and after all the awful rounds of surgery; he'd taken her in,
made her his, and at the end, had ensured that she had a home, a
small lifetime income, and a final cash settlement that was just sitting at the bank waiting to be put either into the Building Society
or to some good use.

She'd loved him so much, had depended upon him so utterly, that
it hadn't ever been anything more than the remotest possibility that
he might one day die and leave her entirely alone with no one to act
as a buffer between her and the rest of the world; no one to place his
hand upon her shoulder reassuringly when her speech—due to fear
or embarrassment or uncertainty—grew unrecognizable as such and
emerged as a flow of half-swallowed, strangling sounds. That gentle
hand had served to slow her down and calm her, enabling her to
articulate carefully as she'd been so painstakingly taught to do.
There was no one to walk with her along the back country roads on
a Sunday afternoon; no one to accompany her to the pub and buy

her a shandy and then sit smiling as she warmed her hands after their brisk ritual Sunday walk; no one to shake his head and laugh over her first attempts at cooking and say, "Never mind, old girl. I'll fetch us some fish and chips," and, reaching for his keys, go off in the car to get them; no one to sit with by the fire in the evening; no company beside her to laugh over the antics of *The Goon Show* on the wireless and, later on, some program on television. It was all gone. And she still hadn't fully accepted it.

She glanced at her watch, returned her cup to the kitchen, and went along to the office to check in with Margaret Evans and find out if there were any particular problems needing attention.

Margaret appeared to most people as a large, rather hard woman with a sharp tongue to match her sharp features and an overly stern way with the residents. Sarah believed that beneath Margaret's efficient brusqueness was a caring person. Having to cope with being permanently short-staffed and inadequately funded placed a tremendous load on her and her husband, Ian, who was in charge of the place. They both seemed to work non-stop, and had never taken more than a four-day holiday away in all the years since the residence had opened.

Sarah said, "Good morning," and Margaret glanced up distractedly, then looked down again at the papers on her desk, replying absently, "Oh, Sarah. Good morning." She finished reading something, then lit a cigarette and at last raised her head.

"Miss Morgan took rather a nasty spill last night," she said, exhaling a thick stream of smoke. "Tried again to go to the lavatory on her own."

"Has she broken anything?"

"Fortunately not," Margaret said, looking sorely put upon. "But she's feeling very sorry for herself this morning, and very angry. You know."

Sarah nodded, understanding exactly what Margaret meant. *Miss Morgan's like me,* she thought. *She refuses to accept things.* Miss Morgan's stroke had left her able to walk only haphazardly at best with the aid of a walker, yet she was determined not to ask for help, with the result that she took spills on an average of once a week.

"I'll look in on her first," Sarah said.

"Good. And when you've got a moment, Mr. MacCreech wants to write another letter."

He was forever writing letters to the editor of some newspaper or another, dictating to anyone who'd take the time to sit down and write for him. A surprising number of his letters got printed and he had the clippings in an album he kept near him at all times.

"Anything else?" Sarah asked.

"Not at the moment. We've got nine who're not down for meals. You might give Cook a hand with the trays if you've got a moment."

"All right." Sarah left the small, smoky office and made her way down the corridor to look in on Miss Morgan.

Margaret watched her go, feeling quietly angry with Sarah, as she always did. She'd long since forgotten what precisely triggered her anger; it just existed. With a sigh, she took a final, hard draw on the cigarette then crushed it out.

Feeling purposeful and useful, Sarah was smiling as she knocked at the open door to the room and approached the bedside.

"Don't come smiling in at me that way!" Miss Morgan snapped, the left half of her face downpulled, rendering her speech intelligible most of the time only to Sarah. "I'm not some reprobate *child* you've to deal with!"

"I've no intention of doing that." Sarah continued to smile. "You know you've taken a spill for no good reason." She placed her hand on the thin, bony shoulder of the elderly woman and at the contact Miss Morgan closed her eyes, giving way to tears. Sarah knew she was raging inside, feeling humiliated and defeated, betrayed by her own body. Miss Morgan had once had money. She was better educated by far than the majority of the others here and had, for thirty-five years, held a senior civil service job in London. But then she'd been retired and had come back to the Midlands thinking to enjoy her retired years gardening and reading, living peacefully. She'd been a volunteer here when Crossroads had first opened and had come three days a week to lend a hand, to read to some and write letters for others, to bring round the food trays and generally bask in sharing her good health and strength. Until the stroke. Now, to her permanent chagrin, she was no longer an agile volunteer but one of what she called the "inmates." Sarah had known her for thirteen years, since the days when she, too, had been a volunteer, and understood the woman's feelings. Miss Morgan was a proud, capable woman who'd been humbled by her body's treachery.

Sarah bent down and put her cheek against the woman's, whispering, "It's all right, dear." Then she straightened and asked, "Did you refuse breakfast?" knowing perfectly well that she had. It was Miss

Morgan's fruitless attempt at retaliation, refusing meals. Getting no response beyond the woman's unyielding state, she said, "I'll go and fetch you something," and went off back to the kitchen to boil an egg, prepare two slices of toast and a small pot of tea. She returned to set the tray on the table across Miss Morgan's bed, knowing she wouldn't eat until Sarah left the room .

"I'll drop back shortly," she said from the door, then continued on to see Hugh MacCreech.

God, but she loved these people, felt so worthwhile being able to be here with them. She was grateful to the Evanses for allowing her to become a full-time staff member after Uncle Arthur's death. Her three-mornings-a-week volunteer work hadn't been enough to sustain her or to keep her mind off the sudden, astonishing emptiness of her life. She was paid very little for her five and a half days' work here but it wasn't the money that mattered, it was the feeling of usefulness, and the freedom to give and take love from these people. When there was a death, as there was more often than she cared to think about, she felt the loss deeply, personally. This was her family now. Probably, she thought, the only family she was ever likely to have. And she constituted the only family most of them had, too. The ones with children wrote their notes and letters but rarely received visitors. Yet they made endless excuses for their children, creating reasons why they didn't come. This justifying bothered Sarah, yet she understood both sides. The children were adults with children of their own, with jobs to attend to, and homes and problems and distance; they couldn't really be blamed. But they could've made more of an effort. She was there, though, she thought. And surely that made up for some of it.

As always, the day went very quickly. Before getting ready to go home, she stopped for half an hour to write Hugh MacCreech's letter to the editor of the Sunday *Telegraph*, criticizing the previous week's editorial on America in Vietnam. It was a strong, well-thought-out argument against American intervention that Sarah was going to have to think about later. He dictated so quickly there wasn't sufficient time between his thoughts and words for her to consider what he was actually saying. When it was done, he said, "Let's have a look then," and held the pages under his large magnifying glass, quickly scanning what she'd written. At last, in a trembling spidery flourish, he signed his name to it. "That'll give them something to think about," he said, watching her fold the letter into an envelope and address it.

"I should think so," she agreed, opening the drawer of his locker for a stamp. "You're down to the last of your stamps. Shall I pick up some more for you?"

Another formality. Of course he wanted her to replenish his supply of stamps. But it would not do for her simply to arrive with them. She had to take the coin purse from the drawer and put it into his hands in order that he might shakily count out the change. Small transactions of considerable importance. She took the money, returned the coin purse to the locker, tucked the stamped envelope into the pocket of her overall, and stood up.

"How's old Arthur getting on these days?" he asked.

"Uncle Arthur's been gone two years now," she reminded him gently.

"That's right, isn't it?" He nodded soberly, his hands doing a quiet dance on top of the neatly folded-back bedclothes. "Shocking, the way the memory plays tricks. He was a good chap, Arthur was. Did you know I worked under him years back?"

"Did you?" She played along, aware he hadn't any idea how many times he'd told her this in the past three years.

"That's right. I did. Clerking in his office."

"I'll be going now," she said. "Is there anything you'd like before I go?"

He raised his eyes to hers, pale blue and sometimes as wide and innocent as a child's, sometimes as piercing and perceptive as those of the young man he'd once been. Now they were simply an old man's tired eyes and, his memory clearing as it was wont to do, he gazed at her for several moments before saying, "Young girl like you, Sarah, you shouldn't be wasting your life here. Ought to be out and about with young people, having a family of your own and enjoying your youth."

"I'm happy here," she said, as she invariably did. "I'll see you in the morning."

"What do you do with yourself?" he asked. "Evenings, weekends? Have you got a young man, Sarah?"

"I have you," she teased with a smile. "Why on earth would I want a young man?"

"We all of us need someone," he said sadly, looking down at his hands.

"That's why I'm here," she said, feeling somehow obliquely threatened. Was he rejecting her?

He shook his head, a slow, bobbing gesture. She didn't want to stay any longer and risk hearing him say something profound and upsetting. She touched his quivering hand, kissed his flaccid cheek, and went off, her smile feeling unnaturally stiff on her face.

It was stupid of her, she thought, to allow things to bring her down so easily, as if these twenty-five residents were all potentially disapproving parents. She fluctuated between playing parent to them, and child. Mr. MacCreech's final words had moved her from parent-in-control to child, and as she stopped to push his letter through the slot outside the post office, she wondered if her future would consist of living out her life at Crossroads, a volunteer until a stroke or a heart attack or some physical failure turned her, as it had Miss Morgan, from outsider to insider. The idea deeply frightened her. *I'm too young*, she thought. *Perhaps he's right. But to him I'm still a child, not a grown woman of thirty-two. Is that the way it seems from seventy-odd looking at thirty-two? Do I appear very young to him?*

She stopped at the greengrocer's for some salad greens and two very expensive imported tomatoes, then went on to the butcher's for a half-pound of mince. She'd make a bolognese for supper, with a salad, and save a bit of the sauce for Sunday's meal. Carrying her string bag of purchases, she made her way home hoping someone from the garage had been to see to the car.

After putting her things down in the kitchen, she went out to try the car, discovering it in the same condition as she'd left it. She'd have to ring Mr. Beaconstead and find out why no one had been round. Returning inside, she hung away her coat then put her handbag down by the steps before going into the kitchen. She stared at the telephone as if it were alive and an enemy as she removed things from the string bag and placed them on the counter. She delayed, thinking she'd get the sauce started and then ring. But by then the garage would be closed. She'd simply have to do it now. She was moving towards the telephone when she heard the slam of a car door and went through to the front of the house to look out of the lounge window and see the young man from this morning lifting the bonnet of her car.

Glad that someone had come, she watched him doing this and that, then stepped back in surprise when he looked over and smiled at her as if he'd known all along she was standing there watching. Now, she supposed, she'd have to say something, and went to the front door and down the path to where he was, to say, "I was just about to ring up."

"Yeah. We had a busy bloody day today. I stopped by on my way home thinking you probably need the car."

"I do like to have it. Although, actually, I can walk to my job."

He came up from under the bonnet and straightened, wiping his hands down the sides of his oil- and dirt-streaked overalls. "That one's gone for a burton. You're going to have to have a new battery." Looking at her, he wondered why she didn't do something to smarten herself up. Bloody unbelievable, he thought, that a woman didn't do something with herself in this day and age. A bit of make-up, some decent-looking gear, a haircut, and she wouldn't be half bad. Women. Mentally he shook his head. Some of them you couldn't do a bloody thing with. He looked at her mouth, having already figured it out that her lip being like that 'n all had to do with the wonky way she talked. Toffee accent, though, even with the peculiar way some of the words came out sounding. Probably had pots of bloody money, what with the house 'n all. *Christ! Give me a bit of lolly and I'll show you what I could do with it. None of this mousing about, that's for bloody sure, mate.*

"Will it take a long time, a new battery?" she was asking.

"Look," he said, cupping his hands around a match to light a cigarette, then, on second thought, offering her one. "Smoke?"

She was freezing, standing out there in just her cardigan for warmth. And she hadn't yet had a chance to have her before-dinner cigarette, so, without thinking, she took one from his pack and said, "Thank you very much," holding one arm wrapped around herself while she leaned towards his cupped hands and the match.

He tossed the match into the gutter before beginning again. "I could do it for you in my own time. It'd cost you less than it would at the garage. Save you a fiver, at least."

"I'm not sure," she hesitated, feeling it might be disloyal to Mr. Beaconstead. But then, five pounds.

"Take me less than an hour. I could fetch the battery from the supply place in Coventry during my lunch hour tomorrow, install it after work, and you'd be all set. I'd just charge you for the battery and my time." He spoke a price and she considered it, starting to shiver.

"Yes, all right," she agreed. "That would be fine."

"Right." He smiled and lowered the bonnet. "Tomorrow, then."

"Yes." She stared at him for a moment then thanked him again for the cigarette before hurrying back inside.

He watched her go, thinking she had a decent enough looking body and probably wasn't anywhere near as old as she came across. He got into his car and checked the time. He had just under an hour to get cleaned up and meet Bobby at the local. He felt a sudden excitement at the prospect of an evening with Bobby. Christ, the lad was bloody gorgeous, even if he did mince about like a bloody ponce. Usually, he couldn't abide the ones that minced and pranced and prissy-lipped their way along. But Bobby, once you got him off on his own, was downright bloody sweet. Even tasted sweet.

She put out the cigarette and quickly chopped an onion, threw it into the pot with the oil, and then began chopping the tomatoes, thinking about that young man. It couldn't really be considered disloyal to Beaconstead. After all, one had to save where one could.

She ate in the kitchen, then cleared up, made a cup of instant coffee and carried it upstairs with her to the bathroom where she started the bath filling and switched on the overhead heater. In the bedroom—still her old, small one because she didn't feel quite right about making Uncle Arthur's room her own—she turned on the electric blanket before quickly undressing. Carrying her dressing-gown and nightdress and a library book, she ran back to the bathroom, her skin goosefleshed from the cold. Out of habit, she locked the bathroom door.

Once in the bath with the coffee conveniently perched on the rim and her book open, she sipped and read and slowly thawed out, finding herself diverted by thoughts of that young man and his scrubbed-clean look, the way he'd smiled. No man of an eligible age had ever smiled at her that way before. It gave her an odd feeling, as if she wasn't someone damaged and quite unpleasant to look at but simply a person, a woman.

Setting the book aside, she looked down the length of her body, not really seeing herself; her eyes simply absorbed the fact of her body's sameness. The coffee finished, she sat gazing into space, aware that the water was beginning to cool, trying to imagine how it might be to have a young man of her own, someone to see in the evening or on a Sunday afternoon. Immediately she discarded the notion as being thoroughly fanciful and well beyond the realm of probability.

People out there in the world, they never saw the person who lived behind the face; they only ever saw the face itself and listened with strained, even pained expressions, to the words that seemed, of their own accord, to grow more distorted than ever, emerging from her scarred mouth in a kind of defiant garble that hadn't anything to do with her will. The truth was she wasn't *seen*. She'd known it from the day the police officer had come to take her out of the house for the first time. The faces of the neighbors who'd collected by the front door had revealed only curiosity and mild revulsion, but no recognition of her. Her mother had told the world that her baby had died at birth; even Uncle Arthur hadn't known she was alive.

Her own mother and father had hated her, were ashamed of her, so ashamed they'd shut her away. She might have died in that room because of their shame. No young man would ever want her, she told herself, but she was fine as she was. And tomorrow, she'd ring the plumber and the painter, too. She'd see to the loo and this bathroom. When the car was fixed, she'd go into town at the weekend to pick out some wallpaper and get some paint color charts.

Of their own volition, her eyes suddenly focused on her body and she studied herself in dismay, looking at the breasts and belly and hair. Awful, dreadful. Her face turned hot on seeing the white reality of her own flesh, and she had that disgusting desire to touch herself again. She wouldn't, she promised herself, sitting up and reaching for her flannel and the soap. It was positively horrid and she always felt so ill afterwards. It was a sickness and she wouldn't.

In bed, she turned on the radio and tried to return to the book but was still unable to concentrate properly. She lit her before-bed cigarette—feeling as guilty as ever, knowing how dangerous it was smoking in bed—and inhaled deeply, remembering how he'd offered her a cigarette. Had anyone been looking, they might have thought the two of them were simply ordinary people standing together on the pavement having a conversation.

No! She redirected her thoughts. She'd stop at the post office in the morning to collect Mr. MacCreech's stamps and buy a packet of Miss Morgan's favorite sweets. Opal Fruits. Thinking of the residents, she smiled. They'd all be tucked up in their beds now, walkers and pushchairs and canes put to one side, hot bedtime drinks consumed, empty cups awaiting collection. The kitchen would be empty, echoey, in readiness for morning.

With a sudden stabbing of insight that came like a pain in her chest, she knew she would in time, without question, find herself tucked up at Crossroads, being administered to by someone who looked to her eyes like a girl at the age of thirty-two. It would come to that. It was merely a matter of time.

Two

WHEN IT GOT TO A QUARTER TO NINE AND BOBBY STILL HADN'T
arrived, Simon dug about in his pocket for some change and went
to the telephone, irritated with himself for being unable simply to
let it pass, to say to hell with it and go home. He was further irritated to have the phone at the kid's digs ring unanswered until, giving up, he replaced the receiver and returned the change to his
pocket. He half-heartedly chatted up the barmaid while he drank
down another half-pint then bid a cheery ta-ra to no one in particular and went out.

The rain was pissing down. He turned up his jacket collar and
sprinted to his car. Bloody bladder ready to burst from all the bitter.
Never mind, he'd go at home. Bitter instead of a meal. He'd missed
tea because of stopping to see to that woman's bloody battery. The
whole bleeding day was a stinking shambles. He was driving too fast
and eased back. Just what he bloody needed, to get stopped and have
them do the breathalyzer; he'd get his license pulled and then he'd
really be in a fine fix.

The hall light was burnt out again and he had to grope his way up
the stairs in the dark, cursing the bloody landlord under his breath
as he pushed on the time-switch landing light, went into the loo,
then emerged to jab his key into the lock, to open the door and survey the place—all of it plainly in view from the doorway:
bed-bloody-sitter with a cooker and two shelves to hold his few bits
and pieces of crockery, a frying pan and a small pot, three mismatched mugs, and some pilfered beer glasses from the local.

Our Simon's done ever so well for himself, he thought, hearing
echoes of his mum's voice as he pushed a shilling into the meter—
his horde of old coins was dwindling rapidly and the bloody landlord
never returned them as Simon repeatedly asked—and got the gas
fire going, then sat down on the floor in front of it to dry himself out.
He was hungry but too pissed off at Bobby and too annoyed with
himself for having tried to ring him up to do anything about it.
There was only a bit of cheese and a few dried-up slices of bread left.

There was a small tin of Nescafé; he could make himself a cup of coffee. But not now, a bit later, he decided, holding his hands out to the blue-flickering jets of fire. For a moment he wished he'd given that barmaid a proper chatting up. He could've had her after time was called. She was there for the having, wasn't she? Half the lads in town had had her. But what for? To get back at Bobby for not bothering to show up? Sod it! He wasn't in the mood for a woman; he'd wanted the lad. Well, that put paid to that, didn't it?

His hands warmed, he got out his pack of Senior Service and lit one, reaching over to the table for the ashtray. He thought he probably should've stuck it out in London like old Teller had wanted him to. The idea that he might've thrown in his hand just at the point when they were getting ready to start taking notice of him drove him wild. He couldn't stand to think he might've called it quits too soon. But all those bloody layabouts emoting and intoning all over the bleeding place. You saw them at every damned audition, every stinking call they showed up in their one "go-see" outfit—usually something velvet. They all affected bloody velvet, or the pseudo-Yank types who tried to pull it off with jeans and that casual look. They didn't have the right kind of bodies or the right kind of jeans for it. You had to have those lean hips and long legs, like the American kids. Too many gone-to-fat arses crammed into tight jeans. It wasn't even erotic, it was just bloody obscene.

And how do you know you're even any damned good, Simon, my-son Fitzgerald? Larking about with amateur bloody productions. Couldn't even get into a stinking rep company for all your supposed bleeding talent. Forget that! Beaconstead pays a fair enough wage and working on the motors is more your style. It's not so bad to be home. At least some of the faces are familiar, and the streets, the shops. But admit it, lad! Once your mum gives it up, you'll head back to London just as bloody fast as you're able.

Well, maybe not. A damned sight less expensive sticking here, isn't it? And there's always Stratford. Give that a try come the spring.

He got up and filled the pot from the basin in the corner then set the water on to boil while he spooned a good measure of the Nescafé into one of the mugs, tossed in two spoons of sugar, realized he'd forgotten to bring up his half-pint and ran downstairs in the dark to find his milk with the help of a lit match.

With the coffee and another cigarette, he returned to sit on the floor in front of the fire, trying to think things through. Mum would be going into that place in another week. Then he'd have to clear out her flat, see to disposing of that mess of knick-knacks and souvenirs she'd been accumulating for the last forty years. He wasn't looking forward to that. But she'd be better off where they could look after her properly. Christ! If the people below hadn't heard her fall, she'd have been for it. Another week in hospital, then she'd go into the residence.

Unexpectedly, he found himself thinking about that peculiar woman, for a moment wishing she were one of the few he sometimes fancied. The lads were playing him up something wicked and that was the truth. They took it like a game, they did. And he hated bloody games. For them it didn't have anything to do with feelings, with caring. It was a power, like; they'd discovered they had it and tried to use it on the ones like Simon who really did care. He had a dream of one day finding one he could live with, get old with. Someone to be a friend, as well. They'd maybe buy a little house in town and have a life together. Settled. Funny about the dream, though, he never could seem to see it with a woman. It was always a lad or another man. He'd tried to see it with a woman but they all had such demands to make, hadn't they? Not just the sex. He didn't mind that part of it so much. In fact, he liked the sex part just as much as he liked it with the lads. When it was right, it was good, sweeter by far than the other. Because they were soft, weren't they? And there were times when he craved that softness, when it was like a killing hunger in him he just had to satisfy. But they wanted so bloody much, women. Possessions. Houses and cars and new clothes. They were always wanting you to provide them with something they wouldn't go out and get for themselves. Oh, at the beginning, they always played it the way they thought you wanted it. More games. Kittens curling up against you, trying to trick you with all their softness. But once they thought they'd got you hooked good and proper, it all changed, didn't it, and out came the demands.

It was one of those—what did they call it?—harelips. That's what it was. A bad one, from the looks of it. He remembered the lad back at the grammar who'd had one. Not nearly so bad as that, though, and he'd talked well enough, except that some of the hard sounds had come out wrong—B's sounding more like M's. Why does she speak so loudly? he wondered. Not overly, but fairly loud. And so carefully. Getting every word out. How did something like that turn your thoughts? he wondered, taking a swallow of the coffee. Was it her mouth, was it because of that she dressed like she did with the shapeless woollen skirt and the cardy, the mouse hair and undressed face?

He smiled, seeing himself sitting her down, tucking a tea towel round her neck and going to work with a pair of tweezers and some make-up. He'd always loved the challenge of a makeover, seeing what you could bring out in people. There'd been that girl in London. What was her name? He couldn't remember. The art student. He'd chatted her up outside that pub on the Fulham Road near World's End. And she'd been right bitchy at the start. "What're you then, one of those hairdressing queens?" He'd laughed and told her he just wanted to have a go at it. "Suit yourself, then." She'd shrugged and let him do up her hair and make up her face. She'd come out looking like a tart, he'd thought. She'd come over all angry and thrown him out. His smile widened. It'd been a lark. Fun. Something good about getting that close, being able to examine the details of a face at such close range: noticing the down on the nape of her neck and the tiny little lashes at the very corners of her eyes. It wasn't nearly so good making up a lad, not nearly. That time he'd made them up for that shoddy bloody amateur production of *A Taste of Honey*. The girl, she hadn't been bad. A bit wooden. But the lad, he'd been a shocker. I could've done it a thousand times better. I knew that part, that lad. No, they said, I was too old. So, ta ever so, I'll do your bleeding make-up. Too old. It didn't rankle quite the way it had. But if he'd been too old then, he was over the bloody hill now, at thirty. And common sense told you to give it up, give over when you've put in six bloody years in London going the rounds, giving out your photographs and made-up résumés, getting passed over every bloody time, week after week, months and years on end, so you were grateful for a crowd scene now and again that paid a tenner to cover the rent and buy you some smokes. Never mind Teller's saying to stick with it, the break'd come. Comes a time when you tell yourself you're wasting your time, mate. Pack it in and go on home, go back to what you know, what they'll pay you good lolly to do. No sin, no shame to packing it in. The sin's in staying, hanging on with that lot of layabouts, all lying through their bloody teeth about the part that's coming in for them or the big audition all set.

It had to do with self-respect, hadn't it? And wanting more in your pocket than the few bob picked up waiting on table or fixing some bloke's carburetor, and wanting something settled even if it's only having a decent place to live and something to drive about in. Six years. Mum going at him like he was a right nana, wasn't he, going off to London to be an actor. Well, she'd been right, eh? And look where they were now: her in hospital, and him in these stinking digs, putting his earnings into the post office account. Saving up for what? Five months back home and less to show for it than he'd had in London. What was it like to have a lip like that? he wondered.

Rushing back inside from the damp cold of the outside loo, she went directly to the telephone to ring the plumber. She promised to drop off the house key on her way to Crossroads and to have a word with him before he did any work on either the upstairs loo or the bath-room. Feeling in control, she next rang the painter but was told by his wife that she'd just missed him. "I'll ask him to stop by this evening, if you like," the wife said, and forgetting that the man from the garage would be coming, Sarah said that would be fine and rang off.

The telephoning having held her back, she had to fly upstairs to dress, foregoing breakfast in order to drop the key off to the plumber, to explain about the broken loo and still get to Crossroads on time. As she was coming in, Margaret was emerging from her office adja-cent to the front door.

"Ah, Sarah. Good morning."

"Good morning. I'm a bit late, I'm afraid."

"Not to worry." Margaret stared at her for a moment, causing Sarah to feel awkward and uncertain. Had she forgotten to brush her hair? Was something about her clothing awry? "We had rather a bad night, I'm afraid," Margaret said, redirecting her eyes down the cor-ridor looking at nothing. "We had two go."

"Oh no."

"Mr Weatherly, and your Miss Morgan."

My Miss Morgan? How odd of Margaret to put it that way. "Miss Morgan," Sarah repeated softly, the impact slowly making itself felt.

"Another stroke," Margaret explained, preparing to move on. "I thought you might like to clear out her things, see to all that."

"Yes, all right. I'll just put away my coat."

Miss Morgan. My Miss Morgan. She went to the staff room to remove her coat, awed as ever by death's waiting claim upon these people—her friends, her family. How dare it keep on happening? Why couldn't the body somehow be taken away or cared for independently of the brain? Miss Morgan's brain had been perfectly all right. She'd not become forgetful, like Mr MacCreech. Blast it! She'd forgotten his stamps. She'd have to go out midday to the post office and get them. And the sweets. She'd left them on the counter in the kitchen. Miss Morgan's Opal Fruits, soft and chewy, the kind that sent tart sweetness over your mouth. She wouldn't be wanting sweets. *I hate this*! she thought, gripped by sadness and anger at the knowledge of another loss. She stood gazing into space for several seconds, wishing she'd had the courage to go to nursing school and get a diploma. She and Uncle Arthur had talked it over, reasoning out the pros and cons. But she couldn't have faced any aspect of it. It was one of the many times she'd been compelled to acknowledge just how much of a coward she was—unable to confront the obstacles standing between her and what she wanted. But all she'd been able to visualize was a group of uniformed student nurses all laughing at her, and an impatient matron being verbally abusive because of Sarah's failure to make herself understood at a crucial moment. Lives that might have been lost because of her inability to communicate properly under stress. All her potential skill and caring of no importance whatsoever in the face of her unpredictable speech patterns and the hearing impairment she suffered as a result of numerous early ear infections. Not only did she fail to speak comprehensibly at times, she also missed quite a bit of what was said in the lower registers. A half-deaf rabbit. The sight of her face in a mirror was enough to make her insides turn to lumps of lead, to make her chest fill with anxiety and despair. Her pulled-back upper lip with its soft exposed inner flesh seemed like something a little indecent that ought to have been hidden. Hating that face, she avoided mirrors and her own image with morbid consistency. If she didn't have to see herself, she could effectively forget for brief periods of time that she had a face at all.

Now Miss Morgan was dead. She'd be buried. There'd be no funeral, no services. There was no one to attend. She felt like putting her fist through the wall in her anger and outrage at the unfairness of it. Instead, she absently smoothed down her hair, tucked in a stray bit at the side, and went out to attend to those of the residents who were bedridden. She greeted them with a smile, touching and patting them, reassured by their responses. Some of them complained, typically, feeling free enough with her to give voice to their petty grievances. Mrs. Swan was out of tissues and had lost her Biro. Mrs. Elgon had misplaced not only her glasses but also the book she'd been reading and shot accusing glances at Mrs. Swan as if privately convinced Mrs. Swan had intentionally hidden her own Biro to direct attention away from her real crime of having stolen Mrs. Elgon's glasses and book. Petty squabbles that went on and on, as if these tiffs were all they had left to live for.

Hugh MacCreech was dozing. She didn't disturb him but went to have a look in on Mr. Sinclair. Skin and bones, he looked like nothing so much as an inquisitive chicken with his head jerking suddenly forward, suddenly back, his round eyes lashless and gaping. He lay propped against the pillows, his oddly too-large hands splayed uselessly on top of the bedclothes like exhausted swimmers, twitching from time to time. He saw only what he chose to recognize, rarely spoke, and had defied all the diagnoses by lasting five months beyond what they'd all believed would be his terminal date. What, she wondered, was keeping him alive, so rigidly erect and seemingly alert in his bed? Spoon-fed like an infant, he soiled the bed even with the nappies he, as did two of the others, wore. He'd even smeared himself foully one morning, and had beamed toothlessly at her and Grace as they'd chided him, cleaning him up.

As she walked from room to room of the sunny, overly warm residence, she was all at once overtaken by a dreadful feeling of unreality. It seemed as if she were moving through an enormous incubator that was attempting to keep alive these aged fledglings. Trussed up like outsized infants, they wet themselves and babbled, they sucked at their fingers and clung to anyone who approached them; they lived on and on inexplicably or died without warning. She felt stifled, a bit ill with the new fear of one morning waking to find herself in the bed next to Mrs. Swan. She simply could not understand this sudden and entirely unreasonable dread when, for all these years, she'd enjoyed the time she'd spent in this place; she'd derived satisfaction both from her own benevolent actions and from doing positive good for others. Now it felt as if she'd simply been playing at some bizarre game, using up time until her turn came to be put in nappies, turned over, alcohol-rubbed and, finally, disposed of.

She stopped at the door to the room Miss Morgan had shared with Miss Spencer, Mrs. Whittaker, and Mrs. Boyle. Spencer, Whittaker, and Boyle being ambulatory, they were downstairs in the lounge with the others where chairs lined three of the walls and the television set was at the far end. On good days, sunlight streamed through the near and far windows, casting into unrelenting definition the wattles and wrinkles and sagging flesh of the dozen and a half old people simply sitting and waiting, open books in the hands of some, knitting in the hands of a few others. One or two of the men still smoked and busied themselves with that. But all of them were waiting, waiting. She could just as easily go along down the corridor, take her seat now, and begin her waiting.

She moved to open the drawer of the locker beside the stripped bed, but couldn't bring herself to touch the contents. So she closed the drawer and left the room. She didn't think she could keep on with this. But she had to do something. If she had nothing to do, she might just as well be dead. She didn't understand why she was so deeply afraid. *I feel ill*, she thought, and realized she was going to be sick.

Pushing into the nearest lavatory, she bent over the toilet and heaved on an empty stomach. Nothing came up but a bit of bitter fluid. She drank some water from her cupped hands then went in search of Margaret.

"You don't look well, Sarah. Are you ill?" Margaret's eyebrows pulled together and Sarah could almost hear her thoughts. If Sarah went home ill, the workload would pile up on the others. And Ian wasn't yet back from his trip to London to give his quarterly progress report to the board of governors. For a moment, in view of all this, Sarah wasn't sure how to answer.

"I feel a bit off," she admitted, reluctant to go home and leave the others to cope with the additional work.

"Come along and have a cup of tea." Margaret extended her arm across Sarah's shoulders, reaching up to do so, and led her along to the kitchen. "You're upset about Miss Morgan," Margaret stated, watching Sarah drink the tea. "You really must learn not to take these things so to heart."

"But one has to care," Sarah said earnestly. "They *need* to be cared for."

You need to be cared for, Margaret thought, restraining her impulse to say so. Who would care about her? It was all too plain to see how poorly she cared for herself. She was a good stone lighter since her uncle had died. "You should eat more," she advised, relaxing. Sarah needed her attention and it gave her rather a good feeling to offer her advice and concern to Sarah. She was so patently hopeless a case that it made Margaret feel decidedly strong and even maternal to take these few minutes to be with her.

"I didn't have time for breakfast, actually," Sarah recalled aloud.

"Well, there you are, you see!" Margaret said a little impatiently, feeling thoroughly justified in her view of Sarah as something just short of a charity case. "Stay right here! I'll have Doreen fix you something. How *can* you expect to do a morning's work with nothing in your stomach?"

"There wasn't time. I had to ring the plumber, then go round with the key. And then ..." She trailed off, hearing how almost simple-minded she sounded. In any case, Margaret had gone bustling out and could now be heard telling Doreen to fix a round of sandwiches for Sarah who'd gone ahead and missed her breakfast again. Did she know how loudly she was speaking? Sarah wondered. Or how it felt to hear her speak that way, as if Sarah were a naughty child? She was anything but a child. Thirty-two years old.

Her thoughts sparking off in odd directions, she tried to visualize what Margaret and Ian did in the evenings, in their free time together. Perhaps they had very little free time, living as they did in the flat here, on call day and night. Her thoughts shifted shockingly to the bodies of the old men, bodies she handled with detached gentleness. Shrivelled pouches of flesh. It hadn't ever before occurred to her to think about the fact that these had once been young men whose flesh had swelled with passion, whose parts had merged with those of willing women. God, how could they bear it? Putting the parts of themselves together. But almost all of them in the residence had. *And no one's ever so much as held my hand. No one ever will. Did anyone ever hold you, Miss Morgan, kiss you and put the parts of himself to the parts of you? Was there someone you loved who died, perhaps, in one of the wars, or who let you go, preferring another? Did you ever wish for children only to find yourself old and past that possibility? I never thought to talk with you about who you were or what you'd hoped for yourself. Perhaps you needed to speak of those things; it might have kept you alive. I don't know. I don't know. I could be losing my reason. Letting things get away from me. Letting the upstairs loo go that way for months. There's no reason for it, no need. Still, I did ring and go round with the key. It'll be repaired; the bathroom will be redone. I'm really not that bad.*

"Eat this now!" Margaret put a plate down on the table in front of Sarah, then sat down opposite, lighting one of her Embassys. She saved the coupons, Sarah knew, and got all sorts of things with them: a lamp one time, and some quite pretty coffee mugs another time. It seemed so sensible of her. Sensible, yes. There was no romance about Margaret, none at all. Everything she did was for a purpose. Sensible like her stout body and solid shoes, like her bluntly cut hair and straight, plain features. Sarah picked up half the sandwich. Cheese. She began to eat.

Margaret smoked her cigarette, arms folded across her wide chest, watching Sarah. Sarah, tall and thin. Yet one didn't realize her height until she stood up and then her height and thinness both seemed somehow more, and less, as well. Seated, she seemed quite small. Small bones. Margaret had seen her in town one Saturday afternoon, had spotted her coming out of Marks and Spencer and go hurrying through the crowd. From the rear she'd looked no less than fifty with her shabby navy overcoat and her string carrier-bag, her low-heeled shoes and heavyweight stockings, her hair hanging in wisps over her coat collar. Yet, face on, she often looked a child with her large deep-blue eyes and pure features. She had a face of extraordinary innocence and surprising intelligence—an unlived-in face, somehow. The pleasant symmetry of her features was jarringly disturbed by the sharp lift of her upper lip. It wasn't at all that ugly, really. She'd seen worse, she thought, harking back to her nurse's training years before in London—nights on the casualty ward, the sights she'd seen then. This woman's minor imperfection was nothing to what she'd seen back then.

Sarah's problem, she thought, lay in her having been raised by a man, without a woman's care. That was it, of course. What did men know about seeing to the needs of a growing girl? It wasn't in the least surprising Sarah was so hopelessly dowdy with her too-long skirts that only accentuated her height, and her sensible shoes and colorless blouses and jumpers. To Margaret's mind, Sarah was the embodiment of a man's interpretation—a bachelor at that—of how a young respectable woman should look. It was positively, pathetic, Margaret thought, indignation momentarily replacing charity as the color of her mood.

"Better?" Margaret asked, openly studying Sarah as she wiped the crumbs from her fingers.

"Yes, much." Sarah smiled. Then, all at once, she remembered that the garage man and the painter and, undoubtedly, the plumber were all due to come at the same time that evening. "I *am* an idiot," she said, quickly explaining. "I simply didn't think."

"I scarcely think you'll need to tell the man how to change the battery," Margaret said sagely. "Just see to the painter. There's no need for you to get into such a flap over things the way you do."

"I do do that, don't I?" she agreed, considering it. "I shouldn't, but I do. It's as if I'm only able to deal with one thing at a time, when I know that's quite absurd. I'm able to deal with whatever needs doing. It's just that I start ... imagining all sorts of problems, I suppose. I don't know. I expect I'm upset just now about Miss Morgan. I hadn't thought it would be so soon. I hadn't anticipated it at all, to be truthful."

"None of us did, Sarah. But she was so wretchedly unhappy. Surely you can see that it's better this way?"

"I suppose," she conceded. "It's just that ... I can't help wondering if this is all there is. You know?" She fixed her wide blue eyes on Margaret's.

"I know. It's inevitable, working in this sort of place. One has to wonder. It wouldn't be quite natural if one didn't."

"If you don't mind," Sarah said hesitantly, "perhaps one of the others could see to clearing out her things. I honestly don't think I'm up to it."

"I'll do it myself." Margaret looked at her mannish wristwatch. "Stay on here for a few more minutes," she said, getting up. "Smoke a cigarette, then get on with the trays. You've got time. And," she added from the door, "do try to remember your breakfast. It's hard work on an empty stomach. You're all right now?" She looked somewhat softened, concerned.

"I'm fine. Thank you very much."

What was to become of her? Margaret wondered, going off down the hall at a brisk pace. She scarcely seemed able to look after herself. Yet she did such a fine job with the residents. Not so much the practical aspects, but she gave them so much of what they really did need: love. Naturally, depending on one's viewpoint, it could appear damned pathetic to some, a young woman like that dedicating herself to caring so deeply for a group of old people all waiting to die. Still, they were the better for it. And where else would Sarah go, after all? What else could she possible do, poor thing?

I'm allowing myself to become like them, Sarah thought, standing by the window with her cigarette. *I've spent so much time with the residents that I'm starting to think and act like them. I've got to find some-*

thing more to do with myself. But what?

Solitary walks in the country when the weather's fine, to park the car and take the two-mile walk along the back roads until I arrive again at the car with my eyes filled with the fields and the mists, all of me almost hurting with feeling for all I see. I get into the car to drive past the pub where we went every Sunday afternoon, Uncle Arthur to have his whisky and I my shandy, in companionable silence studying the people around us before returning home to a late tea. I no longer even bother now to put the car into the garage at nights, but leave it out in the road to rust. What's happening to me? I simply must see to things—to the paint and the wallpaper and the plumbing. I should go ahead and clear out Uncle Arthur's room, have it redecorated and move myself in there. There's no reason not to turn the mattress, put on fresh sheets and make the big bed up for myself. I've never slept in a big bed; I might like that. It's something to do. So little to do.

▽　　　▽　　　▽　　　▽　　　▽

Three

We're going to have to tear back the floorboards and replace some of the piping. Be a good two days before we'll have it set to rights."

"I see." She hadn't realized quite so much work would be involved.

"We'll make a start on it now, then, before I leave, we'll have a look at the bathroom, talk over what it is you think you'd like done in there."

She left him and his mate to get on with it, eyeing as she went the crate containing the new toilet. It seemed exceptionally large, taking up half the hallway. On her way down the stairs, she thought that ripping up the floor would mean having to replace the linoleum. Carpet would be nice. Fresh-painted woodwork with some cheery wallpaper and carpet. Yes. She walked through to the lounge to look out of the window. The old battery was sitting on the pavement and the young man was cleaning something with a rag. She watched, intrigued by his lightness. The evening had already turned dark, yet where he worked it seemed shades brighter. There was something almost angelic about his blond curls and glowing face. Like a religious painting, she thought, then had to smile at this piece of whimsy. A mechanic in overalls was scarcely the subject for a religious rendering. She left the window and went to the kitchen to plug in the kettle. She'd make tea and offer it to the two upstairs and the one outside.

She felt altogether different being surrounded by people. Well, perhaps not precisely surrounded. But having three men at work on various of her belongings did make her feel quite unlike she had previously—as if she was a person of some small importance because she owned things in need of repair. She prepared tea in the good, scarcely used silver teapot, reasoning that they were working hard, after all, and the least she could do was offer a cup of tea.

The plumber and his mate accepted cups of tea and a biscuit each, said, "Ta," and, setting the biscuits in the saucers, placed their tea to one side and got back to work.

The young man from the garage smiled at her from under the propped-open bonnet and said, "No, thank you, luv."

Disappointed, her sense of importance short-lived, she returned inside to stand in the kitchen drinking her own tea, staring into space. Her cigarette burned unnoticed in the ashtray.

Like a kid, Simon thought, getting the last of the corrosion cleaned from the leads. Her face had closed up with that same sort of kid's let-down. He should've taken the tea, he thought, deciding he'd ask for it when he finished the job. Obviously, little things held a lot of store for her. It wasn't right, really, to let someone down on such a small thing if it was no trouble to you and gave them a bit of pleasure.

Holding a fresh cigarette, she was absently touching her lip with a forefinger when the knock came at the front door. Startled, she jerked her hand down as if she'd been caught at some flagrantly illicit activity and hurried to the door to see the garage man standing there smiling at her. Did he always smile? "I'll just fetch my checkbook," she told him. "Do come in."

"Could I wash?" he asked, holding his oily hands out in front of him.

"In the kitchen," she said, rattled. She showed him into the kitchen then left him there while she went upstairs for her checkbook, and returned to find him standing in the middle of the room with his hands now jammed into his pockets, looking about.

"I could do with that cuppa now," he said, hating himself for the way his eyes went straight to her mouth. He imagined everybody must do that to her and he disliked believing himself to be so typical.

"Oh, good." She gave him something like a smile and put down the checkbook and pen. "I'll make a fresh pot," she said, giving the kettle a shake and deciding there was enough water. "It'll only take a moment. Will you sit down?"

"Live here alone?" he asked, pulling one of the chairs back from the table before reaching inside his overalls for his cigarettes.

"It was my uncle's house. He left it to me when he died."

"Big, isn't it?"

"It is, actually." She too looked around, as if for the first time noticing just how big the house really was. Perhaps it was wrong of her to be living alone in a house this size when there was such a chronic shortage of housing. But where else would she live?

"Having some work done, eh?" he said conversationally, fascinated by the way everything he said to her seemed to turn her in a different direction. She was awfully like a kid in a lot of ways, except she didn't sound like one, did she? Didn't look like one, either.

"The upstairs loo," she explained, then flushed as if mentioning loos wasn't done. "I'm going to have the bathroom done too. Everything. The painter's coming round this evening. Uncle Arthur wasn't bothered by the look of things, you see. I mean, he didn't seem to notice the wallpaper or that the woodwork had yellowed."

"I know. My mum's a bit that way." He pushed back his sleeve to look at his watch. A good hour or more before visiting hours.

"Your mother lives in town?" she asked, pouring out the remains of the old tea. She turned on the tap, thinking to rinse the pot, only to discover there wasn't any water. She'd forgotten again. Which meant he'd been unable to wash his hands. She spooned tea into the cold pot not knowing how to apologize, so kept silent.

"She's in hospital, had a heart attack a while back."

"Oh. That is too bad. I'm sorry. Is she quite elderly?"

"Not too. Sixty-eight last birthday. But she's always had a wonky heart."

A wonky heart. She smiled to herself at his putting it that way.

"I've been in London the last six years," he went on, "Been back coming on six months now. It's dead bloody boring after London."

"I imagine it must be. What," she asked, surprised at her boldness, "did you do in London?"

"Acting. Trying, that is." He grinned. "Didn't have too much luck, to be honest."

"You're an *actor*! How super!" She said it with such enthusiasm that it made him feel better somehow about his failed efforts.

"I wasn't bad," he said, trying for objectivity. "But the competition's killing. I didn't have a chance. Took me six years to recognize that fact. It's who you know and where you're seen and what you're wearing, all that muck. I didn't know anybody except my agent, couldn't afford to be seen anywhere, and didn't dress the part, if you know what I mean. So, when Mum had her turn, I decided to chuck the whole bloody lot and come back, stop larking about."

"I expect you're terribly disappointed."

"Oh, I don't know." He paid close attention to his cigarette, tipping the ash off into the ashtray. "It's not as bad as I thought it'd be. You think all the lads'll take the mickey, you know. But there was none of that. It seems as if the old friends're glad enough to see me. That feels right … But it's not the same as it was. It never is, though, is it?"

"I suppose not," she said, having no idea what he meant. She poured the tea and carried the two cups around to the table then, on impulse, said, "Would you care for a sandwich? I expect you've missed your tea."

"I am hungry. Wouldn't mind at all, if it's no trouble."

"Oh, it isn't at all. I'm hungry too."

Feeling useful again, she went to make several rounds of sandwiches with the ham she'd picked up on her way home. But having put the food on the table and watched him start eating, she was overcome by shyness at the thought of having him see how she ate and couldn't bring herself to take a sandwich.

"Go on, luv." He pushed the plate towards her. "Aren't you having any?"

She wanted casually to say something about having changed her mind, but her stomach was contracting hungrily. She'd simply have to contend with it, she told herself, and put half a round on her plate, staring at it for several moments before picking it up and turning slightly away from him as she took a small bite.

She doesn't want me to see, he realized, and felt an inexplicable lumping in his throat. His eyes fixed on her profile, taking in her wispy-looking hair, the appealing shape of her ear, the whiteness of her throat. He was crazily touched by her. No one should have to feel that way, he thought, and wanted to say something to her that would make it better, let her know she didn't have to be ashamed with him because, after all, he wasn't anybody. A failed actor, no one. But she might be even more embarrassed if he said anything or made some reference to what she was trying to hide. So, instead, he said the first thing that came into his mind. "Ever thought about fixing up this place, then selling it and getting something smaller? You'd likely turn a nice profit, and if you took on a place just outside town, say, something needing a bit of fixing up, you'd probably come out nicely."

She forgot herself and turned to look at him. Was he suggesting something beyond the words? "Sell it? But why?"

"Well, it's big, isn't it? And you don't need such a big place, do you? 'Course, if you don't enjoy doing up rooms, there's no sense to it, is there?"

"Do *you* enjoy doing up rooms?" she asked, on her guard against him.

"Never really tried it. I've done a bit of carpentry, a bit of painting. Odd jobs. I might fancy taking on a whole house. Thing is, you save a lot if you do it yourself, the painting and all."

"I can't paint," she said flatly. "And there's a lot needing doing." An actor, she thought, losing track of the conversation. He did look like one with his fine choirboy's features and thick curling hair. An actor playing the part of a mechanic. He looked no older than twenty-two or three. "I don't think I'd care to move," she said after a few seconds. "I've lived here almost all my life."

"Where'd you live before?" he asked, helping himself to another sandwich.

"I was born in London, actually," she said, feeling the tightening start at once; it always did when she approached dangerous topics.

"Isn't that a switch?" He smiled. "You were born there and came here, and I was born here and went there. I'd been born there, luv, I can promise you I'd never've come here."

"You don't like it here?"

"Ah, I don't know. It's all right, I reckon. I like to blame London, you know, as if it's the city's fault I couldn't make a go of it."

That seemed to her a very wise thing to say and she took another bite of her sandwich, considering it.

"You can't," he continued, "blame other people or a city when the fault's your own, can you? It's kidding yourself, isn't it? I mean, if I didn't make a go of it, it's my fault. I gave it my best and that wasn't good enough. I've got, to accept it and get on with things."

She unbent a little now that they were safely away from dangerous subjects such as selling her home, and where she'd been born. "Sometimes," she said thoughtfully, "one *wants* to blame other people. One needs to, really. I mean, there are times when other people *are* responsible ..."

He was looking at her with open interest and, again, she lost track of what she'd intended to say. Someone knocked at the front door. She put down her sandwich and went to open the door to the painter who came in saying, "The wife said you rang about having some rooms done."

"Yes, that's right." Thrown now by the logistics of trying to deal with everyone at once, she showed him into the lounge saying, "If you wouldn't mind waiting, I'll be with you directly." Then she went back to the kitchen, apologetically explaining, "The painter."

"I've got to be going," Simon said, getting up. "Thanks for the tea."

She saw him out, then went in to talk to the painter, in the middle of their slow tour of the house realizing she'd forgotten to give the mechanic his check. She'd have to drop it off to him in the morning on her way to Crossroads.

The painter told her he'd have to sit down and work out a price; he'd get back to her in a day or two with his estimate, as well as some idea of when he might be free to do the work. He'd only just gone when the plumber and his mate came heavily down the stairs.

"We'll be back in the morning," the plumber told her.

"What time?"

"Eight."

Too early, she thought, but said, "That will be fine" and saw them out. Sighing, she returned to the kitchen to finish her sandwich. Too tired to bother hotting up the pot, she drank the cold tea, then rinsed the dishes and went up to have a look at the loo. The old toilet lay on top of some newspapers to one side of the hallway, a pile of rotted floorboards beside it. The loo floor was an exposed area of rusted-looking piping and rough wood underflooring. The tank was still fixed to the wall but its pipe had been capped-off. She closed the door on the mess and went into the bathroom thinking to start the bathwater going, but she felt too tired, so washed instead at the basin, brushed her teeth, then started towards her bedroom, stopping at the door to Uncle Arthur's room. She opened the door to look inside, deciding she would go ahead and redecorate it and make it her own.

Imagine that young man suggesting she sell this place! Someone she didn't know proposing she make drastic changes in her life. For what purpose?

In bed, she lit a cigarette and sat gazing at the far wall, re-examining both the conversation and her feelings, concluding he'd simply been making conversation, being polite.

Doctor John was just leaving as Simon arrived at the hospital and he stopped in the corridor to have a word with Simon.

"She's doing very nicely," John told him. "And how have you been then, Simon?"

"Oh me, I'm fine." And then, not knowing what prompted him to do so, he asked, "You know those harelips? If someone had a really bad one, like this, say"—he pulled at his upper lip to illustrate—"could it be fixed?"

John smiled. "You've met Sarah."

"Sarah?"

"Sarah Breswick. You've met her, have you?"

"Oh, yeah, right. I was just wondering."

"It can be fixed," John said, something subtle changing in his eyes. "I've been after her for a good fifteen years to have it done."

"Fifteen years? And she won't?"

"She's put off by the idea of any more surgery," John said a little guiltily, as if he was telling tales out of school. "I think she feels she's had enough of it to last one lifetime. Good to see you, Simon." He went off down the corridor to look in on another of his patients, leaving Simon to wonder about all the surgery she'd had and what sort. He thought about it throughout his visit with his mother, so that when he found himself out in the carpark, he couldn't remember a word of what he and his mum had talked about. He stopped at the local on his way home thinking to have a quick pint, but saw Bobby slouching against the bar, being chatted up by two raging old queens. In disgust, Simon kept right on walking, through the bar and on out through the opposite exit. It always depressed him to see the ones who'd made themselves into mock women, drooling over young flesh. He'd never be so bloody flagrant! he vowed, climbing into the car, remembering as he did that he'd failed to get his check from that woman. Sarah. The name didn't suit her. Heather, he thought, would've been better. He'd always had a fondness for the name Heather, but hadn't ever met a woman who suited it. She did, though. Funny, that.

Coming on for nine, be saw, checking the time. Still early enough to stop at the house and collect his money. He put the car in gear and headed back across town in a thickening fog that cast pale auras of light like halos, he thought, around the streetlamps.

The downstairs lights were off, but there was one on upstairs and he told himself she couldn't possibly be in bed yet as he raised the front-door knocker.

The sound frightened her, set her heart beating far too fast as she jumped up and grabbed her dressing-gown, pulling it on as she ran down the stairs. Coming to a halt by the door, she called out, "Who is it?"

"Me, Simon. I thought I'd stop for my check."

Oh hell! she thought, despairing over being caught in her night-clothes. He was out there waiting and she couldn't very well turn him away and say she'd pop in at the garage in the morning with the check. Of course she couldn't do that. Mr. Beaconstead would real-ize the young man had been doing a bit of moonlighting and she'd as likely as not get him into trouble. What *could* she have been thinking of? she berated herself as she unlocked the door and, hid-ing as much of herself behind it as possible, said, "Do, please come in. I'm frightfully sorry. If you'll wait just a moment, I'll write it out for you."

She dashed into the kitchen and he stood in the front hall watch-ing her position the checkbook on the table and quickly start writ-ing, then look up asking, "Your name? I'm afraid I don't know it"

"Fitzgerald, luv. Simon."

"Oh!" She returned to writing.

He felt again that sudden softening towards her at the sight of her tatty dressing-gown. What the hell kind of life did she have that she took herself off to bed before nine o'clock at night?

"If I'd known you were getting ready for bed, I'd have waited for it," he called out to her, taking a step closer to the kitchen. "I'm sorry."

"It's quite all right," she said breathlessly, tearing the check from the book and waving it in the air to dry. "I'm sorry for having for-gotten. It was just … so many things going on at once." She came across the kitchen folding the check in half before holding it out to him. "I do hope you didn't have to drive too far out of your way. I am terribly sorry."

Seeing again that image of Bobby being wooed by the two old queens, he accepted the check saying, "Would you fancy coming out tomorrow night for a meal?"

"I beg your pardon?" She looked blankly at him.

"Come out for a meal," he repeated, smiling charmingly. "There's a not bad place I know in Stratford."

"Stratford?"

"I'm inviting you out," he said patiently, tucking the check into his pocket without bothering to look at it. "It's a Friday, so you needn't worry about being out late."

"A Friday," she said stupidly, trying to make sense of this. She felt as if she were about to begin crying. Was it some sort of joke?

"I'll collect you at seven. Okay?"

"All right," she whispered as if hypnotized, her eyes on his shining face.

"Right! I'll be off now, then. Sorry 'bout coming round so late. And thanks for the check." He walked to the door and let himself out. She stood gazing after him from the kitchen doorway. In shock. He'd just invited her out for an evening and she'd accepted. She must be mad! Or he must! Why would he invite her out? How could he want to be seen with her? I can't, she thought. *Call him back and explain you couldn't possibly!* She continued to stand there, hearing the sound of his car starting up and driving away. Too late. She held her hand over her mouth, unable to move. She'd never be able to sleep now, she thought, finally returning upstairs to light a cigarette and sit, shivering, on the side of her bed, trying to understand his possible motives. Kindness. He was being kind. Didn't he know how awful, how cruel it was to play at being kind? She'd suffered horribly in the past at the hands of "kind" people, the ones who'd thought they'd put her at her ease, make her feel comfortable and accepted by inviting her round to tea or dinner. They'd only succeeded in cementing her awareness of just how different and how unacceptable she really was. She again heard Uncle Arthur saying, "You misunderstand, Sarah. Intentionally. They're not setting out to do you harm, they're merely trying to include you. You're getting into the habit, my dear, of playing the recluse. And there's no need for it. It's *you* who's setting yourself apart, no one else. You think all anyone sees when they look at you is your mouth, because it's all *you* see. So, because of it, you will *not* give anyone a chance to know you, *will not* allow yourself to relax and enjoy the company of others."

It wasn't true, she argued with the memory. They *did* see and she loathed having them look at her the way they did, covertly studying her, secretly glad not to look the way she did. No matter how unattractive they might be, at least they looked relatively like most other people. She should have said no, but he'd taken her so by surprise, coming back that way. She hadn't been expecting ... She'd *never* be able to get to sleep now.

▽

What the bloody hell d'you think you're playing at, mate? he asked himself as he climbed into the car. *Out of your bleeding nut, you are! Why'd you go and do that?*

He wasn't so much angry with himself as confounded. Here he was over thirty but with the impulses of a bloody six-year-old. He'd had no intention of doing anything more than collecting what was owed him, and now he had a date on his hands. Not only with a woman, but with *that* one, of all women. Just to get back at Bobby, he told himself, heading home to his bedsitter. *Own up to it, mate! Doing a bit of getting-back-at that no one's going to know about but you. Daft bloody bugger! Well, you're just going to have to see it through now, aren't you? Put on your good gear and go round for her at seven, like you said you would.*

He groaned aloud, imagining her appearing in that woolen skirt and twin set, maybe with pearls and a bit of wrong-color face powder. They'd spend an entire bloody evening struggling to make conversation while she tried not to let him see her drinking or eating. It'd be a bleeding disaster. Jumping right in without a moment's thought. *Well, you just treat her nicely, Simon Fitzgerald!* he warned himself. *You got yourself into it. It's not her fault, is it, you're a bit daft. So give her a pleasant time and that'll be the end of it.*

He made himself a cup of Nescafé while the gas fire took some of the chill off the room then, with a cigarette between his teeth, he sat down on the floor to stare at the reddening elements, smoking and drinking the coffee, feeling a right nana for saying and doing every bloody thing he'd done all evening. Imagine asking Doctor John could they fix up those harelips? And John knowing straight off he was talking about what was her name, Sarah. Bloody Sarah. Go give a kid a name like that and she'll turn out just like the name you gave her, won't she? Call her Sarah, or June, or Jane and she'll come up dead plain every time. Call her Heather, though, and she'll come up soft and nice, with some color to her. If he ever had a kid, which wasn't bloody likely, he wouldn't go giving his kid some daft dull bloody name like Herbert or Samuel, would he? "'Ere you, Bertie!" he said aloud. "Get yourself on in the 'ouse now, our Sam!" He laughed, then said, "Bloody hell!"

Ah, bugger it! he thought, settling down. She wasn't all that bad and they might even have a good time. They'd get a decent meal, in any case, unless the food'd gone off. He'd call midday tomorrow, make a reservation. Maybe she had a dress or something. Dear old thing. He smiled, shaking his head. It was probably the most exciting thing that'd ever happened to her, going out for a meal with a man. She'd probably never been out with a man in her life.

See! Look at it that way, eh, Mate? Doing her a good turn, aren't you, maybe showing her she's not that bad. Maybe talk her into getting her mouth fixed.

He went off into fantasy, imagining himself convincing her to have the surgery done. She'd come out of it looking not half bloody bad. Then he'd make her over and cut her hair. He pictured her all flushed and grateful. He saw her pretty, saw her naked. He could almost feel all that hidden softness. She'd have little breasts, wouldn't she? And soft white thighs. *You'll be lucky, mate! You'd never get that close. Poor old girl probably keeps her clothes on even for the doctor.*

You could get 'em off her, he argued, feeling himself beginning to rise to the challenge. Talk about a bloody favor! Talk about that! Hell! The shock'd bloody *kill* her. But still … He couldn't quite rid himself of an image of her long naked body. He told himself, "Rot!" yet he was challenged undeniably, and intrigued. At last, though, he relegated the idea to the safe area of pure fancy. She was the type that once you got her started, the demands'd come so hard and fast you'd be lucky to get out with your life. That deprived kind, the type with nothing, you gave 'em something and then they wanted the lot. *Just give her the bloody meal and get shot of her. You nit you.*

Four

SHE WAS TRYING, IMPOSSIBLY, TO WORK EFFECTIVELY AND EFFICIENTLY on four hours' sleep, and could feel it taking its toll on her temper, her strength. She felt weak and tired, even angry as she helped Grace get Mr. Sinclair out of his bed and into a bath. These people were so *heavy*. She wondered if outsiders realized just how weighty these frail-seeming, elderly people were. Mr. Sinclair appeared to be a long, terribly pale parcel of thinly fleshed-over bones, yet his weight was substantial. She left Grace to see to his bath while she went back to strip his bed and turn the mattress before putting on the rubber sheet and then the linen. It felt as if she was moving through rapidly setting concrete as her anger came into focus on that fair young man. Simon Fitzgerald. An unlikely name. He'd most probably created it to go along with his externals as an actor. Was it some sort of pretense? she wondered, sighing. Having managed to turn the mattress, she paused before remaking the bed, amassing her energy, summoning up whatever she had of it to get her through this day. It was only just gone eleven; she'd never make it through to seven.

Smoothing out the rubber sheet, she found herself thinking again of years back when Miss Morgan had come here as a volunteer. At nineteen, Sarah had been privately fascinated and intrigued by the older woman. There'd been about Miss Morgan an aura of something like secret satisfaction. Obviously she'd been a very pretty girl, and had lovely features, along with hints of something that might have been passion glinting out from behind the correct gestures, the always-erect spine, the mannerisms undoubtedly acquired at a good school and in a good household. At the end, though, she'd suffered the ministrations of the staff, her vexation all too evident as she'd been stripped, changed, bathed, shifted, and generally handled. She'd borne the intrusions of their hands and eyes and privileged knowledge of her anatomy and bodily functions. Everything that had once been solely her domain had been turned public.

Margaret was right, she thought, tucking in the bedclothes. It was infinitely better that Miss Morgan had gone. Would she herself be allowed to die at an appropriate time, or would she, perhaps, evolve into a female version of Mr. Sinclair? A hen plucked of her feathers, left only with loose, crepey skin and an inane cackle. She'd prefer to die; she'd choose it.

She straightened, surveying the landscape of the bed, made neat once more, and took a second deep breath before returning to assist Grace in getting Mr. Sinclair out of the bath. He didn't want to come out and splashed about happily like a child—a grotesque, preposterous child. It both touched and terrified her. As she and Grace struggled to maneuver his cumbersome weight from the bath, she tried again to understand what it was that seemed to be happening to her. Never had she felt anything even slightly negative about the residents or about her position here. But in the past few days, all she'd felt was a steadily mounting fear and a recognition somehow of her own inevitable end. It alarmed her to such an extent that she found her thinking catapulted into any number of unusual, tangential directions. She thought, unexpectedly and upsettingly, of the surgery, and of having more.

She was certainly no longer a child, no longer quite so fearful of the pungent odor of anesthetic, or the sight of white-garbed figures floating at the periphery of her vision while she was positioned on a table prior to the administering of the anesthetic, from which she would awaken hours later in a state of heart-pounding panic and overwhelming pain. No, there'd be none of that, she reasoned. They called it "cosmetic surgery" these days. And it was a relatively short procedure. John had urged her for years to have it done and had finally given up in the face of her adamant refusal to subject herself to further torture. Her mind might never cease its recoiling at the clear memory of being fed intravenously until the cave of her mouth had healed sufficiently to allow her to swallow slowly small spoonfuls of tasteless mush. The interior landscape of her mouth had become entirely new and somewhat frightening with ridges of tissues and strange, slick areas. No more fissures that allowed food to return out through her nose. She'd relearned how to swallow, how to eat and to speak; she'd been taught like an infant how to shape hard and soft sounds. The echo of her own voice inside her skull had been alien to her ears, as if a small, improbable machine had been turned on and began playing someone else's voice against the roof of her newly reconstructed mouth. Her tongue something thick and all but useless, it had flopped and floundered about in her mouth like a beached fish, until she and her tongue had managed to become accustomed to each other and the sounds slowly began emerging recognizably, making sense not only to her—because, after all, she'd always understood what she'd been saying—but to those around her.

She tried hard not to think about the past; it always upset her. She hated having to face the details, remembered too well, and each time she was tempted—for whatever reason—to risk an encounter with all that, she forced herself away from it, dragging her mind back from the scenario like an exasperated parent with a reluctant child. Part of her, though, longed to settle quietly and re-examine the past in order to try to put it into some sort of viable perspective. But the rest of her was fearful of the disproportionate surging of emotions that attended these short-lived reviews. So, for the most part, she stayed well away.

Yet how, she wondered, might she appear to herself and to others with nothing more, say, than a tiny scar? Her fingertips traced along her upper lip, trying to conjure up an image of herself as relatively complete, only minutely flawed. Something so slight people might- n't even notice ... No. There was no point thinking about it.

She managed to get through the morning. And having seen to the trays for the non-ambulatory residents, she went along with Grace to have her midday meal. Sitting in the staff room with Grace and Mrs. Clayborne, the Friday volunteer, she compared, as she'd done countless times before, Mrs. Clayborne to the residents. A woman in her seventies, she was older than some of those she tended to, yet she appeared much younger and healthier, more alive. It was, in part, a matter of one's health, Sarah thought. Mrs. Clayborne not only had good health, she had an attitude, a certain special some- thing, that would never see her in a place like this. Small, good-humored, busy, she bustled through the place cheering every- one up. She wrote letters for some, or read to a small group in the lounge in an uncommonly appealing, beautifully modulated speak- ing voice. She was a small, full-breasted, slim-waisted woman who dressed and spoke well, with exquisitely tended hands and an uncan- ny aura of sexuality. Her white-gray hair was always superbly dressed and her face, even in repose, wore an expression of contentment.

How on earth did a woman in her seventies manage to transmit so much life?

I'd be like her if I could, Sarah thought admiringly, wishing she wasn't so colorless and fearful. But her several youthful attempts to venture out into the world had showed her in no uncertain terms where her place rightfully was: out of the public eye. Still, there was no harm in imagining herself as someone appealing, even sexually attractive. It was merely a dream after all, and harmless. Dreams were all she had, she admitted, and novels from the library, books about lives better lived than hers.

Her eyes moved to Grace. An angry-seeming, gaunt woman of amazing strength. Sarah had seen her single-handedly lift one of the heavier female residents from her bed and carry her to the bath. One might have thought Grace would handle these people with some of the anger and dissatisfaction permanently on display on her face. Yet she was gentle and almost masculine in the way she silently dealt with the residents, particularly the women. And they all seemed to know and accept that this was Grace's way. Perhaps her physical strength, gentle as it was, made itself felt to them and gave them a sense of safety. The majority of the residents plainly looked forward to Grace's daily arrival, depending upon her to get them started on their slow parade down the corridors with their walkers, or to shift them effortlessly from their beds into their pushchairs. Sarah had only ever heard her speak half a dozen times, aside from a barely audible "Good morning" or "Good evening." She'd seen Grace and Doreen, the cook, in whispered conversation together and knew the two women were friends, and that it had been Doreen who'd found Grace the job here. But what did they talk about? Sarah wondered. And what did Grace have to say when she decided it was time to speak?

Respectful of Grace's silence, Sarah had never attempted to encroach upon the woman's privacy by inviting her into conversation. She simply offered Good mornings and Good evenings and worked with her in almost total silence. There were reasons, Sarah was certain. People always had them for the ways in which they decided to deal with the world. If Grace chose not to speak, it was her right to maintain that, and Sarah could do no more than respect the woman's decision. Yet she did wonder about her, just as she wondered about Mrs. Clayborne, and about Margaret Evans — these women she saw every week of her life, and about whom she knew almost nothing. Were they possibly just waiting for an invitation? They might have a very real desire to talk about themselves, their lives. And it could be that Sarah, by her failure to show any overt interest, had done them a disservice. But how and where did one suddenly begin displaying an interest? It felt too late for that.

Arriving home to see the plumber's small van still parked outside, she let herself in and went up to check their progress. The new toilet was installed and looked oddly small sitting there, like a dwarf in a ballroom, she thought with a smile.

"We're just patching in the floorboards and we'll be done," the plumber told her as his mate carried an armload of the old, rotted floorboards down the stairs and out to the van. "I've a price for you on the bathroom," he said, handing her a folded paper. She unfolded it to see itemized amounts for the fixtures and an amount for labor. It was quite a lot of money and she stared at the figures for several moments, debating. There was more than enough in the bank to cover it: Uncle Arthur's insurance had brought five thousand pounds and he'd left her a cash settlement of almost eighteen hundred pounds more, all of this separate from her lifetime income of four thousand pounds a year.

"When could you start?" she asked. "And how long do you expect it will take?"

"Had a cancellation, as it happens. We could start early Monday and finish by Friday providing all goes to plan. You'll have to have a tiler in. I can recommend one," he offered.

"Yes," she agreed, feeling very bold. "I'd be most grateful if you'd make the arrangement and see to all of it."

"Right you are."

She left him and went to her room to open the wardrobe door. Staring at her meager collection of clothes, she tried to think what would be suitable for her evening out, becoming suddenly enraged at the drab, tasteless contents of the wardrobe. She ought to have had at least one pretty dress. Trembling with frustration, she looked at her wristwatch. Not yet five-thirty and it was Friday, late closing. If she hurried, she could go into town and buy something. But even hurrying, she'd never be able to get into town, shop for a dress, and be back by seven. She became angrier still, and depressed. At last she reached for the one good dress she owned, the black she'd bought for Uncle Arthur's funeral. It was the most expensive garment she'd ever had. Forty-five pounds. It was of a soft black wool with a round collar, tucks hand-sewn down the front, and long sleeves. She remembered the sales lady stopping her as Sarah was taking the dress in to try it on. She'd looked at the tag on the cuff, saying, "You're never a twelve, dear. Give me this and I'll fetch you an eight. I'm sure we still have the eight." And she'd returned with it, smiling as she'd stood watching a doubtful Sarah close herself into the changing room. But it had fitted, the way nothing she'd ever owned had. She removed it now from its hanger and laid it across the bed, forcing herself to disconnect the dress from the occasion for which it had been purchased. It was simply a dress, and because she'd worn it to a funeral didn't make it a garment only to be worn on solemn occasions.

She unearthed the pearl earrings and gold pin, setting them on top of the chest of drawers. She had quite a number of pieces of jewelry that had belonged to her mother, but wearing them always gave her a peculiar feeling of something very like claustrophobia. Nevertheless, she'd wear the earrings and the pin. Plain, unadorned black really would be too funereal.

Next, she looked at her shoes. There were the black patent Bally's that went with the dress. Worn once. They'd pinched her heels, and she regarded them with narrowed eyes, thinking how plain and old-maidish they looked. Black patent court shoes with sensible heels. She clenched her fists and held them against her chest, closing her eyes against the now overwhelming anger she felt at the unfairness and cruelty of this young man's "kindness." If one truly cared about people, she thought miserably, one didn't subject them to this type of agony. Why was he doing this to her? And why hadn't she said no?

Filled with dread, she went downstairs to put on the kettle. She'd have a cup of tea and a cigarette while the plumber and his mate finished upstairs. Then, when they were gone, she'd bathe and get ready. Perspiring heavily despite the freezing draft from the open front door, she stared at her hands while she waited for the kettle to come to the boil, holding them out in front of her to look first at the backs, then at the palms and lastly, closely, at her fingernails which were clipped off squarely so as not to scratch one of the residents inadvertently. Irritably, she reached for her cigarettes to cut short the inspection. No aspect of herself was satisfactory in the least. And his inviting her out to a meal was doing nothing more than compelling her to acknowledge, yet again, her glaring imperfections. She felt as if she hated him, that bright young man with his glowing features and his absurd golden curls.

▽

She didn't actually look half bad, he thought, relieved and pleased. The dress wasn't the most beautiful in the world but it was obviously a good one, even if it was too big. Better any day than the twin set and tweed skirt.

"You look smashing!" He complimented her and watched the color seep into her face, seeing her visibly battle against a desire to look away from him. Bloody painful it was, he thought, and felt sorry for her.

"Thank you," she said almost in a whisper.

"All set then?" he asked.

"I'll just get my coat." She went to the closet off the front hall to lift her navy blue coat from the hanger, and put it on thinking she looked precisely like a bruise, all blue and black, a walking bruise. She picked her handbag up from the hall table, remembered the keys, and then stood waiting to be told what to do.

"Let's go then," he said, extending his arm, indicating she should precede him out. What if he didn't close the door properly? But he shut it solidly so that the lock caught and she walked alongside him to his car, feeling so hollow inside that not only was she not hungry, she actually couldn't even think of eating as she automatically fastened the seat belt around her.

He did up his own belt, got the car started, then offered her a cigarette along with another smile, deciding to play it truthful. If he tried going at it like a proper date, they'd both have a rotten time.

"Nervous, eh?" He smiled at her. "Me, too. I don't do much of this."

Much of what? What did he mean? she wondered.

"I don't," she said slowly, "do any of it."

"How's that?" he asked, lighting her cigarette and then his own before turning to check the road and pulling away from the curb.

"Going out," she explained. "I don't."

"Not at all?" He glanced over at her.

"Not ever," she answered, her eyes fixed on the road ahead.

"Well," he said consideringly, "you've no cause to be nervous. I don't go about with women all that much."

"Sorry?" She looked over at him, confused.

"To tell the truth, I spend more time with the lads."

She still didn't understand what he was saying and sat examining his profile, wanting to believe him cruel but finding nothing about him to validate that.

"I'm what they call," he went on doggedly, "bisexual. But I fancy the lads a sight more than I do women."

"Oh!" She nodded, captivated. She'd read quite a lot about the sexual proclivities of all sorts of characters but had never dreamed of meeting someone who, from the sound of it, had actually made love to both men and women. "I've read about that," she said, losing some of her nervousness and reserve.

"Have you?"

"I read quite a lot, actually."

"What sort of things?"

"Novels, for the most part. I like novels."

"Romances, eh?" he teased.

"Some," she admitted. "But I prefer the more realistic sort. Do you read?"

"Masses. It's what got me interested in acting, reading."

"Yes," she said vaguely, then fell silent, trying to imagine what two men might do to one another in terms of lovemaking. Her only frames of reference were contained within the pages of novels she'd read and she hadn't read all that much about homosexuality. But that wasn't quite the same thing as bisexuality, she didn't think. She was becoming confused again.

Sensing her bewilderment, he said, "Think of me as a friend, not as a man."

"But you *are* a man. How could I possibly not think of you as one?" She was back to wishing she'd said no to this venture, and they'd only been together ten minutes.

"Do you think of yourself as a woman?" he asked, curious to know how she thought of herself.

"Of course, I ..." she began, then stopped. "Actually, I simply think of myself as me."

"And I think of myself as me. So there shouldn't be any problem, should there?"

"I suppose not," she answered, more mystified than before.

"How's the loo coming then?" he asked, switching subjects.

"It's done, but for the redecorating. They'll be starting the bathroom come Monday morning."

"Oh!"

"Installing all new fittings. And a shower. A heated towel rail, too."

"Very posh." He grinned encouragingly at her, finding her heart-breakingly shut away, locked in. "What's your job?" he asked.

"Not very interesting. I do nursing."

"Oh."

Another silence fell; this one lasted until they were coming into Stratford on the roundabout.

"Like Greek food?" he asked, navigating the roundabout, bearing to the left.

"I've never had it."

"Like lamb?"

"I do, yes."

"Like aubergines?"

"I've never had them."

"I think you'll like it," he said somewhat dispiritedly, seeing the evening gaping emptily ahead of him like a wasteland. "It's mostly lamb done up in different ways with vegetables, rice. Smashing sweets," he added enthusiastically. "Baklava. It's made with nuts and honey."

"Sounds very nice," she said politely, thinking she sounded like an elderly nanny, someone accustomed to being polite even in the face of wicked pranks.

The only way to deal with her, he decided, would be to keep her supplied with drink in the hope of loosening her, up. "I'm really not so frightening," he said, then exclaimed, "there's a bit of luck! A parking spot directly across from the restaurant." He put on his indicator and pulled over to allow another car to pass as he prepared to park.

How would *he* know what frightened her? she silently challenged him. He didn't know her.

As they were crossing the road, he turned to her, saying, "You're right tall, aren't you?"

"Yes."

"How tall?"

"Five feet nine inches."

"Crikey! Almost the same as me. I'm just two inches taller than you. But with those shoes on, eh"—he indicated her feet—"you're eye to bloody eye with me."

She had a sudden urge to strike him. She'd hit him and then find some way to get home. She could see herself doing it, then running off up the road. She kept grimly silent as he held open the restaurant door and they went inside to be met with wonderful aromas and a blanket of warm air that enveloped them so that at once she felt hungry and somewhat sleepy, too. He took her coat and draped it over the back of a vacant chair in the small lounge area before going over to make himself known to the hostess. Coming back to sit opposite Sarah, he smiled again, asking, "Will you have a drink?"

What to ask for? She couldn't very well order a shandy in a place like this, could she? And she was unfamiliar with drink, so she said the first thing that came to mind. "Whiskey?" It was something Uncle Arthur used to order.

"Neat?"

"With water, please."

He ordered whiskey for both of them. He hadn't suspected she'd be someone whose tastes ran to whiskey. You couldn't predict, could you? he thought.

While awaiting the drinks, she opened her bag to get out her cigarettes, took one from the pack and then, remembering the several of his she'd smoked, offered him one.

"No, thanks, luv. I'll smoke my own." With another smile he brought out a fresh pack of twenty Senior Service. "I find those too mild," he said of her Rothmans.

He relaxed in his chair, taking stock of her anew. She had more breast than he'd imagined and, for a few seconds, he saw her sitting across from him naked. It wasn't half bad and the surprising stirring he felt at this projected image turned him overheated. He was having very unpredictable reactions to her altogether.

"They have dancing later on," he told her as a girl brought their drinks. "You dance?"

She shook her head. For a moment, watching, he knew exactly how she'd looked as a little girl. "I'll teach you," he said cheerfully. "You'll like it."

She tasted the whiskey, a small sip that seared its way down to her stomach and left a not unpleasant aftertaste in her mouth. She liked drinking, liked the idea that she was sufficiently adult to take one if she cared to. She also liked the atmosphere of this place and admitted to herself that she did enjoy looking at this young man, even if he didn't make very much sense to her. Relaxing, feeling the festive atmosphere penetrating her defenses, she dared to smile at him. He responded with a smile of such dazzling intensity and brightness that her insides seemed to clutch in on themselves and she was all at once very aware of her breasts, and her thighs where they crossed, and her gently swinging foot. She felt, for the first time in her life, very female. And anticipatory. Wondering what would happen.

Five

THE FOOD WAS VERY GOOD AND AFTER A CINNAMON-FLAVORED MOUS-
saka and two glasses of whiskey and several of wine, she felt sufficiently freed from her inhibitions to tell him so.

"See!" He beamed. "You've got to trust my judgment. I wouldn't
bring you to some trucker's caff, would I now?"

"I don't know," she said giddily. "Would you?"

The old drink was going to her head, wasn't it? he thought, pleased
with himself and with her. He admired the shape of her eyes and
their deep blue, almost violet color. "You've got bloody beautiful
eyes," he said. "Did you know that?"

"I do?" Unaccustomed to compliments, she didn't know how to
respond.

"You bloody do."

Thinking of it, suddenly, as a game, she ventured to say, "You've
got a bloody beautiful face," then blushed bright red. In spite of it,
she said, "You do, truly."

Christ! he thought. She was a sweet old thing.

"How old are you, Sarah?" he asked, pouring more wine into their
glasses.

"Thirty-two. And you?"

"Thirty."

"Oh!" It bothered her, being older, but she was glad he wasn't as
young as she'd thought.

"Don't let it worry you," he said, as if reading her mind. "It doesn't
worry me none." In truth, he was surprised to learn she was so young.
He'd been convinced she was nearer forty-two.

Music started up and she turned in her seat to look at the musi-
cians, thoroughly overtaken now by the excitement generated by all
the drink, and the good food, and the fact of her being out in the
world with a young man. She was so overtaken, she managed to
completely forget herself and was quite eager to try dancing, positive
he was right, that she would, indeed, enjoy it. Watching several couples get up to walk out on to the small area cleared for dancing, she

studied the way they went into each other's arms, their smiles and the juxtaposing of their bodies, finding something perfectly congruent in all of it.

"Fancy giving it a try?" he asked, drawing her attention back to him.

She studied him now, taking in the details of his black suit and white, open-throated shirt. He really was very beautiful. She wondered, though, if the two of them mightn't strike the other patrons as a somber-looking pair, both of them being clad in black.

"Come on." he invited, getting up and holding his hand out to her. "It doesn't matter if you're good at it or not. It's a lark just to move about."

She couldn't say no and gave her hand into his, rising from her seat to walk with him to the dancing area where she stood awkwardly waiting again to be told what to do. But there was no telling. He took hold of her right hand, placed his left hand on her waist and, instinctively, she placed her left hand on his arm near the shoulder as she felt his hands directing her. Being touched by him threw her headlong back into confusion. Her feet shuffled without coordination.

"Don't be so stiff," he encouraged, his hand sliding farther around her waist, surprised at how much fabric there was between her and the dress. She was very slim, he discovered, her body lean-feeling under his hand. She wore no perfume, he noticed; there was only a faint scent of soap. Or was it shampoo? Her eyes were moving over the crowd and he took advantage of it to look at her mouth, wondering if it would feel odd to kiss her, to place his mouth on hers and touch his tongue to the pink, exposed satiny underside of her lip. It looked smooth, shiny. It couldn't, he thought, be all that complicated to have it fixed. Just unhook it, sort of, so it didn't pull up that way. She'd be pretty really, with it fixed.

She was moving gracelessly, holding herself rigid and he drew her closer, curious to get some sense of her breasts, and hoping to relax her. Perhaps because she was distracted or had had such a lot to drink, she didn't resist and came up against him, moving with less effort for several moments as if unaware of his having closed the distance between them. Moving his hand up her spine, his fingertips recognized the band of her brassiere as his chest came up against the lovely soft cushion of her breasts. He was quite happy, holding her unexpected fullness to him, until she seemed to suddenly snap back

into her awareness and held herself away from him, her head turning sharply to regard him almost angrily as she returned them to
their distances. It jarred him because he'd been growing nicely warm
and aroused because of her breasts. The softness did it every bloody
time. He just couldn't resist once he'd come into contact with it.

"Please don't!" she said angrily, uncertain why she felt such an
arbitrary and building sense of outrage.

As if he hadn't heard her, his hand left her spine and rose to touch
the ends of her hair. "Soft," he observed. "Lovely soft hair. Smells
nice, too."

"I think I'd like to sit down," she said, wanting him to remove his
hand from her hair, wanting to be safely away from him, at home in
her bed.

"Sorry, luv." He returned his hand to her spine and continued
directing her about in their small space, considering his ever-con-
tradictory desires. It was bloody unbelievable, he thought, that this
woman was awakening more than merely his curiosity.

"Please, could we sit down?" she repeated, positive everyone was
looking at them.

"Oh, sorry, luv." Keeping hold of her hand, he led her back to the
table where he asked, "More wine?"

"I think not, thank you." She hoped he wasn't going to drink too
much. They might be stopped and he'd never pass a breathalyzer
test.

"You don't have to worry," he said. "I'm not going to get drunk. You
seem to worry such a lot," he said, his face very open. "Why?"

She didn't know how to answer that, so said nothing and lit another cigarette instead, then turned to look around at the tables nearby,
noticing a young woman staring fixedly at Simon. Sarah had to look
at him again, recognizing his appeal. Young women would stare at
him. And that young woman in particular had to be wondering what
he was doing here with Sarah. She lowered her eyes to the tabletop.
It felt late, hours past her bedtime. At least she didn't have to work
tomorrow morning. She'd asked Margaret if it would be all right if
she came in in the afternoon instead.

"You grew up in London," he said. "Where?"

"Mayfair," she said automatically.

"Mayfair, eh?" He'd been right. There was money there. "How'd
you come to live here, then?"

"I think I will have some more wine, please."

"Right-o." He refilled her glass, but left his own empty.

She lifted her glass, debating, then thought, What does it matter? and said, "My mother was killed in an air raid when I was seven. My father died abroad, in the army. The only relative who'd have me was Uncle Arthur. The others …"

"Go on, luv."

"My mother had a sister, and Uncle Arthur was the oldest brother. My father had two sisters. But Uncle Arthur was the only one who … wanted me. So, he took me in and I came to live here."

"What happened?" he asked quietly.

"What do you mean, 'what happened?'"

"Tell me about it."

She shook her head, her eyes filling; she felt quite dizzy, disoriented.

"Had a bad time of it, didn't you?" he said softly, touching her hand.

She looked at his hand touching against hers and wanted to weep loudly at the contact. She could almost hear herself emitting loud barking sobs. He really was being very kind, and she was so unused to it she didn't know how to react.

"They *hated* me," she whispered, then held the cigarette to the good side of her mouth to draw hard on it. "She told everyone her baby had died. No one had any idea there was a child in the house. If she hadn't died, I'd have spent my entire life locked up in that room." She had to stop; her chest was starting to heave with the pressure of all the memories rushing back to her.

"*Locked up in a room?* What d'you mean, Sarah?"

"I can't," she whispered so softly that she didn't hear herself, could only feel her lips moving. "I'm sorry. I really can't. Please, I'd like to go home now."

"All right, luv," he said soberly, impressed by the depths of her suddenly revealed unhappiness.

She was shivering as she fastened the seat belt. He saw and said. "I'll have the car warm in a tick. Sarah?" He put his arm on her arm. She didn't move or look up. "I'm sorry if I upset you. I didn't intend to."

"I know that," she said thickly. "I upset myself."

He withdrew his hand and got the car headed out of town towards home. The night was very dark, moonless, and it gave her a strange feeling of isolation to be enclosed in the small car with this man, driving along. She wanted to talk, but couldn't think what to say, so remained quiet until he'd pulled up in front of the house and, all at once reluctant to have the evening end on such a poor note, she asked. "Would you like some coffee?"

"Spot on!" he said cheerily, giving her another of those radiant smiles as he turned off the engine and got his safety belt unhooked.

The house was very cold and she showed him into the lounge, turned on both bars of the electric fire, then said, "I'll just go put on the coffee."

He shrugged off his heavy jacket and sat on his haunches before the fire, warming his hands as he looked around the room. Dark bloody furniture, dark bloody walls. It could be a fine room, he thought, studying its gracious dimensions and the bays of windows at either end. A large, probably sunny, room. He peered around behind the electric fire to see that the fireplace, from the look of it, was functional. If it was up to him, he'd clear out the lot and start anew with some white paint and a decent bit of sunny yellow carpeting.

She returned carrying a tray with the coffee things and he jumped up to pull over a small table, taking the tray from her to set it down. Then, catching hold of her hand, he said, "If you fancy talking about it, it might do you good to get it said."

His hand was very warm, his expression sympathetic. And the effects of the drink were still upon her. She moistened her lower lip wanting to look away from his eyes and his sympathy, carefully extricating her hand in order to pour the coffee. "It's only instant," she said.

"That's fine." He accepted a cup from her and backed his way into one of the dusty armchairs, to watch her sit down and cross her legs, getting a decent viewing of them for the first time. Not half bloody bad, he thought, with nice knees.

Staring at the fire, she lit a cigarette and smoked while he sipped his coffee, watching her. Good hands and good legs, to boot, he thought. A nice nose, too; longish, but nice.

Her eyes remaining on the fire, she said, "I didn't set foot on pavement until I was seven years old. She didn't allow me out. I never saw grass, or other children, not even trees. I remember the first time, how strange it felt to be outside, walking on the pavement and thinking how hard it felt and how furious Mummy would be when she came home and discovered I wasn't there. But I think I knew, really, that she wasn't going to be coming back. And I was glad." She turned to look at him, her eyes hard with years of anger. "I was sorry about Daddy, though. I'd thought perhaps he'd come home and be other than I remembered him. I expect he'd have hated me too, though. They were both so *vain*!" she cried, her emotions threatening to get out of control. "It simply wasn't *on* that they should have a child who wasn't perfect. She was beautiful," she said dully, her eyes now fixed on him the way they'd been fixed on the fire. "Young and very beautiful. Wealthy, both of them. I'm sure it would have killed them to know that most of what they left would go on my surgery, my stays in hospital." Her eyes slid away from his back to the fire. "Almost every penny of it went on me," she said, wishing she could savor the irony of this, but she couldn't. "When the estate was finally cleared, Uncle Arthur needed most of the money to pay the bills for the surgeon, the hospital, the therapists, the tutors, and all. He was willing to pay for the additional surgery out of his own pocket but I refused. I didn't *want* any more. I thought I was past caring at that point."

"You 'thought'?"

"I don't know," she said, rather blankly, looking about for an ashtray. Finding one, she positioned it on her knee, then looked at him again. "I've never spoken of it. Not to anyone. I have no idea why I'm telling you."

"I asked you to, remember?"

"Who are you that I should tell you my secrets?"

"A friend," he said simply.

"A friend. I haven't any friends. I prefer it that way."

"Truthfully?"

"No, not truthfully. It's simply the way it's turned out." She sighed and turned the ashtray on her knee. "Why did you ask me out?"

"I don't know why," he admitted. "It was just an impulse, eh? I'm not sorry I did, though. Are you sorry you came?"

"I don't know. It's so tiring … talking, trying to think."

"That's because you're not used to it, are you?"

She looked up again saying, "Sorry. What did you say? I have a hearing problem."

"I said it's just because you're not used to it."

"Used to what?"

"To talking," he reminded her, half-smiling.

"Yes. That's right. I'm not." She studied his face, feeling terribly tired. "You think I'm mad," she accused. "Or perhaps you think you're being charitable."

"Neither one," he said comfortably. "I think I like you, that's all."

"You *like* me? What on earth is there for you to like about me?"

"Well, for one thing," he said, setting his cup and saucer on the floor to free his hands for a cigarette, "you're different, aren't you? And I was straight with you, telling you about myself."

"Yes, you were, weren't you? Is that something it's difficult for you to do?"

"It isn't easy. I mean, it's never easy having to explain yourself, is it?"

"No. No, it isn't."

"And," he pursued it, deciding the worst that could happen would be she'd toss him out on his ear, "you wouldn't be half bad, if you paid a bit of attention to yourself, did something with your hair, for starters. Some make-up and a few new clothes."

"Why should I?" she challenged, an excited thumping starting up in her chest.

"Why not?" he counter-challenged. "Why be just plain if you can be a smasher?"

"A *smasher?*" She began to laugh. "I'm hardly anyone's idea of a raving beauty." She wanted to hold on to the feeling of glee but it was already evaporating.

"How would *you* know? Probably never even look in the mirror, do you?"

"You're quite right. I don't."

"I like you," he said. "I'm enjoying talking with you this way."

"You make love with men," she said consideringly. "It's my understanding that men who do that prefer the company of other men."

"Yeah, but I'm not a hundred per cent, see? I'm more fifty-fifty. I fancy women, too."

"I've read about that," she said again. "I have actually."

"What about you?" he asked.

"What about me?"

"You haven't ever, have you?"

She should have been angry or embarrassed or shocked, she thought, but she wasn't. It seemed so dismal an admission. "No," she said. "But then who'd have me?"

"I would," he said in so low a voice that she missed it.

"Sorry?"

"Lots of lads would," he amended. "If you gave yourself half a chance."

"Rubbish! Some more coffee?"

"No, thanks. I'd better get along home now."

"Yes, of course." She returned the ashtray to the table alongside her untouched coffee and stood up as he pulled on his jacket, then walked with him to the front door. Her every action struck her as strange, new. Her hand on the latch, she asked, "Do you live alone?"

"That's right."

"Yes," she said, going vague again, as if confirming some undisclosed thought of her own. "I don't suppose you'd care to come on Sunday? To lunch?"

"What time?"

"You mean you would?"

"Sure."

"Well, one o'clock then."

"Smashing! One o'clock."

She opened the door and he moved to the threshold, then stopped and touched her hand where it held the latch open. "Thanks for coming out. It was good, wasn't it?"

She nodded, disconcerted. "Yes, it was. Thank you very much."

His hand left hers and he gave her a final smile. "Ta-ra, then."

"Yes. Goodnight."

They stood looking at each other for a moment, then he turned to go and she began closing the door. Halfway down the path, he turned back to wave and she waved him off before closing and bolting the door. Leaning against it, she listened to him drive off, feeling positively exhausted. Yet that excited thumping kept on in her chest.

Finally, she pushed away from the door and returned to the lounge to turn off the fire, then she carried the coffee things to the kitchen, checked to make sure the back door was securely fastened, and switched off the downstairs lights. She craved rest, but her head was so filled with thoughts and reactions she doubted whether she'd be able to sleep. I like you, he'd said. And he'd promised to come to Sunday lunch. She'd go to the butcher's in the morning and get a small roast. Something to look forward to.

She undressed and, in her slip stood holding her nightgown, remembering how he'd held her for those few moments on the dance floor. It had been a feeling so good and so satisfying she might have been content to remain close to him indefinitely. Until she'd remembered herself, and him, where they were, and the necessary distance between them. But still it had been such a superb feeling. There had been moments off and on throughout the entire evening when she hadn't felt a freak at all but simply female, a woman and aware as she'd never been of the parts of herself and a definite growing longing to know all sorts of things, to experience the potential of her femaleness.

"Oh rubbish!" she said aloud, shaking off the reverie. After all, he fancied men. And that was all right, even safe perhaps. A friend was infinitely preferable to the vast, desperate sameness of the scope of her days.

▽

He drove home feeling very chipper, as if he'd really accomplished something worthwhile. She was right intelligent, he thought, and interesting, too. But what was all that about being locked away? He'd have to ask her, once they got to know each other better. And maybe he could talk her into letting him have a go at her hair and some make-up, even into going shopping for some decent looking gear.

Hark at you, mate! He laughed. *Carrying on like a bleeding kid. Well, never mind, eh?* It was nice having someone to talk with. And he liked dancing; they'd go again sometime. Maybe practice up a bit at her place; he'd teach her some steps. When she'd relaxed, she hadn't been all that bad.

No bloody light yet, he found, groping his way up the stairs in the dark. Bloody landlord. Someone would break his bleeding neck falling down the stairs and it'd serve him bloody right if he found himself with a big bloody lawsuit on his hands, the miserable blighter, too cheap to put in a stinking light bulb.

Sunday lunch. He'd get a bottle of wine and some flowers. Do it up proper.

As he was brushing his teeth, he suddenly stopped, wondering why he was getting so het up over this woman. Unable to think of a reason, he shrugged, rinsed his mouth, and climbed into bed leaving the fire on. It'd run itself out past the two five-pence pieces he'd put in—the last of his shilling collection was gone—and keep the room warm until he fell asleep.

In the dark, with a cigarette, the room tinted a pleasant orange from the fire, he reviewed the evening, focusing on those few moments when he'd drawn her in and elatedly discovered the secret wealth of her breasts. Bloody wonderful creatures, soft women. If only they hadn't so many other daft damned ideas in their heads. But she wasn't like the others, was she? And realizing what he'd got her to admit, he felt an electric jolt. He'd actually got her to admit she was a virgin.

Christ! I've never done a virgin, he thought, feeling a little frightened at the prospect. Not a female virgin. He'd never actually done a lad either, come to think of it. Was them that did him. He'd bloody hated it, too, that part of it. The other was fine, beautiful. But that part of it, never. He always wondered did women feel the same way he did about letting somebody inside them? No, it wasn't the same, nowhere near the same. Still, he reasoned, it had to hurt, didn't it, if it was something you'd never done before? Had to. It stood to reason, he thought, and was intimidated by the idea of inflicting pain on anyone, anyone at all. He could never do that. There was no point even in thinking about it.

But those lovely breasts, and the soft curve of her hips. Christ! A virgin?

We'll be friends, he decided. *I fancy that. Friends.*

Six

THE PROSPECT OF HAVING SOMEONE COME TO VISIT PROMPTED HER TO go through the downstairs rooms hoovering and dusting, making an effort to brighten up the place. She succeeded only in confirming her opinion that the house was in dire need of redecorating and no amount of cleaning would remedy the basic lack of color and warmth. The dining room, unused for well over two years, was the dusty repository of odds and ends. Since she didn't feel she could invite the young man to partake of a Sunday lunch at the kitchen table, she went ahead and got the dining room ready as best she could, clearing an accumulation of books and old newspapers from the sideboard, bringing out the good china and silver to give them a wash and a polishing. Charged with energy, she was, however, defeated by the unrelenting darkness and bulk of the old furniture. It would all have to go, she decided once and for all. She'd go into town next weekend and see to ordering a few new things.

The roast in the oven, she flew upstairs to have one of her last baths in the old tub. As she scrubbed herself, she tried to picture the room as it would be after the renovation. She was much enamored of the idea of a shower, particularly for those evenings when she came in worn out from a day's work and didn't feel like waiting for a bath to run. Then, caught up in a burst of enthusiasm for change, she went wrapped in a towel to take a look at Uncle Arthur's room. Now was as good a time as any to make the transfer. Of course, she chided herself, she should have thought of it before her bath. Still, it was unlikely she'd get all that dirty simply changing the linen and moving her things from one room to another. Not bothering with underwear, she, buttoned on the old cotton dress she wore for the housework and changed the bed, then plugged in the electric blanket in readiness for the night: she'd only have to turn it on. In another few minutes she'd moved her clothes into the wardrobe Uncle Arthur had had built in years ago. Her few things looked quite lost hanging in there. The books were easily transported to the bedside table. Noticing she'd less than half an hour before Simon was due to arrive, she told herself she'd have to see to her chest of drawers later. It wouldn't do at all to have Simon come early and catch her flitting about in an old dress held closed with a safety pin, and no underwear.

On an outrageous impulse, she took off the dress and gazed at her naked image in the full-length mirror on the inside of the wardrobe door in an attempt to see herself the way, say, Simon might. Keeping her eyes carefully away from her face, she stepped closer to the mirror to study her shoulders and throat, then her breasts. Her eyes refused to go lower than her midriff. Absurd! she told herself, wondering none the less if her breasts didn't look altogether out of place on her thin frame. Big, silly looking things, she thought, venturing to lift them with her hands. Like monstrous swellings, they hung quite heavily. Suddenly repelled by the image of a skinny wretch of a woman holding her breasts forward like some sort of offerings, she literally ran from the mirror to collect her undergarments and quickly dressed, bending to enclose her breasts in the brassiere, relieved to have them properly hidden. As she pulled on the remainder of her clothes, there was a low buzzing in her ears, and a shocked monologue in her brain commented on the freakishness of her behavior. What on earth could she be thinking of touching herself that way in broad daylight, in full view of the windows? Anyone across the road, or passing below might have seen her. And as if, in fact, she'd been witnessed, she made her way, head down, to the kitchen to attend, considerably less than wholeheartedly, to the final preparations for the meal. On an objective level, she saw that her encounter with the mirror had made her aware of how much thinner she was than she'd been prior to Uncle Arthur's death. Her breasts were smaller than they'd been, which didn't upset her in the least. She'd always had horribly mixed feelings about having breasts at all. The fact that she now had less than before wasn't a loss. But her ribs showed, and her shoulder bones. And that did bother her, because she hadn't until that moment taken stock of how little concerned she usually was with food, with taking the trouble to prepare meals for herself. Often as not she didn't bother, but ate sandwiches or opened a tin of soup, or beans, or spaghetti. Now, here she was preparing an entire meal complete with broiled grapefruit halves for starters, and for dessert, a trifle far too large for only two people. But he was a good eater, she recollected. He'd eaten all those sandwiches that evening. And Friday, he'd managed to consume an impressive quantity of food.

Perhaps she hadn't made enough, she was thinking when his knock came at the front door.

He was disappointed to see her back in the old twin set and tweed skirt; he'd been hoping for some kind of minor miracle that would have, overnight, altered her view of herself. Stupid! he thought now, holding the flowers out to her as he came through the door. "Thought you might like these," he said. "Brought some wine, as well."

"How nice!" she said, looking and sounding as if she meant it. "They're so pretty." Forgetting to take his jacket, she went to the kitchen to find a vase and place the delicate freesias in water. They were hothouse grown surely, she thought, admiring their rich yellow as she carried the vase through to place it on the dining table.

He'd opened the cloakroom door and hung away his jacket, she saw, coming out of the dining room, and opened her mouth to apologize for her bad manners. But he said, "It's all right," as if he had again known what she'd been about to say, and smiled at her, his eyes hastily sliding over her breasts before going back to her eyes.

"Would you care for a glass of sherry, perhaps?" she asked, acting from the memory of her few experiences with hostesses.

"I don't think so, ta. I'll wait for the wine." He still had hold of the bottle and held it out to her, asking, "Have you room in your fridge?"

"Oh, I think so."

"Smells good," he said, following her into the kitchen, pulling out one of the chairs to sit down while she fitted the wine into the refrigerator then checked the roast in the oven and turned the potatoes.

"I hope it's good," she said, straightening to look at him, not knowing what to say or do next. He was so wonderful to look at: like a splendid painting by an old master, or a perfect sunny afternoon. She might happily have gazed at him forever, but that freakish something inside her suddenly cautioned her that beneath his clothing he was equipped in the selfsame fashion as every other man in the world and it was highly doubtful that he'd be a loose handful of near-weightless, shriveled flesh. The blood flew to her head in such a rush that it was quite painful.

"You're being nervous again," he said not unkindly. "I'm the same as I was Friday. There's no need for it."

"I've never entertained anyone on my own," she said, looking down at her hands where they sat folded together on top of the counter.

"I wouldn't risk entertaining anyone in my bloody bedsitter, that's for sure." He laughed, hoping to ease her.

Still serious, she asked, "Is it so awful, your place?"

"Yeah. Bloody awful. I could do better, I suppose. But I don't like to spend the money. I mean, I don't object to spending money if I've got it; it's just spending it for digs. You know?"

"No, actually."

"I'd rather spend it on clothes, or a good meal, or a gift for someone I like, than give it to some bloody negligent landlord."

"I see." She cleared her throat. "I've got the fire on in the lounge. We could go in there."

"I'm just as happy here, if it's all the same to you. I like a kitchen. Always warm, isn't it?"

"I suppose it is." Nonplused, she continued to stand on the far side of the counter, wishing she had some small measure of ability with people. She was as uncertain of him now as she'd been at the start of the week. Only a week, she thought, taken aback by the realization. Less than a week, just a few days. Yet he did seem familiar to her. "The roast will be done in another fifteen minutes or so," she said for want of anything better.

"Why not come and sit down?" he suggested, moving his chair around and reaching to pull a chair out for her.

She came from behind the counter, sat down, then at once got up and went for her cigarettes and an ashtray, collecting them from the top of the refrigerator. In the thin sunlight coming through the window, he thought her eyes seemed even bluer, deeper and darker. Her white-tipped eyelashes were so fair they were almost invisible. With a bit of mascara, he thought, her eyes'd be gorgeous, and he wished he'd stopped at the chemist's yesterday to pick up some bits and pieces of make-up. He sensed she'd let him do her over and his hands itched to apply a bit of color to her cheeks and lips.

"You're staring at me," she said hoarsely. "It makes me frightfully uncomfortable."

"Sorry." He lit a cigarette, unthinkingly continuing to stare at her. "I was just thinking how much I'd like to see you with some make-up."

"I wouldn't have the faintest idea what to do with it."

"Oh, I'd do it for you. I'm keen on doing make-up. Hair, too. Wouldn't half mind having a go at your hair."

Her hand rose to her hair while her eyes probed his. "Is it awful?" she asked. "Is it quite awful?"

"Not awful. It just *isn't*, is it?"

"Isn't what?"

"Isn't anything." He laughed softly so that she saw rather than heard the sound of it. "You're really kind of pretty," he said, "all things considered."

"All things considered," she repeated, knowing he meant her mouth, and automatically turned so that her left profile was presented to him.

"You oughtn't to do that," he said, putting his hand on her arm. "It don't bother me. I'm used to you now."

"It bothers *me*!" she said more hotly than she'd intended. "And *how* are you 'used' to me?"

Innocently, he said, "Just that I'm getting to know you. We're getting to know one another. Haven't you ever thought about how you only notice the strange sort of things about people until you've begun to know them and then, once you have, you don't even think about what's different or strange?"

"I'm strange-looking to you?" She could feel a pulsing in her throat.

"Nah. Didn't I just say you're pretty? Quite pretty."

"I think," she said slowly, "you're simply trying to be kind."

"I'm not!" He looked offended that she'd think so. "I'm only telling the truth."

"The roast must be done." She jumped up.

"I'll open the wine," he said, going after her around to the far side of the kitchen to get the wine from the refrigerator.

She was so involved in her thoughts and trepidations, she was completely unaware of him as she lifted the roast from the oven, set it down on top of the stove, and turned to reach for the ladle to spoon the potatoes out of the pan. They collided as he put the bottle on the counter and turned to ask her for a corkscrew. Trapped, with the oven open behind her, she was forced to bear his too-close presence and witness the slight narrowing of his eyes as he again scrutinized her face. Going with his impulse, he gave her a quick kiss on the mouth. It felt perfectly all right, he thought. You wouldn't notice the lip at all.

"What are you *doing*?" she cried, leaning away from him, franticaly turning to close the oven door and then confront him from the safe distance of the sink, breathing hard, her hands shaking and thighs trembling.

"Giving you a kiss, eh?" he said blithely. "Got a corkscrew, luv?"

"Top drawer of the sideboard," she answered mechanically, gaping at him as he breezed out to get it. He'd actually kissed her, put his mouth to hers, and seemed not in the least bothered by having done it. How could he stomach it? she wondered, caught between humiliation and astonishment. Obviously, he could deal with it very well indeed. He came back humming to himself—she failed to hear the sounds, but gathered from the movements of his lips and the rhythmical bobbing of his head that this was what he was doing—as he set to work uncorking the wine.

Unnerved, she fumbled the roast on to the platter and somehow got the vegetables into their various dishes, then carried the roast to the dining room with him following, the wine in one hand, a dish of vegetables in the other. Everything on the table, she stood surveying the array of food, asking, "Would you care to carve?"

"Me?" He gave her an amused smile. She was quickly learning that his smiles—like those of passing strangers—fell into a variety of categories. This one was indulgent and amused. "I'm bloody hopeless," he said. "Unless you don't mind having a joint or a bird hacked to bits."

"I'm not much better," she confessed. "Do please sit down and I'll get on with it."

"You sound like old Doctor John getting set for an op."

"Do you know him?" She looked over, the carving tools held mid-air.

"He tends my mum."

"He's ... was my doctor. Uncle Arthur's, too."

"Was he the one looked after you? You know?"

"Oh, no. Specialists. First in London and then, later, in Birmingham."

"What was done?" he asked, hoping she wouldn't decide to go getting upset again.

"The roof of one's mouth," she explained, cutting thin slices from the roast and setting them on his plate, "is formed by two plates, as it were, and the nasal septum all growing in together, joining. A cleft palate, which is what I had"—she glanced over again as she passed him the plate, then continued on with her schoolteacherish little lecture—"is the result of arrested closure taking place around the second month or so of fetal development. There are degrees and degrees, of course. Mine, evidently, was severe.

"When the infant is born it usually suffers from severe respiratory distress. Great difficulty breathing," she explained. "It also cannot swallow, you see, so any sort of nourishment given comes back out through the nose." She paused, laid down the carving tools, and slid into her seat.

"Go on," he said, passing her the sprouts.

"As I was given to understand," she said, watching him help himself to large quantities of the potatoes and the peas before passing the dishes over to her, "some surgery was done almost immediately following my birth. Temporary measures."

"And then?" he prompted, noticing she'd gone very stiff and was sitting well away from the back of her chair, her hands resting half-clenched either side of her plate.

"I had," she said, losing sight of what she'd been telling him, "constant ear infections, frightful pain in my ears. She kept insisting I was simply pretending, seeking attention. Several times she had a doctor in, medicines were prescribed, this and that. Apparently, she was told repeatedly that I needed additional corrective surgery. But she ... didn't have it done. She hoped I'd die, I believe. I do believe that."

He stared at her, trying to absorb all this.

"You don't believe me, do you?" she said quietly. "It sounds highly melodramatic and improbable. But it's all quite true, I assure you. I have a letter upstairs she wrote to Uncle Arthur telling him that the baby, sadly, hadn't survived the birth. I remember her. *Very* clearly. I remember her face horribly twisted, and her screaming at me as she slammed a tray of food down on the table in that room, and her cursing me as if I hadn't any wits at all and didn't understand what she was saying." Her eyes had locked on a point halfway between where he sat and the windows and, unblinking, she said, "I used to wonder what it was I'd done to make her hate me so. I tried desperately to make her *love* me," she nearly choked getting the word out. Emitting a startling bark of laughter, her eyes returned to his face and she said, "I was deformed and that simply wasn't good enough."

"I'm sorry," he said, his eyes on his heaped plate, his appetite dwindling fast. "I'm dead sorry."

"Why on earth are *you* sorry?" she asked without sarcasm. "None of it's to do with you."

"It's to do with me," he said simply, "'cause now I know you, don't I? And I like you. We're friends. So naturally I'm sorry you've had such a lot of unpleasantness."

He meant it! she thought, stunned, her anger defused. He really did mean what he was saying.

"I've put you off your meal," she said guiltily, without appetite looking down at her own plate.

"I'll get to it in a minute or two," he said, summoning up the thinnest yet of his smiles. "Takes a lot to put me right the way off my food."

"I keep having the feeling you're … making light of me somehow. Seriously now, why ever would you give a damn one way or another what had or hadn't happened to me?"

"You're different now than you were when you came round to the garage a few days back."

"I'm always different out there." She waved her hand towards the curtained windows. "But this is my home. Here, I can be whatever way I choose."

He nodded. "That makes sense, I suppose. I'll tell you what." He picked up his knife and fork and began cutting his meat. "After we've done in here, I'll help you clear, then we'll cut your hair."

"We'll *cut* my *hair?*"

"I'm bloody good at it," he said around a mouthful of food. "This is smashing! Delicious!"

"Thank you. Are you in the habit of going around cutting women's hair?"

"Not a habit exactly. It's just something I fancy doing now and then. Give it a try, why don't you? Bet you a fiver you like the way it comes out."

"I think not. But thank you all the same."

"All right." He shrugged with equanimity. "You're welcome to change your mind, though."

She ate a few bites and was on the verge of relaxing her guard when he said, "Why don't you have it fixed if it bothers you such a lot?"

Slowly she put down her knife and fork, then laced her fingers together in her lap, saying, "I'd be grateful if you'd change the subject. I really don't care to discuss it. I shouldn't have said anything, but you did ask."

"Look, luv, I'm sorry if I upset you. But a lot upsets you, doesn't it?"

"Yes. Almost everything, actually."

"Makes it bloody difficult to talk to you."

"*I'm* sorry if that's the case. I'm unaccustomed to … any of this."

"See, you're worrying too much again. Nothing's all that important really."

"*Everything,*" she disagreed, "is that important. We have different considerations, you and I."

"Oh, I don't know. I don't see as how they're all so different. But listen." He lowered his voice so that the rest of his words were lost to her.

"Sorry? I didn't hear."

"I said, if you want me to bugger off, I'll go."

"Bugger off? You mean leave?"

"Right."

"You wish to leave?"

"I'm *asking* if you *want* me to."

Her hands unknotted and she moved them back to her knife and fork. "I don't want that," she said, trying to get herself to pick up the utensils, but her hands were refusing. It had all turned horribly wrong and she hadn't any idea how to turn it right again. She could only think how hopeless she was; she hadn't the remotest idea how to deal with the most ordinary situations.

Seeing her distress, he said, "Maybe I really should go. I'm nervous now about what it's safe to say, and you're worried about that, too, aren't you?"

She got up so quickly she upset the chair in her rush to leave the room. She flew into the kitchen, but felt trapped the instant she was inside, so continued out through the back door to stand in the cold thinking he'd invaded her life. He'd inveigled an invitation from her and she'd given it; now she was caught up in her tangled thoughts and thoroughly undignified behavior, and couldn't see any way to extricate herself save by asking him, yes, please, to leave.

"You crying, luv?" he asked softly from behind her.

Barely hearing him, she shook her head, and turned to face him.

"It's bloody freezing out here," he said, his eyes gone sad. "Why don't you come back inside?"

"In a moment."

He thought she looked altogether too frail standing out there, her hands hanging limply by her sides, her expression so distraught and confused, her eyes so bloody enormous that, again, he had that strong intimation of how she'd looked as a child.

"Look." He stepped down to stand near her. "I'm not taking the mickey or any of that. I know I'm curious. Always have been. Mum was forever giving me one across the ear for being where I wasn't supposed to be, looking where I wasn't supposed to look. I didn't mean you no harm. Now the meal's gone cold, and here we are standing out in the bloody cold and I don't even know why except that I asked you some questions you didn't like to answer. Couldn't we go back indoors?" He reached to take hold of her hand, finding it cold and unresponsive, but she didn't resist and allowed him to direct her back into the kitchen. He closed the door and then, feeling sorry for both of them, he put his arms around her and rested his head on her shoulder. Who was comforting whom? he wondered. Here he'd gone ahead thinking to give her a hug and cheer her up, and it was he who felt the comfort while she remained wooden, her arms still hanging at her sides.

She was so astounded by his presuming to embrace her, by his size and feel, and the scent of his hair and skin, that she simply couldn't move. For a few moments, she felt so deeply moved by him, by his earnest efforts to be understanding and to make sense of her, that she wanted somehow to contain him inside her so that for the rest of her life she might retain and savor his warmth and bewildering presence.

Realizing his gesture was having no effect, he lifted his head, keeping his arms loosely around her, and said, "Come on, luv. Let's cheer each other up. We'll go upstairs and cut your hair. Or"— he looked across at the far side of the room —"if you'd rather, we can do it down here."

To his amazement, she said, "All right. If you're so keen. Why not?" Her voice was deeper and softer than before; the words flowed with what sounded like greater ease. "Why the bloody hell not!"

"Scissors," he said, removing his arms from around her so that she was aware of how cold she was. "Got a pair?"

"Upstairs. I expect it really would be more sensible to do it in the bathroom."

"Tell you what," he said, back to being eager again. "You go get the scissors and I'll put the food back in the oven to keep warm."

"As you like." She left him there and went upstairs to get the scissors from the medicine chest, then brought a chair from the spare bedroom into the bathroom before fetching a towel from the airing cupboard.

She stood behind the chair and listened to him come up the stairs, waiting for him to appear in the doorway. When he did, he gave her one of his most enthusiastic smiles and unbuttoned his cuffs, then pushed up his sleeves.

"We'd best wash it first," he said.

"Wash it?"

"Right. We'll bring the chair over by the sink here and you can sit while I do it."

"You're going to wash my hair?" She sounded, she thought, like a fool, a simple-minded fool.

"Where's your shampoo, all that lot?"

Fascinated by the way things were going, she got out the shampoo and the rinsing glass and set them on the rim of the basin, then stood back to hear his further instructions.

"You'll get your gear all wet." He indicated her twin set.

She looked down at herself. "Shall I take them off?"

That stopped him. He'd imagined she'd be morbidly shy and here she was offering to take off her jumpers. "Well," he said, unsure, "it would be better, but ..."

He preferred to make love to men, she told herself. Could that be possible? She was curious, and felt both imperiled and yet totally safe. He wasn't interested in her, she thought, and unbuttoned her cardigan, removed it, and laid it over the back of the chair. How dangerous could this be? she asked herself, pulling the jumper off over her head and setting it on top of the cardigan.

"Well, all right then," he said, trying not to look but failing. A quick glimpse of white underwear, very white skin, then he shifted his eyes as he moved the chair over by the sink. "Come and sit down then," he said. She came and sat watching him with those large blue eyes as he got the basin filled then reached for the rinsing glass. She leaned forward and bent her head and he experienced a moment of exquisite satisfaction in lifting the hair away from the nape of her neck, revealing the soft, downy flesh there. He longed to rest his cheek against the back of her neck, touch his lips to it.

It was, she decided, the most pleasant experience she'd ever had, having his hands lathering her hair and massaging her scalp. She ignored the discomfort of her position and the hardness of the basin rim pressing into her upper chest.

"Hair like a baby's," he murmured, running fresh water to rinse her hair, relishing its fine silken texture in his hands. All the soap out, he reached for the towel. "You can sit up now," he told her, and vigorously rubbed her hair, then whipped away the towel to find her smiling. "Liked that, did you?"

"I did, yes."

"Just you wait," he promised. "It'll be smashing." Fastening a dry towel around her neck, he drew the comb through her hair, then picked up the scissors.

There were moments when his face came so close to hers she could feel his breath striking lightly against her cheek, her neck, and she felt suspended, like someone in a dream, perhaps, or a coma. It was an intimacy she'd never known. His approving comments whispered aloud to himself, his nods and sudden smiles brought her a new sense of herself as someone indeed possessed of potential. Here he was, proving it. When he stepped away finally, saying, "That's it, then!" and shook his head before removing the towel from around her neck, she felt both disappointed that it was over, and expectant.

"Have a look! Go on!"

She got up, touching her hand to the back of her hair. Short, very short. She approached the mirror with sudden misgivings. It was very likely the end of the marvelous closeness they'd shared for the past half hour or so.

"Well?" he asked. "What d'you think? Like it?"

"I don't know," she answered, trying to familiarize herself with the image in the mirror: a face framed by short hair. "You've given me a kind of urchin look," she said, feeling her mouth readying itself to smile.

"Some softness around your face. *Do* you like it?"

"I think I do, actually. I'm going to have to get used to it."

"Here, you've got hair all over." He began dusting snippets from her shoulders with his fingertips, his hand craving the feel of her carefully contained breasts. His open hand came flatly to rest for a moment at the edge of the concealing slip. Her eyes widened, attaching themselves apprehensively to his. Was the safety she'd been feeling completely illusory? she wondered, her breath stopping for a few seconds. Then he laughed jubilantly and tapped her lightly on the tip of her nose with his forefinger, saying, "Talc'll do the trick. Got any?"

"Somewhere." She looked around, a little lost, her breathing starting up again.

"I'll go down and get the food back out of the oven. Hungry now?"

She'd turned again to the mirror; her hand tentatively touched the side of her hair.

"Hungry now?" he asked again, more loudly, thinking he'd better get out of there that instant before he did something else, made a move and spoiled everything.

"I am, yes."

"Right-o. I'll get the food. Hurry up!" he called, skipping away down the stairs, thinking he'd known it'd be great. He'd get some make-up at the chemist's and they'd do her up next.

She reached for her jumper, realizing as she did, that it was the first time ever she'd looked into a mirror and failed to see only her deformed mouth.

Seven

On the run, Margaret told Sarah, "We've got two new ones coming in today. A woman who'll be taking over Morgan's place, and one who'll go in with Elgon and Swan."

"What sort of condition?" Sarah asked.

"One's ambulatory, late sixties, cardiac. The other's a partial, mid-seventies, arteriosclerosis. Short-term, both of them." Short-term was Margaret's idiosyncratic way of saying that neither of the women was expected to last longer than three months. "I'll go ahead and see to Morgan's replacement, if you'll see to the other ..."

"Which one will be going in with Elgon and Swan?"

"Let's put the partial in there and the ambulatory in with Spencer and Whittaker, Morgan's old place. The ages are a good fit that way, I think."

Margaret went on her way up to the first floor where the ambulatory residents were housed, and Sarah continued down the corridor to the non-ambulatory wing. She was performing on an automatic level, her mind reluctant to involve itself in these routine chores. She was anxious to examine every aspect of her extraordinary weekend, and disappointed that Margaret hadn't had anything more to say about Sarah's new haircut than, "There's a change for the better."

As she made up the bed for the new resident, she cautioned herself against becoming infected by Simon's tendency towards over-enthusiasm. She could see how effortlessly one might slide along into a kind of feckless optimism under his influence, thereby blinding one's self to life's less salubrious aspects.

But an embrace and a kiss, two meals taken together, and the haircutting in the bathroom all constituted quite a few very intimate moments. She felt as if she'd been very hungry and had asked simply for bread, to be given not merely just a bite or two, but loaves and loaves of it, far more than she could ever possibly consume before it all turned hard and stale and inedible. It seemed, from novels she'd read recently, that people went out with a lovehunger and glutted themselves on the first go-round so that, ever after, their appetites were jaded and not quite healthy. More and more marriages seemed to be ending in divorce and surely that had to be a direct result of setting one's expectations and sights so high that one was never capable of achieving any sort of satisfaction at all because nothing would do, nothing quite reached those lofty expectations.

And some of it, she thought, had to do with everything being so incredibly *accessible*. The invitation of women seemed implicit in their clothes and the lacquered piles of their hair, their glistening red mouths, and their lazy gestures. She didn't condemn; she simply wondered if it all wasn't too easy.

She'd have to take care to keep her wits about her, she thought, as she went about the day's tasks. She'd have to take care not to be unduly influenced by Simon's declarations or intentions, or easily misunderstood acts. And yet she did wish he'd said he'd ring her during the week, or that he'd thought to invite her out again for the following weekend. But he hadn't. He'd touched her hand before leaving and thanked her for the meal and for allowing him to cut her hair. "Ta-ra then," he'd said, and gone off.

Ah well, she told herself, it wasn't likely he'd come round again, considering how poorly she'd behaved. But it was something very nice that she'd remember—a totally unexpected bit of pleasantness. She'd tasted Greek food, and danced, and been kissed on the mouth; she'd had a man into her home. That was a lot, really. Certainly more than she'd ever hoped might happen to her.

Mid-morning, Margaret summoned her to see to the settling in of one of the new arrivals and Sarah made her way to the main entry to see Simon holding on to the hand of a small, still-pretty woman in a pushchair. To be perfectly fair, she thought, he seemed equally surprised to see her.

Breaking into one of his most engaging smiles, he exclaimed, "Here! This is a surprise, isn't it?" To his mother, he said, "This here's my friend, Sarah. This here's my mum," he told Sarah. The two women looked at each other with curiosity.

Thrown, Sarah moved to the rear of the pushchair, then, on second thoughts, stopped to ask Mrs. Fitzgerald if she mightn't prefer to walk to her room.

"I'd be glad to get shot of this," Mrs. Fitzgerald said spiritedly, getting up to cast a disdainful glance at the pushchair. "You go along then, Simon, luv," she told her son. "I'll be fine now."

"Well, all right, then, Mum." He looked doubtful as he kissed her cheek. "You'll look after her, won't you?" he asked Sarah, who responded with the usual politely assuring lines addressed to the relatives of residents. Her arm around Mrs. Fitzgerald's shoulders, she turned to direct the woman down the corridor towards the lift.

"See you Sunday then, Mum," Simon called out after them. "Ta-ra, Sarah."

She had the queerest feeling being in charge of Simon's mother, as if far more had been entrusted to her than just another aged resident.

"How d'you know Simon then?" Mrs. Fitzgerald asked, looking up at her.

"From the garage. He did some work on my motor."

"Oh?"

"What do you prefer to be called?" Sarah asked, her hand aware of the prominence of the bones in the woman's shoulders. As always, she was somewhat defeated and more than a little cowed by the fragility of these people, and how easily their bones could be broken, how subject they were to so many ailments. Hypothermia was the primary concern of the residence, which was why the building was maintained year round at seventy-five degrees.

"Lizzie's what they've always called me," the woman answered.

"Lizzie," Sarah repeated, aware that Mrs. Fitzgerald was staring at her mouth.

"Had an aunt years ago with a lip like that," she said bluntly. "Didn't talk so well as you do, though."

"No?" Sarah liked her for her directness.

"Not at all. Aunt Grace. She spent her life with her hand over her mouth, she did. The thing of it was, though, it was both sides of her mouth. Looked right dreadful, she did. Whatever do you think of *that?*"

"It happens."

"Does it now? Is that a fact?"

"It's rather uncommon, but it does happen. Here we are." She led Lizzie into the large sunny room where Miss Spencer and Mrs. Whittaker were preparing for their afternoon lie-down. "This is Mrs. Fitzgerald," Sarah introduced her. The two women came over smiling, eager to welcome a new face. "I'll leave you to settle in, Lizzie," Sarah said, knowing the two women would do an infinitely better job making her feel comfortable than Sarah ever could. It had to do

with her being considered too young to be credited with compre-
hending the special problems, the particular losses and gains these
people had sustained to arrive at this point. "Tea's at four," she said,
depositing Lizzie's suitcase on the bed. "If you've any problems at all,
ring, and someone will come."

"You're here every day, are you?" Lizzie asked, thinking what a nice
girl she was, and so kind.

"Sarah's here right enough," Miss Spencer said, capturing Lizzie's
attention. "You'll see plenty of her. Have you come from home or
from hospital?" she asked, anxious to hear all the medical details.
One could learn such a lot, hearing what the newcomers were
plagued with.

For her part, Lizzie was keen on getting the gen about this Sarah,
as well as about this place. Turning to answer Miss Spencer's questions, her eyes remained on Sarah as she moved towards the door.
As Sarah disappeared into the hallway, Lizzie said, "Ever so nice,
isn't she?"

"Oh yes, ever so," Miss Spencer agreed quickly, then asked again if
Lizzie was coming from home or from hospital.

Sarah went downstairs to the staff room for her belated mid-morning cup of tea and cigarette. She very much liked what she'd so far
seen of Simon's mother, and thought she must have been lovely as a
girl, with her red hair and green eyes. Simon looked like her, with
the same small pointed nose and shapely mouth. Perhaps he'd ring
this evening, she thought, now that it seemed they had something
to talk about.

He went off back to his job feeling easier about his mum being in the
residence now that he knew Sarah was there to look after her. It
seemed fitting somehow that Sarah should work at that place. He
had no idea why he thought this; it was just a sense of rightness he'd
had seeing her come striding down the corridor towards them. The
way she'd walked, and how she'd looked in her white overall had
impressed him. She'd seemed someone with a purpose and destina-
tion and he'd had an entirely new view of her. And he admired the
way she'd taken over with Mum, putting her at ease. He could tell
his mum had taken to her right off. He imagined they all did, the old
ones. She'd seemed so immediately caring.

He'd been right, too, about her hair. She looked tons better with it short. He made a mental note to stop by the chemist's and pick up a lipstick, mascara, and some eye shadow. He'd pop round that evening and talk her into letting him do her up. She was bound to let him, wasn't she, now that he'd done her hair. And maybe later on he'd go and fetch some fish and chips; they'd eat together and talk about his mum.

As he was about to run over to the chemist's, Beaconstead came out so say, "Here, Fitzgerald, there's a bloke on the blower for you. Make it sharpish like. You know I don't care for you lads getting calls here."

"Must be about Mum," he said, hurrying inside to the office to hear old Teller on the line from London saying, "You're bloody hard to get hold of, old darling. I've called round half the damned country trying to pin you down."

"Find me? What for?"

"I've got something for you. If it's not too late. I've already wasted all of Friday last trying to track you down."

"Something for me?" He felt suddenly hot and unable to breathe. Was it finally going to happen?

"I've got you an advert. Television. Three days filming."

"For me? It's a cert?"

"If you can get yourself down here straight away. The chap just wants a few words with you to satisfy himself you match up to your photos, that sort of nonsense. You know how it goes."

"I don't bloody *believe* it!" he exclaimed, already thinking of what he'd tell Beaconstead. Could he be straight with him? he wondered. *He wasn't a bad bloke. And the customers like me. I'll just be straight with him and tell him the truth.*

"Sixty for the three days," Teller went on. "As well, as expenses. They're shooting in Cornwall."

Barely able to contain his excitement, he asked, "What sort of advert?"

"Cadbury's chocolate. They're doing a series of costume adverts and the chap picked you straight off, says you're perfect for what they have in mind. If it goes well, he might decide to use you again." A warning note crept into his tone.

"It'll go well. What time am I to be down there?"

"Could you be here for four?"

He looked over at the clock. It was just coming up to one. He'd

have time to go home, shave, and throw on his good gear. If he
drove hard, he'd make it. "Your office?"

"That's right."

"Okay."

"Don't let me down now, will you? I held out for you, Simon, and
got him up on the money, too. Take it seriously, will you?"

"Don't you worry. I'll be there!"

He rang off and ran to catch Beaconstead just as he was climbing
into his car to go home for his meal. He always waited until after the
lads had had theirs.

"Listen!" Simon said, out of breath. "I've got a chance at an advert
on the telly. If I can be there this afternoon by four, I've got it. I can
be back here ready for work Friday morning. And whatever's not
done, I'll clear off over the weekend. I'll stay late Friday and come
in Saturday and Sunday, too, so's not to let anyone down."

"An advert on the telly?" Beaconstead began to smile. "You,
Simon?"

"Bloody fantastic, isn't it? I'm being straight with you 'cause I don't
want to … I just don't fancy lying, that's all. They want me there by
four this afternoon."

Beaconstead pushed back his sleeve to look at his watch, "You'll
have to get a move on then, won't you?"

"Beautiful!" Simon gave him an exultant smile, then tore off
towards his car. Beaconstead watched him go, a bit bewildered, yet
feeling something like reflected glory. The lad had himself an advert
on the telly, he thought, putting the car in gear. Wait until June
heard that! She was always going on about what a lovely-looking lad
he was. He was shaking his head as he reversed out into the road.

As he tore down the M-1, he couldn't help thinking Sarah had
brought him luck. After all this time, when he'd finally given it up
as a bad lot, to get an advert. The best possible bit of luck in the
world, an advert, because of the exposure. Everyone got to see your
face. It could be the start of all sorts of things, some real work, maybe
even parts on the telly or in films. All sorts of things. He flashed his
lights at a bloke dawdling in the fast lane and shot past at a hundred,
then swerved back into the center lane, easing down to ninety.
Overcome by excitement, he felt higher than he ever had, and felt,

too, something like love for Sarah because he believed she'd brought him luck. He'd get some good make-up for her while he was in London, and maybe a little gift.

As he was nearing the Watford turnoff, he suddenly realized he hadn't anywhere to stay the night, and ran down the list of people he knew, trying to think of who might put him up. Come the morning, he'd be on his way to Cornwall and the advert, if all went well. Old Teller'd be happy enough to put him up for the night. What the hell! he thought. It wouldn't kill him playing house for a night with old Teller.

▽

Without knowing she was going to do it, she returned home to ring the surgeon's office in Birmingham, and asked to speak with him.

"Who is calling?" she was asked.

She gave her name.

"Have you been to see doctor before?"

"I have, yes. But quite a long time ago."

"Hold on just a moment, would you, please?"

She sat holding the receiver to her ear with a wet hand. What was she doing? She suddenly wanted to ring off. But how could she when she'd already given her name? The voice came on the line again saying, "I have your file. Doctor's in surgery just now. Could I take a message or get him to ring you back?"

"Well, the thing is"—she wet her lips—"I wanted to have a word with him about … about the surgery. He did say I could have it done at any time, that it wasn't a terribly complicated procedure."

"If you'll leave your number, I'll have him ring you."

She rang off feeling dizzy and frightened, telling herself she was merely making enquiries. It wasn't something she *had* to do. Unsteadily, she got up to go and have a look at the bathroom, see what had been done.

The basin had been removed, the pipes capped off. Part of the floor was torn up. She wasn't going to be able to bathe for days. She hadn't given any thought to that at all and the very consideration of it now made her feel in need of a wash. She could, of course, use the facilities at Crossroads, but she disliked the idea of it—picturing the old women crowding in to stare at her while she tried to bathe.

Shaky, irritated, she made tea and some toast, but couldn't eat.

Back at Crossroads, she stood by the staff-room window with a cigarette while Grace and Doreen sat at the table holding a muted conversation Sarah heard none of. She felt shattered and tried to understand why it seemed as if her entire world—admittedly limited as it was—had been completely overturned, sent chaotic. It was Simon, of course; she'd allowed him in and now everything was changing. She'd have to discontinue seeing him. It was obviously too upsetting to her equilibrium to have him around.

Yet when the telephone rang that evening, she flew to answer, hoping it would be him, having forgotten completely about the doctor.

"Sarah? Dr. Naughton here. I understand you rang?"

"Oh. Yes, I did, actually. I wanted to talk to you …"

"You wish to have your mouth seen to. Good girl! I could see you on Thursday at three. Is that convenient?"

"Yes, all right," she said, feeling pressured into agreeing, and unduly frightened.

"I am glad you've decided, Sarah. There's really no need, in this day and age, to go about with something so easily corrected. A few days in hospital and you'll be off home. We'll discuss the details on Thursday."

He said good-bye, and rang off. She stood staring at the telephone, trembling. "No need," "so easily corrected," "a few days in hospital." She was terrified, unreasonably, irrationally terrified. Anything could happen. There'd be anesthetic. She might never regain consciousness, might die while he was performing his uncomplicated bit of surgical procedure. *Anything* might happen. She suddenly, desperately wished Simon would telephone. She wanted someone to talk to, someone to comfort her and make light of her fears.

She sat out the evening until the plumbers left, waiting, hoping he'd ring. Too distraught to eat or even to consider it, she waited. Finally, she bid goodnight to the plumbers, locked up after them, then wandered into the kitchen thinking she really should eat. She hadn't had anything since Sunday afternoon. But the thought of opening her mouth and putting food in, chewing and swallowing, enervated and sickened her. She wished she could lie down and never get up again. In the space of just a week, her life had managed to get completely out of her control. And she didn't know exactly how it had happened or even if she really wanted to resume control.

▽

I do owe him something after all, Simon told himself, his hand obliviously stroking Teller's hair as his face contorted with pleasure. The old dear really did have a talent for it. He thought of Sarah, then of his mum. He'd ring Crossroads in the morning, see if he couldn't have a word with Mum and maybe leave a message with her for Sarah, explaining. His hand went to the back of Teller's head, fingers tensing. *Christ! Brought me luck you did, Sarah.*

▽

Margaret said, "It's quite impossible. Couldn't you ring back later this afternoon when they're down in the lounge?"

"I won't be able to," Simon said.

"Could I give your mother some message?"

He didn't like the tone of her voice or the impatient way in which she was trying to get rid of him.

"Just tell her I rang, eh, to see how she was getting on."

"Of course."

Too bad, he thought, gathering up his gear. Teller was going to drive down with him to put in an appearance, then take the train back to London later. Overtaken again by elation, he told himself Sarah would understand. He'd pop over Friday if it wasn't too late, to tell her all about it, to tell her how she'd brought him his first bit of good luck.

"Just play it their way, won't you?" Teller said.

"Not to worry!" Simon gave him a smile. Poor old Teller, always worrying. "You're a bit like Sarah," he said, then had to tell him all about her.

▽

"We'll do a small graft," Dr. Naughton was explaining, "from the upper thigh."

"I see," she said, again wondering why Simon hadn't rung up or dropped in. Perhaps he'd been amusing himself after all, using her as a diversion.

"If we could get you in early on Saturday, we could prepare the graft, then perform the surgery on Sunday and have you home for Thursday. That way, you'd miss a fortnight's work all together. I understand how concerned you are about that. There'll be a bit of swelling and some soreness for a fortnight or so, but nothing to prevent you from going on about your business."

"Saturday?" she asked. "This next Saturday?"

"Why delay?" He leaned back in his chair. She thought he seemed little altered in the fifteen years since she'd last seen him, and she wondered how she must appear to him. Very old and very stupid, she thought. "If you wouldn't mind," he went on, "I'd like to take a photograph of you before you leave today, and then another following the surgery."

"Why?"

"For my records."

"Oh. All right."

"Sarah," he said, leaning towards her across the desk, "there's nothing to fear. It's my opinion that you've done yourself a great disservice delaying so long."

"Well, perhaps," she conceded. "But I couldn't, you see."

"I understand."

Did he? she wondered. "It's just that it all … alarms me. The needles and the anesthetic, being in hospital. I become afraid I'll never come out again."

"I assure you you'll come out again." He smiled. "Perhaps sooner than you'll care to."

What did that mean? she wondered, watching him get up and walk around from behind his desk. He put his arm around her shoulders as he directed her into a small anteroom where he positioned her on a high stool in a very bright light and took her photograph.

She was so patently nervous he felt sorry for her, and knew he'd done absolutely the right thing in going ahead and arranging a room for her in hospital, getting a time set for the operation. Had he waited, he doubted whether she'd have come back for a second consultation. This way, he'd taken the choice out of her hands. He saw her to the door saying, "Saturday morning. Try to be in by nine. Will you be able to manage that?"

Swallowing hard, feeling too vulnerable and deeply afraid, she nodded. "I'll manage it," she said and left to go, shivering, out to her car. She felt condemned, terminal, and sensed she was about to make a further, irrevocable change to her life. She was doubtful of her ability to deal with all the changes there were bound to be, knowing she'd shaped her life, her days around her so-visible flaw, using her mouth as a kind of protective armor to shield and insulate her from the world. With the flaw removed, there'd be an entirely new set of problems to contend with. At that moment, she didn't feel she had either the courage or the energy to cope, and allocated the blame to Simon: for having come smiling into her life and forcing her out of her safe hiding and into the undoubtedly dangerous and dimensionless unfamiliarity of caring for a specific someone. It could no longer be the amorphous benignity of caring for a group of unlikely surrogate mothers and fathers. She'd been safe and comfortably cushioned in that, but he'd brought himself into her life like a mirror, to reflect the drab emptiness of the nest she'd created.

Back home, she sat before the fire in the lounge slowly going through the pages of the album her parents had kept throughout the first three years of their marriage, at once relocating her pain at the sight of the one slightly out of focus snap of her pregnant mother. This photograph was the only evidence of Sarah's presence in their lives. There was one additional photograph after it and then the record ended. A dozen or so blank pages remained, along with a half-empty packet of gold-foil corners that might have been used to contain further documentation of how their existence had been undone by the birth of their defective daughter.

She sat with the album folded open across her lap, gazing at the bars of the electric fire, wanting to cry but unable to do so. She closed the album, replaced it in the drawer of the desk where it lived from year to year, and went to prepare herself some eggs. She had to eat, she knew, or she'd be too weak to withstand the shock to her system the surgery was bound to be.

To her confusion and relief, she found herself noiselessly crying into her scrambled eggs. And, giving in to it, she ate the eggs and toast without tasting them, feeling free at the very least, as she'd told Simon, to do whatever she chose within the confines of this house. That much hadn't changed. But why hadn't he come back or telephoned?

Kindness, she again concluded. That damnable, treacherous kindness people played with so thoughtlessly, so recklessly, never considering how damaging their acts might be to the supposed beneficiaries. She wanted, as she had the night he'd taken her to Stratford, to hit him, to strike him just as hard as she could in order to illustrate graphically the extent of the turmoil his acts had created within her.

Instead, she cried some more, then drew the blinds across the kitchen windows and, shuddering with the cold, bathed at the sink.

$\triangledown$ $\triangledown$ $\triangledown$ $\triangledown$ $\triangledown$

Eight

By Friday evening the plumbers had finished and, encompassed by the four torn-up walls of the bathroom, the new shower/bath enclosure stood—awaiting tiling—along with the new basin and heated towel rail. It seemed unbelievable that the installation of these few things had managed to create such an impression of destruction. The shiny new fittings looked ludicrously out of place against the patched-over walls and large areas of exposed plaster, the dangling strips of old wallpaper. The tiler, it had been promised, was to come Monday in her absence. She'd left the plumber the house key to pass along to him.

Bathing in the new tub, she sat looking at the ravaged walls feeling oddly as she had as a small child, hiding behind the blackout curtains during the evenings, peeking out at the daily renewed devastation during the mornings. The room did look as if it had been blasted. Its new contents appeared temporary, ill-placed. She felt a depression so consuming it overwhelmed and displaced her fear of what the morning would bring.

Drying herself, she turned to watch the water sliding noiselessly away down the drain — unlike the old bath from which the water had rushed and chugged like an ancient train. She felt tired, deeply, achingly tired. And terribly old. Her bed, that large, still unfamiliar arena of her dreams, awaited her, warmed well in advance; she'd turned on the electric underblanket immediately upon arriving home. She craved sleep in order to obliterate her feeling of betrayal at Simon's absence and his failure to contact her. She felt betrayed, too, by what she considered her sudden, absurdly late-blossoming vanity.

What else could it be called, after all, but vanity? Why else, at thirty-two, was she going to all the trouble of having cosmetic surgery, if not for the sake of her hitherto undiscovered vanity? In the moment of partially exposing herself to Simon's eyes by removing some of her clothes, she'd been acknowledging the existence of her curiosity and desire, her previously suppressed longing to be touched and held and

treated in a sexual fashion. And what she'd now embarked upon, however mistakenly, was all towards that end. What good was it to lie to
herself about it?

Imbecile! she berated herself for thinking such idiotic rubbish. He
fancied men. He'd made quite a point of telling her that. And why
on earth should she, even for a moment, believe he'd want her?
Because he'd touched her several times, and kissed her once? Sheer
vain stupidity and ignorance! An aging spinster's concept of
romance.

In her nightgown she cleaned the bath, then rinsed out her stockings and pants, draped them over the heated towel rail to dry, turned
out the bathroom and landing lights and ran to slide into the warm
bed. She sighed deeply, luxuriously, before swallowing a sleeping
tablet. Then, with a cigarette, she lay staring at the ceiling, allowing
her thoughts to range off directionlessly. She imagined Simon coming to the front door, and the astonishment on his face at finding her
suddenly beautiful. *Beautiful!* She laughed loudly, briefly. Opening
the door to him. Opening her arms and legs to him. This thought
caused her several moments of pure anguish. That she could be so
influenced in her fantasizing by what she'd read in books struck her
as not only simple-minded, but alarming.

Yet something had made itself known to her in the course of her
somewhat drunken dinner that evening in Stratford. She'd studied
his lovely features and thought how wonderful it would be to have a
child, a child of his, with his same lightness and fine features and
glorious smile. In those few moments, she'd understood why women
chose to have children. She'd been able to see that the reasons were
numerous: someone to love unreservedly, someone to return—however, briefly—that love, someone to relieve the unending emptiness
of the days, someone to lend its mother credibility and accord her a
measure of public respect if for no other reason than because of her
body's capabilities. All of this was provided, of course, that the
mother was a married woman and not suspected of being a bit mad;
provided, too, there was a man who was willing to make an entrance
into the woman's body and place a child there. This final glimpse of
reality put a firm stop to her dreaming. It was one thing to furtively
touch herself in an attempted projection at simulated sensations, but
quite another to actually have a man view her naked and, finding
her reasonably acceptable, choose to indulge himself within the
confines of her body. She could readily sense how pleasurable it

might be. But the actual, more technical aspects of the act only distressed her. It had to be, novels notwithstanding, a messy, painful business at best, one it was most unlikely Simon was interested in performing with her.

She smoked out her cigarette and lit another, deciding that perhaps one sleeping tablet mightn't be sufficient, so she took a second. She rechecked the alarm clock several times before relaxing against the pillows, enjoying her cigarette, and waiting for the tablets to slow her system down, to dull her thoughts, and to take her away from herself.

▽

He loved every minute of it. The experience fully lived up to his expectations, and he reveled in the costume fittings, the make-up sessions, the attentions paid him by the crew and the director. So easy, so bloody easy. A lark, it was. And getting paid sixty quid on top of it was too much. He'd have done it for naught, he thought, delivering his lines, carefully handling the chocolate so the "Cadbury" part showed plainly. It was colder than bloody hell but the weather held good; the sun stayed out, and by the third afternoon, it was done. Lots of back-slapping and hand-shaking, swapping of telephone numbers. New mates. He'd spent the previous night with the camera man, and had had a smashing time of it altogether. He piled into the car convinced he'd be called back for a second advert. Hadn't the director as much as said they'd be in touch about another?

Back at the hotel he had a quick wash to get off the make-up, then rang Teller to thank him again and let him know he was on his way home. After a quick look-round to make sure he hadn't forgotten anything, he checked out, handed in the room key and ran out to the car, anxious to get going. A good six hours' driving ahead of him, at least. He'd ring Sarah first chance he got tomorrow, although he doubted he'd have a minute free what with three and a half days' work awaiting him. Still, he'd ring or go round and tell her about it—all but the bits about Teller and the cameraman. No point in telling too much. He had the strange feeling that none of this, his first professional experience, would be completely real until he'd told it to Sarah, and wondered why he thought that. Never mind, though. She'd enjoy hearing, he knew.

Just outside London, he stopped to have some bangers and chips at a Grenada stop on the M-1 and sat eating, thinking again how she'd taken off her things in the bathroom. Maybe she'd expected him to do something. Yet when he'd touched her ever so slightly, nowhere even near the breast, really, the way her eyes had gone wide had told him she hadn't been expecting anything. He didn't know what to make of her or of his continued thinking about her. But picturing her locked up in a room made his insides go tight and his jaw lock with rage at the idea that people could be so bloody rotten and cruel to a kid. He couldn't conceive of anyone being so purposely evil.

Back in the car, some miles on, he thought about her again and this time she was sitting naked on the chair in the bathroom. It gave him an erection which so surprised and distracted him that he had to think of something unpleasant in order to send himself down, and allow him to concentrate on his driving.

By the time he'd taken the A-426 turnoff he'd decided he wanted to make love to her. There was no logical explanation for it; he just wanted her. Wanting her, of course, presented him with the not inconsiderable problem of her virginity. He couldn't imagine forcing himself inside the body of a woman who'd never done it before. Still, he shrugged, things had a way of working out.

What attracted him, he thought, were those glimpses he kept having of her as a child, and also how she'd be if she took a bit of interest and got herself fixed up. She was smart, wasn't she, with that toff accent and the brainy way she talked, using all those big words. When he told her something—like about her hair that time—she didn't get all silly or angry the way a lot of women would but just asked him did he really think so. She was nice that way. And she took him seriously, didn't she, which was more than he could say for a lot of others. Bobby, for instance, and even old Teller sometimes, treated him as if he didn't have a bloody brain in his head. She wasn't like that. She was all kinds of ways, wasn't she? Like a kid sometimes, and other times like a teacher, the way she'd explained about how the mouth got formed and all that. She had nice-looking skin, lovely-looking skin, all silky-like on her shoulders and neck. She'd be like that all over.

▽

She was gliding smoothly into the dark envelope of sleep and wasn't sure if it really was a knocking at the front door, or a dream noise, or perhaps something out in the road. Never mind, she thought. Never mind. Whatever it was, her descent into this embracing peacefulness couldn't be interrupted.

▽

He worked until midnight on Thursday, then was run off his feet all the next morning. Midday, Beaconstead approached him to say, "Leave off with that lot and come home to lunch with me. I want to hear all about your advert."

It was quite a departure and, being incapable of refusing a well-meant invitation, Simon went along to sit at the kitchen table with the man and his wife, June, drumming up the energy to tell them about the filming while they ate beans on toast and drank watery orange squash. The two of them listened intently, nodding and smiling approvingly so that he warmed to it and threw himself wholeheartedly into the telling, pausing to praise Mrs. B's beans on toast—which he could well have done without, being all too reminiscent of his hungrier days in London.

In the afternoon, he worked extra hard, hoping to have Sunday afternoon free so that he could maybe invite Sarah out for a walk, or fetch something in from the Chinese takeaway. He worked until nine-thirty Friday evening, locked the place up and, still in his overalls, drove to her house knowing she'd most likely have gone to bed. The place was completely dark. Nevertheless, he felt unreasonably let down at getting no response to his knock. If she was asleep, he reasoned, he really didn't want to wake her. So, he gave it a quiet try, waited, then turned and went back to the car and drove to the local near his digs to have a slice of their liver patty—homemade and very tasty—and a couple of pints of bitter. Back at the bedsitter, he fed pennies into the ancient heater in the bathroom so he could have a bath and rid himself of the day's grime.

Saturday evening he tried again with the same result.

Sunday, he went to Crossroads to have tea with his mum, circuitously getting around to asking about Sarah only to have his mother inform him, "She's gone off for a fortnight. Didn't you know?" She told him with an almost proprietary air, as if her knowledge of Sarah's comings and goings was her personally privileged information.

"Oh yeah? Where's she gone to then?" he asked casually, unwittingly feeding his mother's recently acquired fondness for bits of gossip.

"Don't know," Lizzie admitted, somewhat peeved. Everyone was curious about where Sarah had gone off to, but no one seemed to know.

"Well," he said, discomfited, sensing something amiss. "How're you liking it here then, eh, Mum?"

"It's all right," she said, playing it down, and both of them knew it. "Lovely and warm, at least. You know I like a warm place. And we're to have a proper Christmas dinner, Simon, with *festivities*." She stressed the word, savoring its significance.

"Festivities, eh?" He grinned at her. "Dancing girls and all that lot, eh?"

"Go on!" She laughed, pleased, giving him a shove on the arm. "Such a tease, you are. Tell me all about your advert. When's it going to be on? Did they pay you a lot of money? We'll all watch for it, you know," she said proudly. His being in an advert had given her popularity quite a boost.

He told her about it, all the while wondering where Sarah could have gone, and if she'd really gone anywhere at all or had simply decided to take to herself for a fortnight, maybe seeing to the painting.

He drove past the house again after leaving his mother, only to find her car gone and the house locked up tight with an air of emptiness about it. Well, blow me! he thought, looking up at the windows. She'd really gone off. He went back to the car wondering guiltily if he'd had any part in her going off so suddenly. Had she gone on her own, or had someone gone with her? Nah! he thought. She didn't have any friends, did she? She'd said so. Which, all in all, made the idea of her going off alone somewhere seem altogether sad.

Why had he told her it was uncomplicated? Perhaps to his mind it was. But he hadn't warned her of the sensations she'd feel during the taking of the graft. Not pain—there wasn't any because they'd locally anaesthetized the area—but the sick horror of feeling blood running down her numbed thigh. She'd felt that, all right. Spread, draped, on an examining table, with her shaved leg bent up, she'd had to turn her head away thinking she'd faint if she actually had to see them shearing off the patch of skin. She'd listened to the murmured comment of the young doctor and the nurse while the doctor, a not very friendly stranger, had talked to the nurse about Sarah and Sarah's flesh as if she weren't human but simply a mass of problematical tissues lumped on the examining table. And the blood ran trickling down her thigh. He'd kept mopping, murmuring, talking through his teeth before finally asking the nurse for the jar—or whatever it was—and going on to complain about the stink of the liquid preservative. "Some new stuff, is it?" he'd asked the nurse, the two of them then engaging in a silly-sounding discussion of the liquid while he'd cleaned the area and bandaged it. But not thoroughly.

"You'll have a scar," he'd told her before going off and leaving her sitting stranded on the edge of the examining table, her eyes inexorably fused to the small, labeled bottle sitting awaiting collection. A sickly pale wafer of her flesh suspended in clear liquid. Could it possibly be of any use? she'd wondered. It hadn't looked like human flesh so much as some rare biological specimen worthy of scientific interest.

Upon being returned to the ward, she couldn't dispute the darkened streams of evidence staining her leg. She'd had to ask the sister on duty if it would be all right for her to go to the bathroom to clean her leg. The sister, heart-warmingly, had shaken her head saying, "I'll fetch a basin of warm water and get you cleaned up." What she'd really seemed to be saying was how shoddily the job had been done.

Well after the fact, her thigh pained her, as did her entire head. She felt as if she'd been struck full in the mouth by a brick, and gingerly touched the thick wrapping of gauze bandages, apprehensive of what might be revealed once they were removed. She sipped liquids cautiously through a glass straw inserted in the small hole left in the bandages for this purpose, heedful of Dr. Naughton's warnings not to move her lips if at all possible. He'd spoken of invisible sutures, and severed muscles, and other things that had barely penetrated the nauseating, foggy aftermath of the anesthetic.

Having relived fully the childhood terrors, she'd awakened from the surgery back behind her curtained-off area in the ward. A sister had come to give her an injection of something, had touched a gentle hand to her forehead and whispered, "You'll sleep again now, dear," then gone off. And she had slept again. She'd done little else her entire time so far in hospital.

Tomorrow morning, Dr. Naughton would be coming to remove the bandages and she was positive their removal was premature. Her mouth felt critically injured. Surely she couldn't be ready to leave; it seemed too soon, much too soon.

But after breakfast the next morning—hers consisting of lukewarm tea through the straw, and some juice, followed by something the sister assured her was a liquid nutritive that was foul-tasting and thick—Dr. Naughton was there, attended by a sister who carried a tray of forbidding scalpels and scissors: a gleaming array of surgical utensils. He cut away the bandages, then remained bent over, peering at Sarah closely so that she could see the pores in his face and the hairs in his nostrils. His hand on her chin turned her head slightly to this side, then that, his expression almost grave. Then straightening with a sigh, he said, "I'm most satisfied. Would you care to see?"

She whispered, "No," and he smiled, saying, "As you wish. I'd like to change the dressing on your thigh, see how that's coming along."

She lay back and closed her eyes while the hospital gown was lifted back over her belly. Tears sprang up as he unpeeled the tape, then applied something cool to the burned-feeling area.

"Coming along very nicely," he commented. "I'll use a small plaster. Keep it on another day or two, then let it have air." Lowering the gown, he indicated she should sit up and he perched on the side of the bed to talk to her. The sister went off with the tray so that they were alone within the curtained-off area.

"I've left you the mirror," he said diplomatically, having guessed she'd prefer to look at herself without benefit of observers. "You're going to have to try," he said softly but seriously, "to stop thinking of yourself as someone unsightly and disfigured. I know that's easier said than done. It's been a very long time, after all. But I'm confident you'll feel the bit of pain's been worthwhile in view of the results. I'll be expecting you in a month's time for an office visit, and another photograph for my records. Is there anything you'd care to ask me?"

"Is it all right now for me to ... use my mouth?"

"Just be mindful of the fact that the mending process is still going on. Much of the swelling and soreness should be gone in a few days. I'll see to it you've a prescription for painkillers, should you need them. Try to rest now. If there's any problem, ring me. Otherwise, once you're home, stay indoors and take things easily for the next week or so. I'd feel a good deal happier if you'd take a full fortnight's rest at home, but since you've made it clear that you won't, I won't push for it."

"Thank you," she said inadequately, feeling the pain with every slight movement of her lips.

"The difference," he said, standing up, "is formidable. I'm very pleased indeed. Enjoy it, Sarah." He disappeared through the curtains and she lay breathing with difficulty, after a time reaching for the mirror, holding it face down in her lap for several minutes as she listened to the other women on the ward chatting together. She lit a cigarette. The smoke stung and burned her entire mouth. She extinguished it, took a deep breath and held it while she picked up the mirror. Very swollen, but an ordinary looking mouth, like any-one else's but for two thin red lines of scar tissue he'd assured her would fade to nothing. She stared at herself for a long time, then put down the mirror and held both hands cupped over her mouth as if to protect it from her tears.

Every evening after work he stopped outside the house hoping she'd be there. And finally, that Friday when he pulled up, there were lights on. He was wildly excited as he ran up the path and knocked at the door, then waited, listening closely for sounds of movement inside.

She thought it was the painter who'd promised to start on the bathroom that evening and went downstairs to open the door, star-tled to find Simon standing there. His expectant smile going, his eyes widened as his mouth dropped open and he said softly, "You had it done. Christ! Is *that* where you were then?"

She nodded, her heartbeat erratic.

He shook his head, wet his lips, shook his head again, then said, "It's smashing, isn't it? Can I come inside?"

"I'm supposed to be resting," she said unconvincingly, wanting him both to go away and to come inside.

"I'll just stay a minute."

"All right." She stepped away from the door, feeling most precari-ously balanced as she went into the lounge and automatically bent to turn on the electric fire.

"Sorry about the gear," he said, indicating his overalls. "I came straight from my job. I've been by every night."

"Have you?" She looked up at him, surprised. This knowledge made her feel better at once.

"Have you eaten? D'you fancy something? Are you still recovering like?"

"I'm not hungry. I'm supposed to be resting," she said again.

"You're pissed off with me," he said, squatting by the fire and looking over at her. "What for?"

"I'm not at all," she lied, wondering why it was that his swearing never bothered her when anyone else's use of the same language would have offended her.

"Sure you are," he argued. "I know why." He understood suddenly. "It's 'cause I didn't ring you, or come round. I tried leaving a message. I mean, I thought I'd leave one with Mum. But I rang there, see, and the one who's in charge, you know her, the sergeant, I call her, she went on at me about how it was too early in the day, wasn't it, and couldn't I ring back later in the afternoon. But I couldn't because I got a part in an advert, Sarah. I actually got a job and I had to go down to Cornwall for three days to do the filming. *That's* why I didn't come round. Not because I didn't like you or didn't want to come. You thought I was blowin' air into my own sails, didn't you? Thought I was just larkin' about with you, making myself feel good. I wouldn't do that," he said unhappily, "I'd never."

"You got an acting job!" She wanted to smile, but felt, in advance, her facial muscles protesting. "How super!"

"Shall I make us some tea?" he offered hopefully.

"All right. If you like."

"You're supposed to be resting up?"

"Yes, actually."

"In bed and all that?"

"Not necessarily."

"It does look smashing," he said. "But you know something?"

"What?"

"I liked you just as well with it the other way."

It closed her throat. She looked away wishing she had her cigarettes near to hand. She told herself she didn't want him there saying the things he did, whether or not he was sincere.

"I'll get the tea, eh?" he said after a moment, and went out, quietly closing the door, leaving behind his scent: a combination of dirt and oil, cigarettes and maleness.

She moved to cross her legs, felt the still-smarting patch of flesh and remained as she was, listening to him moving about in the kitchen, listening with great care as if fearful she might miss some important sound, for a moment cursing her faulty hearing. Then she consulted her watch, wondering when the painter would arrive. She wasn't sure how she felt about having the painter find her and Simon together.

By the time Simon came back, she'd managed to regain the better part of her composure and thanked him very formally for the tea. He stepped out into the hall to remove his overalls, then, in his jeans and grotty work jumper perched on the edge of one of the armchairs, sipping at his tea.

She was aware as she hadn't previously been of his body, his wide shoulders and full chest, his fairly narrow hips and slim thighs. For several seconds she had an insane desire to see him naked, convinced he'd be even more beautiful without his clothes.

"Will you get more parts now, do you think?" she asked at last, desperate to break the lengthening silence.

"Hope so. It's hard to say, though."

"Oh, I expect you will. You look the sort one sees on television."

"You think so?" he asked brightly.

"Oh, yes. Most assuredly."

"You had right toffee-nosed tutors, didn't you?" he asked.

"I'm afraid I don't follow."

"Your accent," he explained.

"Oh! Well, yes, I suppose I did. Does it bother you?" she asked, in the same way she'd asked did he think her hair was awful.

"Nah! I like it, really. How'd they do it, then?"

"Do what?"

"The op."

"Oh! They took a skin graft from my thigh, then severed the lip, did a bit of this and that, then patched it all over with the graft."

"Christ! It hurt, eh?"

"The graft bothered me most. Not that I felt it. Just the sensation of all the blood running down ... It made me feel ill."

He wanted to go over, lift her skirt and kiss her on the thigh where they'd cut her, and had to fight down the impulse to ask her to let him see. He felt overcome with emotion, completely awestruck by what she'd done. It'd been the truth when he'd said he'd liked her as she'd been. Of course, she'd never believe that, he thought, and wished he knew how to say it so she would believe him. But how could you tell someone a thing like that without making her feel she'd gone through a lot of pain and trouble for no good reason?

"I meant to get you the make-up," he told her, "but there wasn't a chance. And then, when I heard you'd gone off for a fortnight, well, I thought ... I thought maybe ... I thought it maybe had something to do with me, see, and I didn't know if you'd be all that keen to have me coming round with make-up and all."

"Even if I had gone away somewhere, why would you think it had anything to do with you?"

"I don't rightly know. It's just the way I felt, isn't it?"

She suddenly realized that he wasn't a terribly intelligent man. This perception was shocking, stunning. She'd never in her life made a comparison like it: determining that, of the two of them, she was by far the more intelligent. It gave her the oddest feeling. He was beautiful; he was simple, straightforward and direct, and not overly intelligent. She, on the other hand, was unattractive, complicated, devious, and highly intelligent. How extraordinary! she thought, unsure of where to go or what to do with this monumental piece of insight. But it seemed to move her even farther from him. How could the two of them ever possibly hope to find some common ground upon which to stand?

"I'm sorry," she said gently, as if speaking to one of the residents. "I had no idea that you might feel that way. It did, in one sense, have to do with you," she admitted, closely watching his face. "Meeting you, and our going out together, made me see I'd been neglectful ... cowardly, I suppose. Because there really wasn't a valid reason for my not having it done, for presenting myself ... that is to say ..."

"I know." He smiled. "And why shouldn't you, if it's what you wanted to do?"

"Precisely!" She tried to smile back at him.

"Hurts to do that, eh?" he observed sympathetically.

"Slightly."

"I expect you're not up to eating all that much."

"Not really," she apologized. "Not for a few more days, at least."

"Eggs, then," he said, inspired. "They're easy."

"Simon," she began, then stopped.

"Go on. What were you going to say?"

"Nothing. It wasn't important."

"My mum's dead keen on you," he said cheerfully. "She said they all are, over there. Says you're ever such a kind girl," he mimicked an elderly woman's voice. "Ever so kind, she is, Sarah. An angel, she is, an absolute angel."

"What?" Her face turned red. "Angel?"

"She is and all," he said in that same voice. "A true angel, our Sarah. *Ever* so kind."

"Oh stop! That's such rubbish."

"It isn't though, is it?" he said quietly, in his own voice. "It's like you love them all. And they know you do."

"I *do* love them, All of them."

"Gave me quite a turn seeing you over there the other week."

"Did it? Why?"

"Don't know, really. Just that I wasn't expecting to see you, I reckon."

"She's very dear, your mother," she said, in a hushed tone, looking directly into his eyes.

"Yeah, she is, isn't she?"

She looked at his blond curling hair and round brown eyes and felt a clutching in her chest, a feeling that might be caring. It made her suspicious and afraid so that she didn't know what to do, distrusting herself and him. He was still highly suspect. And she now had, to her own mind, become overly susceptible to his appeal. She wished she had the courage to ask him to go and not come back. But it was too late and she was far too curious to find out what would happen to do that. So, she sipped her tea, mindful of her too-tender mouth, knowing she was just going to have to wait and see, and found herself filling slowly with a kind of awful expectation.

Nine

Y OU KNOW, WE'VE NEVER ONCE BEEN HERE ON OUR OWN, BUT FOR that Sunday." He stepped back to study the effect of the dark gray eye shadow. "There's always some bloke about, tearing out the bloody pipes, or papering some wall, or painting some bloody thing."

"It's true, isn't it? I hadn't thought of that."

Nodding approvingly at the effect he was creating, he moved in again to wipe off the excess shadow with a bit of cotton wool, saying, "Keep your eyes closed a moment." He was pleased that her eyelids didn't flutter at all; it seemed proof of her trust in him. They'd progressed nicely, he thought, since a fortnight earlier when he'd come round hoping she'd be home. He'd fallen into the habit of stopping by most evenings after work to have a cup of tea, or share a meal from the Chinese takeaway or the fish and chip shop. It gave him a good feeling knowing he'd see her at the end of each day. It was something to look forward to. With Christmas just a fortnight off, he planned to buy her something soft to wear, maybe one of those cashmere jumpers he'd seen in Jaeger's. He had the sixty he'd made on the advert, minus old Teller's ten per cent, and it didn't seem right to put that money into his post office account. It was pleasure money, happy money for spending on something special that would make old Sarah's face go all soft and surprised.

She sat contentedly, enjoying the quick light strokes around her eyes as he applied this and that. He'd come in with his collection of brushes and puffs, little jars and pots and tubes, looking like nothing so much as an eager schoolboy. She couldn't possibly have refused to indulge him in this.

"I hope," she said half-seriously, "you don't expect me to go through all this every morning when I'm tearing about, trying to get to Crossroads on time."

"Once you get the hang of it, you'll have it on in ten minutes. There's nothing to it. Open your eyes now and let's have a look."

She did as he asked to see him studying her intently, his head slightly to one side.

"Simon, how do you know ... decide, I suppose ... What I mean to say is ... whether it's a man or a woman ... ?"

"It's something I feel." He recapped the eye shadow and reached for the mascara. "It's not so much deciding really, as how a lad looks to me. Or a girl."

"How do you mean 'looks'?"

"I don't know. Just if someone looks right, if it's someone I'd like looking at."

"Is it ... ? Do you feel the same way about girls, women?"

"That's different, isn't it?"

"Is it?" His logic was hard to follow.

"I know how women are, don't I?" he said patiently. "What they expect. Most of them, leastways. You're asking me about the sex part of it, aren't you?"

"I suppose I am," she said, refusing to be put off by his directness.

"The thing is I've never fancied being used like a woman, see. I don't mind the other. In fact, I like it. But I don't like *that*. You don't know what I'm going on about, do you?" he asked, seeing the confusion creasing her forehead. "I'm not good at explaining things. Look straight ahead now and try not to blink." He began applying mascara to her lashes, sounding pleased as he said, "Got bloody long lashes, haven't you?"

"Have I?"

"You bloody do, luv."

His smiling face was inches from hers, so close she could see the slight incoming growth of his beard, the shadings of brown to his eyes—ranging from dark chocolate to gold—and his thick, golden lashes. The eyes of a child. She found him exquisitely touching. "Go on," she encouraged, trying to keep still as he'd asked. "Will you tell me more? That is, if it doesn't bother you to talk about it."

"I'm not bothered. Leastwise, not with you. I like talking with you. Never have talked with anyone the way I do with you; it's dead easy."

"Thank you."

"I don't know," he said thoughtfully. "When I think about being with another lad, it's simple like, 'cause we're the same, aren't we? So we know where we stand. Oh, some of the lads, some of the young ones, they're like girls, making demands, making a show of having your attention. But the older ones, they're happy just to spend the time, aren't they? There's none of that raving and carrying on. It's just some time together, knowing what we both want. I mean, say I'm with a lad, eh? He's not going to be with me for a night, then go expecting me to *love* him, is he? He knows it's what it is. But women now, they think if a bloke wants to make love, it means he loves them. And they've got all these rules, haven't they, and things they expect you to do. It's like, if you're a good lad and say what they want, do what they want, then for a reward, like, they'll let you. I can't be bothered with all the fuss, the pretending. All I want is to spend some time and have a bit of pleasure out of it. I mean, it's fun, isn't it? A bit of this, a bit of that. No harm's done, no one's hurt. I'm not out to hurt anybody. And I hate playing bloody games."

"Have you ever loved anyone, Simon?" she asked, treading incautiously in dangerous territory.

"Oh, Mum," he answered without hesitation. "And you, I reckon. That's about it, really."

"Me?" She was sure she was misinterpreting what he was saying. "Are you serious?"

In answer, he ducked down and gave her one of his now-familiar little kisses on her mouth. And, as happened every time without fail, something inside her rose in eagerness. "Yeah, I'm serious. Hold still now. I haven't finished." Returning to his work with the mascara, his face went blank with concentration.

"Why do you say that?" she asked thickly.

"'Cause I'm happy with you, for one. You're not like all the others; you're different. Don't blink for a bit, luv, let it dry." Rewinding the mascara applicator into the tube, he straightened. "It's smashing! Your mouth still sore, or can I put on the lipstick? I got one the perfect color for you."

"It's not sore in the least now."

He bent again, looking closely at her mouth. "It does make a big difference, 'specially now it's all fading, not so red. Got a lovely mouth now, you have, Sarah. Really."

"You're only being kind," she said softly, flushing. He was too close; anything might happen.

"Nah," he said dismissingly. "It's the truth. I fancy kissing you all the time now." His face was only inches from hers. She couldn't speak, or even breathe, her eyes riveted to his. Wanting something to happen, waiting for it. If he touched or kissed her, she might simply turn to liquid and melt away. But he was motionless, simply gazing at her at this impossibly close range.

Her lips parted slightly and he looked into her eyes, then at her mouth. A sudden rush of desire overcame him. "I really do love you," he said so quietly that she read the words rather than heard them. She felt herself moving forward blindly, closing the distance. Feeling as if she were suffocating, she received the pressure of his mouth on hers. There was a dazzling burst of color behind her closed eyelids as she lifted her hands to his face, instinctively opening her mouth to deepen and prolong the kiss, to experience its giddying intensity. Her tongue danced forward to taste his, to know the silken interior of his mouth. A small gasp of astonished pleasure escaped her at the touch of his hand on her breast. She sat away from him in breathless confusion, to examine his smile before looking down to follow his hand's unhurried progress over her breasts, all of her turned outwards in anticipation. Then he stopped. "I'd better get this lipstick on you," he said, looking somewhat dazed, "before it's too late for stopping." He wanted to put her down right there on the floor and touch her all over.

Dumbly, she nodded. "Yes. All right." That low humming had started up again in her skull, her skin felt electrified, and her breasts were chafed, somehow, by their containment, as if they might burst from her clothing and offer themselves into his hands.

He uncapped the lipstick, in a low voice saying, "I fancy you, Sarah."

"What? I'm sorry?"

"I said," he raised his voice and looked straight at her, "I *fancy* you."

"I know," she said, speaking from an entirely new plane of herself, one she'd been unaware existed until this moment, a plane where she was capable of saying and doing almost anything.

"But we're never on our own, are we?"

"No."

"I go touching you and the next thing either of us knows, old Jimmy down there'll come popping in asking about this or that."

"He always leaves right on nine."

He stared at her a moment longer, then set to work applying the lipstick. Finished, he said, "I want you to be truthful now. Don't go jumping up saying you don't like the look of it just 'cause you're not used to it."

"All right," she promised distantly, wondering if they'd really just made the agreement she thought they had. She stood up to confront the medicine chest mirror, failing, for a few moments, to recognize herself. Then, taking in the burnished look of her cheeks and mouth, the exaggerated enlargement of her eyes, she didn't know how to react. Mainly, she felt like weeping. She also felt definitely cheated, thinking she might have looked this way for years instead of learning the true definition of her features when it felt far too late in the day. And, finally, she felt something very like love for this young man for giving her such an exceptional gift: an acceptable image of herself.

"You don't like it, do you? I can tell."

"No, no. I do, actually. It's just …" She shrugged, her hands lifting helplessly. "If I were twenty, perhaps. But now …"

"Don't be daft, Sarah! You were twenty, I wouldn't be here, would I, wouldn't be bothering. It's the right time so long as you feel it is."

"Do you mean the things you say?" she asked, unable to look away from the mirror. The image of this stranger was most appealing.

"Course I do. What d'you think I am anyhow?"

She didn't answer. Perhaps, he thought, she hadn't heard. She turned from the mirror to survey the assortment of cosmetics sitting on the rim of the basin, saying, "You must let me pay you for all this, Simon."

"Not bloody likely! I wanted to get you them. You won't go paying me."

"Don't be angry," she said, feeling unequipped to deal with him or with her emotions.

"Don't you know how to be when someone gives you a gift?"

"No," she said, lost. "I don't think I do."

Softening, he said, "You just say thank you and that's the end of it."

"Thank you."

"I don't know why I feel like I do about you," he said, looking as bewildered as she felt. "It's not the way I ever felt about anybody else. The times I didn't come round, I felt guilty, as if I was missing out. It's like I want to be here all the time. And I don't know why."

"I enjoy having you here." Her voice had gone thicker still. "Shall we go down"—he cleared her throat—"and have some coffee?"

"Hang on just a minute." He put his hand on her arm, forgetting what he wanted to say to her. Smiling instead, he said. "You do look nice. Right nice."

She reached past him to open the door. As they were going down the stairs, she became aware she was trembling and that her stomach muscles were aching from having held herself so tightly together.

"Why don't you go ahead into the lounge and turn on the fire?" she suggested. "I'll put on the kettle. I expect Jimmy would like some coffee, too."

She opened the kitchen door and smiled at the sight of the newly papered walls—wonderful yellow flowers with dream-like drifts of green leaves—and the gleam of brightly white high-gloss enamel on the ceiling and woodwork.

"You've almost finished," she said, squeezing past Jimmy on the ladder to get to the kettle. "It looks splendid."

"Come up nice, didn't it?" he agreed, unsmiling. In the week he'd been at work in the house, she'd yet to see him smile. And while in the past she might have accepted that, she now found herself wondering why he chose to face life with such sobriety. It was Simon, she thought. He'd changed her, and kept on changing her.

Having given Jimmy his coffee, she carried the other two mugs through to the lounge to see Simon in his favorite spot, crouched in front of the fire. He looked like a big, golden cat. She passed the cup into his hands, then set her own coffee on the table and, on impulse, went to the desk to get out the album. "I thought perhaps you might like to see this," she said, as she sat down on the floor near him.

"What's this then, the old family album?"

"That's right," she said, her throat hurting.

"Let's have a look." He took it from her, setting his coffee down to lift the cover and glance over at her for a moment before redirecting his eyes to the photographs.

"That's my father." She pointed, and on the next page, indicated her mother.

He stared at the photograph of a slim young woman with a very beautiful face, clad in a thirties' outfit of wide-legged trousers of some shiny fabric and a short, puffed-sleeve blouse. She had blonde, shoulder-length hair that curved under at the edges, and was an absolute stunner, he thought. She looked like a bloody film star. He went on, turning the pages, trying to gather some kind of feeling about these people. The father was a stiff-upper-lip sort with a thin mustache and too-narrow shoulders, all rigged out in golfing gear, then later on, in uniform. But it was the mother that intrigued him, the woman who had been Sarah's mother. He couldn't connect them.

"Beautiful she was, eh?" he said, after a time.

"Oh yes," she said in a strangled voice. "Very."

"And they kept you locked away," he said wonderingly. "Can't imagine that. You must've hated her."

Hate? "I *loved* her!" she cried, breaking into tears, wishing she'd never brought out the album. "I loved her and she kept me hidden away like a disease she didn't want anyone to know she'd had. I went to her over and over and over again. Every time the door to that room opened and I saw her, I went hurrying to her, hoping to please her somehow, get her to love me. I couldn't understand how she could be my mother and so beautiful and not want me to love her."

"Here, here." He draped his arm around her shoulders, reaching for his handkerchief and giving it to her, always undone by the sight of a woman crying.

"I was so small," she said, glad of his immediate sympathy, yet suspicious of it. "They thought I was only three or four ... when they found me. I kept trying to explain to them that I was seven. And then, when they managed to get hold of Uncle Arthur and he came ... He came and was so kind." She could see it all, every detail, every word sharply clear. The tall, gray-haired man stooping down to take hold of her hand. So dignified, yet there was something merry in his eyes as he'd said, "Sarah, how very happy I am to meet you, my dear." Then he'd stood nodding his head while she'd babbled at him, looking for all the world as if he'd understood what it was she was trying to tell him. *Take me with you, please. I hate it here at the shelter. All the others make such fun of me. No one understands. Want me, please.*

"It was months, *years* before I understood he was someone gentle and caring. And when at last I could recognize that, it was the oddest thing. I began to grow." She turned, wet-eyed, to look at him. "I began growing, getting taller. It was as if her keeping me shut away, not wanting me to love her and her not loving me, had prevented me from growing properly. When I started to trust Uncle Arthur, and started believing that he really did want me and intended to keep me with him, I grew. He used to laugh about it." She smiled a quivery smile. "He'd tell his friends, 'How extraordinary, but my Sarah's shot up seven inches in as many months.' He *loved* me," she cried, the tears starting up again. "But it took me such a long time to believe that."

"Sarah, luv," he said quietly, drawing her closer, "what are you trying to say to me?"

She dropped her head, watching her fingers twist his handkerchief into knots. "I'm frightened. I feel as if I trust you ... as if I want to trust you. And I'm afraid ... You'll hurt me. It'll happen ... between us ... and then you'll go off to someone else and I'll have ... I won't be able ..."

"Hold on now," he tried to interrupt.

"No! Hear me out. I must say what I'm thinking. I could ... I could get pregnant," she said, agonized at having to put this into words, as if their getting into bed together was an established fact. "I could. And if I did, I'd never be able ..."

"If you do," he said calmly, "we'll get married."

"Oh, don't *say* things like that! It makes me feel like one of those women you're always talking about, the ones with all the dreadful 'demands' to make."

"I know you're not like that," he said reasonably, feeling most comfortable with this decision he'd made on the spur of the moment. He liked the projected image of the two of them together, because there was no need for pretending with her, no need for playing games. "You're not like the girls hanging about the local, are you, or the ones who'll do bloody anything to net a lad. You're different. And I wouldn't mind a kid. So, whatever happens, you're not to worry."

"I'm never going to be like you, Simon." She lifted her head to look at him. "I wish to God I could be, but I know myself, and how I am. You're such a happy person. I envy you. I do so envy you. I don't really understand happiness, what it takes to face every situation with assurance, taking things as they come, feeling confident that you can cope because you've been tested before and you've succeeded, so you know you'll succeed again."

"You worry too much, you do. There's nothing to being happy. It's just letting it happen, that's all. I'm happy, right enough, for the most part. Lately, the truth be told, I've been happiest with you. I don't rightly know why. It doesn't even matter, really. If I'm happy with you, that's smashing. I'll be happy with you. I know you're smarter than me. I know that. But the way I figure it though, see, I'm better at having fun in life, and you're smarter. So, it all balances out like, see?"

"You think so?"

"Yeah. That's the way I see it. Here!" He picked up the album and tossed it into a corner. "You ought to get shot of that, for starters. Why'd you want to keep something around that's so bloody depressing for you?"

"I don't know. To remember them, I suppose."

"That's where you're wrong, see? What's the good of remembering if it just makes you miserable? If it was me, I'd trot it out to the dustbin sharpish like. It's just reminding yourself how you can't be happy 'cause you didn't start out happy. And that's all wrong, isn't it?"

"You make things sound so simple."

"Things *are* simple, luv. It's you doing the complicating, worrying and thinking about things all the time. Get shot of all that lot and start fresh."

"I wish I could."

"Come on now," he coaxed, tightening his arm around her. "Blow your nose, then give us a kiss and put that behind you."

She dried her face, then allowed his hand on her chin to turn her head. His kiss was light, sweet. Dropping her head to his shoulder, she breathed deeply, wanting to believe but feeling bedeviled by her doubts and fears. She wished they'd simply go away and leave her; she wished she had the courage to tell him all of it—about how the experience had stunted her in so many ways that she was almost eighteen when her body suddenly, one day, turned over and became a woman's, and about how it wasn't until she was nearly twenty that she'd finally had what seemed a woman's body. She wanted to tell him everything.

They jumped apart, startled, as Jimmy knocked on the lounge door, then poked his head in to say, "I'm off now, Mrs. Breswick."

"Thank you, Jimmy." She'd given up trying to stop him calling her that.

"See you tomorrow evening, then. 'Night. 'Night then, Simon."

"Ta-ra, Jim."

He closed the door and they listened to him letting himself out. Once the front door closed, she said, "I didn't know you two knew each other."

"We were mates at the grammar, me 'n Jim."

"I see." She looked down at her lap.

"Well." He drank down the coffee and got up. "I'd best be getting along."

"I'll see you out," she said routinely, and got to her feet. She turned off the fire before walking past him to the door, reaching into the cloakroom for his jacket. She was reluctant to have him go, yet uncertain how to convey to him that she wanted him to stay. As she handed him his jacket, she saw he was staring at her as if making up his mind about something.

"Ask me to stay, Sarah."

She looked at him, wetting her lips, unable to get the words out. "I uh ..." She gazed at the floor, casting about for the right thing to say.

"Look, I'm just as scared," he admitted. "And you've never. I've never been with a woman who hasn't ever. We could just cuddle, if you like."

She cleared her throat, eyes still on the floor, then made herself raise her head. "I thought I'd take a shower," she said. And then, to her mind having made the invitation explicit, she turned and started slowly up the stairs.

$\triangledown \qquad \triangledown \qquad \triangledown \qquad \triangledown \qquad \triangledown$

Ten

HE WATCHED HER GO, THEN PUT HIS JACKET BACK IN THE CLOAKROOM before going into the kitchen, pausing a moment to admire the improvements and taking care not to touch the wet paint. Shivering in the chill, he stripped down to wash at the sink, clenching his jaws to keep his teeth from chattering. What this house really needed, he thought, wincing as he applied his soapy hands to his body, was some bloody central heating.

She stood inside the locked bathroom holding her nightdress and dressing gown, listening. Unable to hear anything, she wondered if he'd gone home after all. She told herself it didn't matter and draped her nightdress over the towel rack to keep warm, then undressed and pulled on her bath cap before climbing under the shower. He must have left and she simply hadn't heard. Again, she cursed her faulty hearing. Had she heard him going, she'd have gone down and asked him to stay. She felt suddenly doomed to half-gestures, to living out her life as a *demi-vierge*, as a result of her infrequent, half-mad night-time self-investigations. She'd gone so far, upon one occasion she wished desperately she could erase from her memory, as to force her fingers up into herself in an attempt to approximate a feeling she thought she mightn't ever know. She'd succeeded only in creating a rending pain and making herself bleed. It was a vile memory she kept sequestered in the least accessible regions of her mind. She was, she thought, an obscene and fuddled spinster casting wishful dreams about a man whose constancy was doubtful at best.

Dried, she pulled on her nightdress, brushed her hair without con-sulting the mirror, then slung her dressing gown over her arm, turned off the light and overhead heater and unlocked the door. She stopped at the sight of the light spilling from her bedroom. She had-n't left it on, which could only mean … She took several steps, com-ing to a halt in the bedroom doorway to see him installed in her bed, smiling at her.

"I … uh, thought you'd … gone, actually," she said, taking her time closing the door. She felt as if she were having some sort of heart seizure.

"Why'd you think that?" He sat up and moved over to make room for her, anxious to see her, finally, without clothes.

"I didn't, ah ..." She had to stop and take a breath. "I didn't hear you go."

"That's because I didn't go, did I?"

She couldn't move—turned to stone on the spot—thinking of his nakedness beneath the bedclothes. He'd expect her to be naked, too. *I really couldn't*, she thought, deciding perhaps she'd have a cigarette. He seemed to have brought hers up from the lounge. So thoughtful. He was forever doing considerate things like that. How could she possibly suspect him of duplicity when he'd yet to show himself as anything but direct and generous and kind?

"Come here then." He held his hand out to her. "I'll take it off for you."

"I don't think I can."

"Come on." He smiled, curling his extended fingers.

All she had to do was put out her hand, put it in his and everything would happen. She lifted her leaden arm to find her hand warmly, firmly enclosed in his, being drawn over so that she had to sit or risk toppling down upon him. She sat. He took hold of the bottom of the nightdress and she shifted to free it from beneath her, raised her arms obediently and it was gone. She was naked and he was looking at her, his features somehow altered. It took every ounce of her strength not to cover herself and run out of the room. Her heart was fluttering, her throat hurt and she couldn't seem to breathe.

He couldn't believe how nicely she was made: her skin had a kind of soft shine to it, all white with tracings of blue, and a lovely pink color to her nipples.

When he put his arms around her, moving her forward against his chest, it seemed to her the most intensely pleasurable moment of her life, one that had her drawing small, inadequate breaths as she felt his warmth seeping into her, becoming hers. His hands glided over her back.

"Lovely," he murmured and lay back, holding her to him, engaging her in a second of those deep, giddying kisses. "Come on, lie down with me," he said, smiling, watching her face closely, no longer afraid. She was simply a woman after all, lovely and soft, with such pale, innocent breasts. "Lovely breasts," he said, his hand between their bodies closing firmly over her left breast.

His kisses on her throat and ears brought back that low humming in her head. She watched him lower his head over her breasts, utterly removed from thought, completely absorbed in his interest in her. Her eyes wanted to close at the twisty inner sensations generated by his hands and then his mouth grazing against her breasts, at the sudden jolt to her interior when his lips fastened to her nipple, sucking at her, his tongue painting circles. He glanced up at her, then went on with it, causing something down low inside her to contract, creating a seeping wetness at the tops of her thighs. She hoped and prayed it wasn't a period starting, she'd die of the shame if it was. Her fingers languidly wove through his hair; curls wound themselves around her fingers. How wonderful, how simply wonderful to have this happening! She closed her eyes finally to better appreciate the sensations aroused by his mouth, his tongue, his hand stroking down her belly. Should she open her legs? It seemed as if she should; his hand appeared to want to come in between her thighs. She let her knees part and his hand slipped up; his fingers moved here, there, causing her belly to quiver and her throat to open around an animal-like sound of pure pleasure. She could hear its echo inside her head as she spread her thighs further, giving herself up. Her hands were eager for the muscled swell of his upper arm, the taut smoothness of his shoulder, the rippling planes of his back. It seemed astonishing that his flesh, his body should provide her with such a wealth of pleasure. She wanted more kisses and placed her hands over the sides of his face. Her eyes very wide, she directed his mouth back to hers.

He felt as if he'd unwittingly turned some hidden switch in her that neither of them had suspected existed, and witnessed the abandoning of her reservations with sheer delight, sensing he was at last reaching the real Sarah, the woman who lived hidden inside the woman. It was very exciting. He was eager to know how she'd be, to know where he might take her, and dizzily relieved to meet no resistance to his probing fingers. It would be all right. He stopped thinking.

For a time—she hadn't any idea how long—he let his weight bear down on her while they kissed, her legs trapped either side of him so that she felt gapingly open. She wanted him to go on kissing her and, at the same time, to have him push himself all the way into her, and her body squirmed under his in anticipation of that. She wondered if he'd do it, if that was more or less how it got done. But he

sat away off her, keeping hold of one of her hands, his eyes following his free hand as it molded her shoulder, then traveled first to one
breast and then the other, down across her belly and up the length
of her inner thighs. As if to himself, he said, "I love it that you're so
wet," as his slippery fingers slid over her, her body somehow drawing
him in. He let go of her hand to shift down, urging her thighs wide,
gratified by her innocence and willingness. He had to take the time
to admire her, moved as always by the delicate vulnerability of a
woman's construction. He loved this part of it almost better than
anything else, he thought, his fingers caressing the incredible softness of her inner thigh, for a moment tracing the slightly puckered
area where the graft had been taken.

Before she had any chance to react or possibly question his actions,
he'd put his mouth to her and touched her with his tongue in a fashion that made her want to scream. Like some sort of subtle surgery,
it rendered her instantly, entirely submissive to his mouth, causing
her to cry out, "Simon! You're … *Simon!*"

"You want me to stop, luv?" he asked, afraid he'd gone too far, too
fast.

She stared down the length of her body at him, in part wanting to
find this aspect of the performance grotesque. But what he'd been
doing had felt so good, had excited her so tremendously that she did-
n't care what it looked like.

"I … No," she whispered. "No, I don't."

He kept on until he'd succeeded in generating a tremendous pressure in her groin, one that had her lifting blindly, her thighs tensely
spread, a rhythm and determination in her hips had her writhing
madly until, caught near the apex of something that promised to be
better than anything she'd ever conceived of, she went absolutely
rigid, holding poised at the brink. She told herself she didn't care,
that nothing else mattered. This would be finer, more explosive
than any feeling she'd ever created for herself and her entire being
was ready. But he stopped, asking, "Is it all right?" as he positioned
himself between her legs.

"Yes, yes," she whispered, ardent, urgent. She held herself open to
accept him, feeling there was something perfect, yet unearthly in his
bringing himself into her. With surprising ease, she was able to
accommodate him. Why had she thought it would be painful? Her
body was capable, evidently, of a very great deal. She held him and
helped him, blindly searching to retrieve that magnificent physical

sense of anticipation. She heard his indecipherable whispers against her ear as he thrust into her—an elusive percussive tempo she could-n't seem to match—until his motions seemed to be cresting and she felt him leap suddenly and, trembling, dissolve in her. He kissed her softly, tiredly, then lay with his face against her neck, serene within her enclosing arms, whispering beyond the range of her hearing, "I love you, Sarah." She felt only the soft gusts of his breath against her ear, battling off her welling disappointment, glad to hold him, to be able to feel his substance and the smooth texture of his skin, breath-ing in the heat of their two bodies. Well, now she knew, she thought. But was this all there was? What had happened to that exquisite, fine-edged tension that had collected just beneath the sur-face of her skin, merely waiting to be released?

She could, nevertheless, make sense of a number of things that had previously been incomprehensible to her: the behavior of couples she'd seen, of teenagers, even of the residents. She thought of Miss Morgan and hoped she'd known something of this. She smiled at his hand closed possessively over her breast, his knee wedged between her thighs. At least he'd found her desirable, not ugly. She slipped her hand between their bodies and closed it around him, in a state of amazement at discovering a small sense of power inside at having him grow into her hand. She lifted open eagerly to contain him again, lying side by side, glad at having become the repository for all his so-welcome affection. Perhaps he'd bring the feeling back for her.

Her body feeling strained and overfull, jittery, she stealthily lit a cig-arette and lay watching him sleep, fascinated by the quiet rise and fall of his chest. She wanted to be able to keep him with her always, to spend the rest of her life studying each new aspect of his face and manner, to hear his voice, feel his flesh, have him touch and hold her in any fashion whatsoever. A series of almost violent sexual atti-tudes clicked through her brain. She could see herself, slick with perspiration and grimacing with need, straining against him in an effort to rid herself of the pulsing pressure of her desires.

Into his dreaming sleep, she whispered, "I love you. I love you so much." Watching him shift, settling against her, she dared to touch her fingertips to his jaw, then his shoulder. She smoked out the cigarette then curved herself against his back, closing her eyes. Without effort, exhausted, she slipped into sleep.

She didn't hear him go. When she awoke, he was gone. For a few moments, she felt afraid. Perhaps he'd left out of displeasure at something she'd said or done, or because of her failure to completely lose herself as he had. But, reasoning it through, she concluded he'd gone home to tidy himself up before going to his job. He did start at eight, after all. And she wasn't due at Crossroads until half eight. She got up to go into the bathroom to wash her face, brush her teeth, and then, upon consideration, wash between her legs. She was surprised at her soreness and the ache in her thighs, yet smiled at this evidence of their activities. In an instant, she relived all that had happened, saw him putting himself inside her and felt the heat of renewed desire overtake her. She risked a look in the mirror to see that the mascara he'd put on her had left jet smudges beneath her eyes and she opened the medicine chest to find a bit of cotton wool and some oil to clean his hard work from her eyes, She'd have a go at the make-up on her own, she decided, to please him.

She felt very well, all things considered. Not even the freezing downpour could affect her sense of well-being, of something like rebirth. She drove to Crossroads humming and pulled in, puzzled by the sight of Simon's car parked in one of the visitor's slots. Getting out, she stood a moment looking at it, then hurried inside. Margaret Evans called out to her as she was going past the office.

"A bit of bad news, I'm afraid," Margaret said, regarding her, Sarah thought, with an odd look of sympathy and something else she couldn't entirely decipher, but that might have been suspicion. "We lost Mrs. Fitzgerald last night."

"Oh, no!" Her thoughts suddenly accelerated, colliding. "That's why. Simon ... I must ..."

"Steady on," Margaret said. Doing her mental arithmetic quickly, she summed up the situation and felt faintly disgusted as she pointed Sarah into the chair opposite the desk. The redness around Sarah's mouth and chin seemed blatant signposts of just what Sarah had been up to. The slut! Margaret thought, then hastily amended that to, The poor fool. She'd allowed herself to be interfered with. "Sit down a minute," she said. "Grace is having a word with your young man. We tried reaching him all evening, then gave up as the landlord was becoming exceedingly annoyed. We tried again this morning, and he's only just now arrived. I think it might be best to give him some time alone. Have a cigarette, Sarah. Would you like me to fetch you a cup of tea? You're not going to faint, are you?"

"No." She swallowed, not entirely sure she wasn't going to faint. She felt very nauseated as she opened her bag for a cigarette. A double loss. Not only someone she'd known, but someone whose son she'd known most intimately through the night. If Simon hadn't been with her, if he'd been at home, they'd have been able to contact him to let him know about Lizzie. She felt guilty, confused, and upset.

"Stay here and I'll fetch us both tea," Margaret volunteered, prompted by her ungenerous thoughts to press Sarah's shoulder reassuringly in passing. She was certain Sarah and that Fitzgerald lad had been up to all kinds of things and it was, she thought, disgusting. Obviously, he was simply using Sarah. Why would a young man like that want anything to do with someone like her? Really, she was such a fool!

Sarah lowered her head to her knees, concentrating on not being sick, swallowing the bitter fluid that kept rushing to fill the floor of her mouth. The back of her neck was icy cold. Her hands whitely gripped her knees as her stomach turned to what felt like aspic. She tried to tell herself she'd known Lizzie wouldn't last. She'd known; she'd been told. But of all times, all nights. If only they'd been together before, or after … She pressed her hands against her temples, grateful for the shocking coldness against her too-hot face. She didn't dare sit up; she knew she'd be sick and hadn't the strength to run down the hall to one of the lavatories.

Margaret dispassionately placed a hand on Sarah's head, asking, "Are you all right?" sounding a shade more impatient than usual.

Am I all right? she wondered, and risked slowly straightening to say, "I'm all right."

"Here, drink some tea." Margaret sat down watching Sarah's every move. "I've never seen anyone go quite that color," she said. "Perhaps you'd do well to lie down for a while."

"No, I'll be fine." Why, she wondered, was Margaret acting so annoyed?

"Well, drink the tea then and have a cigarette or something."

My young man, that's what she called him. And she's behaving so angri-ly. Did she know? Did everyone know? Did it *matter* if people knew? Feeling a burst of her own anger, she thought it was her right to do what she chose and not only was it none of Margaret's business, but Margaret wasn't in a position either to judge or to display anger. She picked up the cup, her hands shaking so badly the tea sloshed into the saucer. But the first swallow helped settle her stomach and the second seemed to stabilize her body temperature. She felt warm again and lit a cigarette, very aware of Margaret's eyes on her.

"Have people been talking?" she asked at last.

Taken aback by this unexpected directness, Margaret said dismiss-ingly, "Not particularly. You might just say it's been noticed."

"I see."

"People do notice these things, you know. It's no good pretending they don't or won't."

"Do you think of yourself as my friend, Margaret?"

"Of course I do." She looked most offended to think Sarah might not think so.

Sarah wasn't sure she believed her, but couldn't contain her need to express her shock. "Everything seems changed. Before, the deaths ... it all seemed so personal. My personal losses. But this isn't like that. And Simon was ... They were so close. I don't think he could've been prepared for this."

"He was told." Margaret lit an Embassy and turned aside to exhale a thick cloud of smoke. "John had a good long talk with him after her first attack. He was most definitely told."

"I see. I hadn't realized that."

Relenting somewhat, she said, "Sarah, there's really no need to worry yourself about people talking, that sort of thing. After all, nei-ther of you is married. It's not as if you were carrying on outrageous-ly in public or anything like that. When you've finished the tea, stay the day or go off home; as you choose. Things are quiet just now so there'll be no harm done if we're without you for the day."

"Where is he?"

"In the lounge," Margaret answered, irritated that Sarah didn't choose to recognize the generosity of her offer.

Sarah told herself she was being overly sensitive and that Margaret was merely trying to be kind. "I'll go have a word with him," she said, "and see if he'd prefer to be on his own."

"That's wise," Margaret said coolly.

He was sitting in a chair, alone in the center of the row of chairs along the far wall, smoking a cigarette and gazing into space. Unsure of what to say or do, she went over and sat in the chair next to his.

After a time, he reached for her hand and held it while he smoked several cigarettes, continuing to stare into space. She sat quietly. Two or three times people came to the doorway, looked in, then went away.

Scarcely aware of her, he was remembering some things, considering others. At one point, he thought Sarah was probably feeling guilty because he hadn't been at his digs to take the call, had he? He'd been with her. And she was bound to be feeling badly about that. He'd have to set it to rights, say something about how Mum would've been glad he'd been with someone instead of on his tod. This led him to recall what his mother had actually said when he'd mentioned he'd been seeing quite a lot of Sarah. She'd given him a long look, then said, "She's not very pretty, is she?" to which he'd responded with laughter. Perhaps she'd heard the echo of her words and hoped to modify them by adding, "She's certainly nice enough. I'll say that for her. Such a kind girl. They're all mad for her here. It's just that I thought … Well, never mind what I thought. It's up to you, isn't it, to decide what you want. I never could turn you away from something once you'd made up your mind."

What had come through in this conversation had been her disappointment at his choosing to be with Sarah. Mum had spent the better part of his lifetime telling him he was special and therefore deserving of someone equally special. And she'd been trying to tell him that Sarah, although nice and ever so kind, was unspecial. But that was just mum-chat. And if he'd ever taken it to heart, he'd have ended up properly turned around, thinking he was too good for everybody. Nah, she'd meant well. But things were different now than when she was young, weren't they? You didn't go about things the same way. He'd say something to Sarah later, when they were off on their own, to make her feel better. She looked right down in the mouth, he thought, glancing sidelong at her before returning to his rambling thoughts.

Funny thing about Sarah, he thought, his attention momentarily arrested by her presence at his side. He didn't think of her, or feel about her, the way he'd have done about most any other woman once he'd had them. Last night hadn't been good for her, he knew, he hadn't brought her off, and he was in no great hurry to make love to her again, but his pleasure in her company remained. He'd been a little afraid that would go once he'd been to bed with her. But, if anything, he felt better than ever with her now. Maybe it was because she wasn't coming at him all-over eager, full of her own importance just 'cause they'd done it. And she wasn't making a lot of silly bloody noise about how they shouldn't've and she was sorry 'n all. She was the same as ever, except even quieter. She was some-one who gave him room for thinking, for breathing. Here she was being respectful of his feelings just now, and not saying a lot of fool-ishness about his mum. He'd spoken more truthfully than he'd real-ized, saying he loved her. He hadn't planned it or anything, it'd just come out when she'd asked him. But it was the truth. She felt like a mate and, not some damned weight he'd have to drag about with him until he got fed up and had to let her go. And he liked the look of her, with her nice soft breasts and warm belly; he liked the way she'd let go of herself to let him touch her.

Mentally shifting again, he pictured his drafty bedsitter and sud-denly didn't want to go back there ever again. What with Mum gone and all, he really couldn't take the idea of groping his way through the dark bloody front entry and up the stairs to shove five-p pieces into the bloody meter to take some of the chill off the damned place. Bloody depressing, it was.

"Sarah," he said at last, "could I come and stay with you?"

"Stay with me?" Her head was suddenly filled with visions of the neighbors clucking and gossiping, of being the chief topic of con-versation up and down the road, everyone watching her and Simon's comings and goings and reporting on them.

"I don't fancy going back to that bloody bedsitter. Especially now."

"Yes, well." She looked away from him for a moment, considering. How would it seem, his moving into her house the day after his mother's death? People wouldn't understand. She looked back at him knowing he was awaiting her answer, knowing, too, that he'd abide by whatever decision she made and respect it. Yet she felt pres-sured both by his having asked and her own recently acquired desire to have him with her. If she said yes, she'd be flaunting every con-vention, everything she'd been taught was proper. But wasn't it hyp-ocritical to have gone as far as she already had and then start draw-ing lines? And if she said no, she risked losing the only man who'd ever shown the slightest bit of interest in her.

"All right," she said. He nodded and gave her hand a slight squeeze.

"Right then. I'd better get on with the arrangements and all that lot about Mum. I haven't rung Beaconstead yet either. He'll think I've done a flit, if I don't ring him. Christ! It feels like too bloody much to do all at once. There's the insurance and her post office savings. I'll have to see Doctor John, get the death certificate."

"I'll be glad to help in whatever way I'm able."

"It isn't like I didn't know she wasn't going to make it or anything. I knew, right enough. I just thought maybe she'd last through to Christmas. I bought her a present 'n all. Well." He sighed, trying to be philosophical, "I'd best get on with it, I reckon."

"I suppose," she agreed, feeling there was something missing, something of significance absent from this exchange.

"I'll be round with my gear this evening, then."

"Yes."

He gave her hand another squeeze, then got up and left. She watched him go, thinking he was using her. She didn't want to think this way but couldn't help it. She was afraid that he'd use her and when she had nothing left to offer, he'd go on to someone or somewhere else. He'd go off and somehow she'd have to cope.

She was making a big mistake, her inner voice warned as she got up wearily to take her things to the staff room. But whether it was a mistake or not, it was too late to change her mind.

Eleven

It wasn't at all the way she'd thought it would be. She tried, to no avail, to console herself with the fact that little, ever, had come about as she'd expected. But having Simon in the house was, for the most part, merely having Simon in the house. Complaining that he slept better on his own, he'd appropriated her old bedroom and had chosen to spend the majority of his nights there so far. She never knew when she might emerge from her nightly bath or shower to find him ensconced in her bed, eagerly urging her out of her nightdress. When she most wanted him, he seemed least inclined. They shared the house and the chores. He brought in groceries without having been asked, and took out the trash. He shared in the washing-up, the cleaning and, very occasionally, he shared her bed. Aside from being able to depend on him for Sunday lunch, she couldn't be certain from one day to the next if she'd see him at all. They lived this way for the two and a half weeks preceding Christmas.

On Christmas Day, she prepared a roasting chicken ready for the oven, then the two of them went off to serve lunch to the residents, following which, with the aid of a handful of volunteers, it was planned they'd serve those of the staff members who lived in. It was an opportunity to observe Simon at his charming best, teasing the elderly women, telling bawdy jokes to the men. He had them laughing and singing along to Christmas carols; he had them entranced. They plainly adored him.

As they were filling plates in the kitchen and passing them through the hatch to the volunteers, Margaret asked in a quiet aside, "Is it real, the charm, or does he put it on?"

"I believe it's real," Sarah answered truthfully. "He seems to be enjoying himself. It's the happiest I've seen him since his mother died."

"There's always that," Margaret said enigmatically, then went off to deliver the filled plates to two of the residents.

Pilfering a roasted parsnip from the pan, Sarah worked on at decorating the plates with the tiny portions of food she'd long since become accustomed to putting out for the residents. She glanced up now and then to watch Simon literally dancing among the tables, pouring sweet or dry sherry—a bottle in each hand—into the out-held glasses of those of the ambulatory residents who were able to join in the festivities. She had no idea what to make of him. He seemed now the way he'd been when they'd met and she wondered if he'd drummed up some spirit for the occasion. After all, he was a kind soul and he wouldn't like to see these people sitting in glum silence over their Christmas dinners. Yet it irked her mildly that she was unable to distinguish between real and simulated when it came to his moods.

As they were leaving, Margaret presented them each with gifts and then; atypically, embraced Sarah and planted a kiss on her cheek before stepping away to extend her hand to Simon, wishing them both a happy Christmas.

"How thoughtful of them to have a gift for you," Sarah said in the car.

"Yeah, that's right. They didn't know I'd be coming, did they?"

"No, they didn't."

"I don't like her," he said. It was the first time Sarah had ever heard him speak of disliking someone.

"Why?"

"She's dodgy, that one. I don't trust her."

"But why?"

"Don't know why. It's just how I feel, isn't it?"

Back at the house, before taking off her coat, she got the chicken into the oven and the vegetables going. Finally, she removed her coat and went into the lounge to find Simon on his haunches in front of the fire.

"I fixed you a drink," he said, pointing to the mantelpiece.

She picked it up, then sat down with it, smiling uncertainly at him.

"Cheers, luv!" He leaned over to clink glasses with her, then sat back again looking at her with an unreadable expression, watching her take a sip before setting the glass down on the table to light a cigarette. "I expect I've been right boring the past fortnight," he apologized.

"I understand, Simon."

"Here, give us a kiss." He grinned, kneewalking over to her, and leaned on her knees to kiss her. Then settling with his head on her lap, he said, "I wish you'd make up your mind to get shot of this bloody barn, and buy something smaller, with a bit of character to it. Now it's been done up, I wager you'd get a good twenty thousand for it. More than enough to buy a smaller house to fix up."

"I'm not altogether sure I'd care to move." Hesitantly, she stroked his hair. She wanted him to hold her and make love to her, to reassure her as to the wisdom of having him there. She wanted him to rid her of her doubts and uncertainty, to tell her he loved her.

"Tell you what." He sat up. "We'll have a bit of a look round at what's going, keep a watch and if something comes up, we'll talk about it again."

"Yes, all right." She took another, slightly larger swallow of the drink. Gin and bitter lemon. It was quite pleasant.

"You're not pregnant or anything, are you?" he asked, reaching back for his drink. "You're dead quiet, a bit pale, too."

"I'm not," she said, somewhat remotely. She'd had her period the week before, and had suffered through four days hoping each night he wouldn't pick that night to decide he wanted to make love to her. Yet, she'd been curious to know what he'd have done had he discovered it. She couldn't believe he'd have wanted to make love to her while she was bleeding, but that in no way, prevented her from wondering, as well as from being let down that he'd made no advances. Counting, she realized they'd only made love a total of three times since he'd come to stay at the house. She had expected they'd manage it every night, or even more often. But now, she was reconciling herself to the fact that that wasn't going to be the case. She hadn't any more clues to the reasons why he did or didn't choose to make love, and suspected he didn't approach her because she hadn't quite sufficient appeal for him. She'd tried doing the make-up on her own but had only botched it, looking, at the end of her half-hour session, like the Madwoman of Chaillot. And she'd at once cleaned off the whole mess. She simply had no ability with make-up.

He got up and drew the curtains over the windows on the street side of the room.

"It's quite a sunny day, actually," she began, wondering what he was up to.

"I know." He looked intent, she thought, as she watched him come back across the room and tried to fathom why he did the things he did. "I fancy doing this," he said, back on his knees before her, pushing the skirt of her black dress up over her thighs, looking hungrily at her legs.

"Simon, I really don't think …"

"Let's get shot of this," he said, pulling her forward to get at the zipper of her dress.

It was both exciting and frightening. Too confused to protest, she could do no more than watch as he deftly got her out of the dress and her slip, then reached behind her to unhook her brassiere. Within minutes, she found herself naked in the armchair, hoping to God no one would decide to take a short cut across the rear of her property and decide to look through the windows. She felt utterly wanton and faintly degraded as he pulled her forward in the chair and began caressing her breasts and belly, then buried his face between her thighs. She wanted to ask him why they couldn't have gone upstairs, or why he hadn't given her some warning. She closed her eyes to the indignity of seeing herself with one leg draped over his shoulders and both hands wound into his hair as his up-reaching fingers teased her nipples and his tongue probed insistently. He sent her moaning and shuddering into what she thought of in one last lucid moment as sweet agony. She danced, then died.

He rested for some time with his cheek against her bare thigh, his fingers stroking where his mouth had been, then he murmured, "Be a luv," and took her place in the chair. Directing her down to her knees before him, he made it clear what he wanted her to do.

It was absolute debauchery! she thought, but did it, grateful to be able to reciprocate the aching pleasure he'd given her. And he praised her, saying, "Christ! You've got a bloody talent for it. A bloody *talent!*"

She didn't mind it in the least. In fact, it was really quite exciting. But when she stopped, he looked almost pained. "I don't think I uh … I'd really rather you didn't …" She couldn't bring herself to ask him not to finish in her mouth and hoped he wouldn't insist because she thought she'd be violently sick if he did.

"Oh, luv." He smiled, understanding. "I wouldn't with you. I never would. Come on up here, come on!"

He had her straddle his lap and said, "Happy Christmas," as he brought himself into her. She remained pliant, and when it was done, lay against his chest while he caressed the length of her naked back and buttocks. She wanted to cry; she also wanted to believe this was the sort of things lovers did, but she couldn't and felt only sad.

"You're upset," he said, surprised, easing her away to examine her features. "Why?"

"It's just that all this ..."

"There's no written rule it has to be in bed, Sarah. No written rules altogether. Couldn't you just forget yourself?" he asked softly, deriving tremendous pleasure from the warm weight of her breast in his hand, and from the knowledge that he'd finally managed to send her over.

"I'm trying. But I can't go at things quite the way you can. What I mean to say is, it's rather titillating to read about this sort of thing in novels, but when it's real, when one's involved, it's not the same. I suppose," she allowed, "I have somewhat preconceived notions."

"Look, Sarah. I was straight with you from the start. Maybe I didn't say it all that well, but the truth is it's not all the time with me. It doesn't mean I don't care for you, 'cause I do, see. It's just that I am what I am. I've gone for months, sometimes, without having a woman. When I've got the feeling, I want to enjoy it. A lot of waiting, playing at rules, like, and the feeling's gone. I love you," he said, his hand continuing its protracted tour of her breasts. "I really do love you. I can't make all sorts of promises, but I'll stick with you. And whatever happens, I'll always come back to you."

"You mean you're going to leave?"

"I might sometime. I can't say, can I? Things happen. You've got to understand that."

"I don't think I understand any of what you're trying to say."

"I'm saying there might be times when something else comes up."

"I see. I think I'd like to get dressed," she said, preparing to climb off his lap.

"Hang on a minute," he said, stopping her. "I know the way things are, Sarah. I know the way *I* am, just like you say you know how you are. I wouldn't hurt you for the world. But what you might *think*, that'd hurt you, wouldn't it? And that's what I'm trying to tell you." He kissed her throat, then her shoulder, trying with his hands and these kisses to tell her what he couldn't put into words. "When it's right, see, I'm better than the best. It's just that I can't count on the feeling. So, what I'm trying to say is, I've got to go with it when it comes. And if there's someone you fancy, it doesn't have anything to do with us, does it?"

"But there *is* no one else. You know that."

"I don't mean now. I mean sometime."

"What you're saying is that you'll go on about your business as before, and I'm to avail myself of whatever comes along, should anything come along, and should I care to."

"Yeah, that sounds about right."

Gracelessly, she climbed off his lap and picked up her clothes. Holding them in front of her, she went to the door and stopped to look back at him. He was doing up his zipper. She felt like a whore. She ran upstairs to the bathroom, locking the door after her. Too shaken to cry, she got under the shower to try to wash off the feeling. Going back over what he'd said, she arrived at the conclusion that he'd proposed a *laissez-faire* arrangement and it was up to her whether or not she went along with it.

All her instincts told her it wouldn't work. To live subject to his whims was all but unthinkable. It left no room for her thoughts, her feelings, her whims. How could she possibly live that way?

Dressed, she stood in her bedroom looking out of the window, feeling a dreadful sense of finality about everything. How truly terrible to have him come into her life and show her so much of what she'd missed, and then qualify every bit of it with stipulations! How even more terrible to allow herself to be changed because of her attraction to him. And yet, she reasoned, none of the changes were to the bad. What did she want? she wondered, her eyes tracking the passage of a car on the main road. Possession. Having been shown the underside of intimacy, she now wanted to be the sole possessor of his attentions and affection. He'd said, "I love you." But what was it worth? He'd said, "I can't make all sorts of promises but I'll stick with you." Wasn't that of some value?

"Sarah?"

She turned to see him standing in the doorway, looking worried.

"It's very difficult for me," she said quietly, her hand on the curtain. "I *want* to understand, to be adult in my decisions. But it's so *difficult*. Why the *hell* did you have to be the way you are? If you were at least drawn to other women, I could understand that because I know I'm not beautiful and couldn't possibly compete. But how do I compete with other men, Simon? I wish to God I knew what to do. I love you. It's not something I've done before and I don't say it lightly. You stay away from me for a week, then get me to behave in ways that run strongly against the grain. I don't know how to *deal* with you."

"I don't know," he said. "I can't help the way I am, can I?"

"I don't suppose you can. But I can't help the way *I* am. So what are we to do?"

"Let's try it on, give it some time. I've never lived with a woman. I'm not finding it easy, either, knowing you're expecting me to want to be with you. It's hard, knowing people expect things. But I want to try. I'd really like us to have a kid."

"Simon, if I agreed, first of all, to sell this house and move into a smaller one, and then you went off, I don't know what I'd do. This house is all I've got left. It's not the finest place in the world, I grant you, but it's familiar. And secondly, much of what I just said applies to a child. What would I do if you went off and left me with a child? You suggest things and I take you literally. Perhaps, I shouldn't. And it isn't that I have expectations of you. It's that I never know what I *should* expect."

"I can't make promises I know I won't be able to keep."

"No, I realize that."

"But I'll put my money into a place we buy. I'll be getting the insurance and Mum's post office savings."

She sighed, understanding that he was saying he was prepared to invest what he had in some sort of future for the two of them. What more could she ask? "All right," she said. "We'll try."

"Smashing!" He stepped away from the door revealing the gift-wrapped box he'd been holding behind him. "This is for you, Sarah. Open it!"

A deep blue, long-sleeved cashmere jumper. She held its softness in her hands, once again undone by his generosity. "This is beautiful," she said, "the most beautiful thing I've ever had."

"It's cashmere," he said happily, proudly.

"Yes, I know. Thank you." She put the jumper down on the bed to hug and kiss him, deciding then that she'd have him whatever way she could. Having him even part-time was infinitely better than not having him at all. "Come down and let me give you your gift," she said, taking his hand. "If you don't care for it, you needn't feel embarrassed about exchanging it for something you like."

Throughout the meal he kept looking at and exclaiming over the gold link bracelet she'd given him, pausing repeatedly to turn it on his wrist, and saying several times, "It's dead posh, isn't it? Best present I ever got." He called her, "My clever old Sarah," and said, "My good luck is what you are." All of it served to illustrate that she'd been—as he'd accused before—creating things to worry about.

After dinner, they sat together on the floor by the fire, watching television. And when the program ended, taking her resolve firmly in hand, she asked, "Are you going to sleep with me tonight? You needn't if you don't care to. I'd just like to know."

Delighted and, surprisingly, aroused by this display of forthrightness, he laughed. "Bloody right! Now you're getting it, aren't you? Come on!" And off they went to bed.

She was learning.

▽

In mid-January, Teller rang Simon at the garage to say, "I've got you an important audition. For a new series. They've seen the Cadbury's advert and they're very keen on you."

"A series?"

"Television. Thirteen weeks. If you land this one, you'll be made. When can you get here?"

"When do they want to see me?"

"I can set it up for tomorrow afternoon. And I'd count on being called back at least twice. You know how they are, old darling. They do like to play it out."

"I'll ring you back and let you know."

"Soon as you can. We don't want to waste any time. And Simon?"

"Yeah?"

"This is *serious*."

"Yeah."

"My reputation's at stake on this. I'm counting on you not to let me down."

"I'll ring you back."

Beaconstead expressed misgivings. "We can't have you getting into the habit of taking days off at a stretch, lad."

"Maybe I'd better pack it in then," Simon said thoughtfully.

"Be sorry to lose you," he said, reconsidering.

"Look, it's a chance at a series. If it comes off, it'll put paid to my job here anyway, so I might as well take my cards now and no hard feelings."

"All right, then. But if it doesn't work out, come see me, and we'll fix something for you."

"Fair enough." They shook hands. Beaconstead agreed to send on his cards and his wages and Simon went home to tell Sarah.

"You've *given up* your job?"

"It's a chance at a whole bleeding *series*!" he shouted, furious with her for not bothering with his good news but picking up only on the part about his job. "You think I want to spend my whole bloody life with my head under the bonnet of some bleeding *Mini?*"

"No. But … I mean … I thought you'd given up acting."

"Well, I haven't, have I? And Teller's coming through for me, isn't he? What'm I supposed to do, tell him to shove his sodding audition up his bloody arse?"

"Please don't shout and curse at me. If it's something you're pleased about, then of course I'm happy for you. There's no need to be abusive."

"I'm not being bloody abusive. I come in with my good news and all you hear is that I've put paid to my job. Like a bloody *mother!*"

"Simon, I'm sorry. Please do stop bellowing at me. When is the audition?"

"Tomorrow. I'm stopping for three or four days in London. All right?"

"Yes, of course."

"Bloody hell!" he muttered, reluctant to surrender his anger too easily. "I thought you were my *mate*, not my bloody *mother.*"

"Look, I've said I'm sorry. But I am *not* going to go on and on saying it simply to appease you. You took me off guard saying that you'd given up your job when it is, after all, only an audition and not something you've actually got."

"I'll get it," he said confidently. "They've already seen the Cadbury's advert and they're dead keen on me."

"I hope you do get it. If it's what you want."

"Course it's what I bloody want. Thirteen weeks on a series and there'd be no looking back, would there? I'd be set. Bloody money coming out my ears and jobs all over the stinking place."

"Good! Splendid! I wish you the best of luck. I've a headache. I'm going to take some Aspro and lie down for a bit."

He let her go, then relenting, went after her into the kitchen saying, "I'll go fetch us something to eat. If you've a headache, you won't want to be cooking."

It was his way of apologizing, she knew. She drank the last of the water, then said, "That would be nice, if you wouldn't mind."

"What's your fancy? Chinese? Fish and chips? Bangers and chips?"

"Fish and chips, I think. I'm not in the mood for Chinese."

"Right. You go have your lie-down and I'll nip over to the chip shop." He went to the door, turned around, came back and put his arms around her. "I'm sorry, luv. I didn't mean to go raving at you. It's just that I was so pleased and it seemed like all you were concerned with was the bloody job. Maybe it's risky," he said, staring past her shoulder, his hand seeking out the soft place at the nape of her neck, "but the way I figure it, everything's risky, isn't it? You got to take the chance if it's coming your way. And you've brought me luck, haven't you? I *know* this is it! I can feel it!"

"I hope so," she said inadequately as he released her and went off whistling. "I do hope so."

▽

On her way to Crossroads the following morning, she found herself contemplating the prospect of three days alone with some measure of relief, and wondered if wives felt this way when their husbands went off.

As she was going past the office, Margaret smiled and invited her to come and sit down for a minute, saying, "I scarcely seem to see you these days. You're always rushing off home."

"I'll have a little more free time for a few days. Simon's gone off to London for an audition. An important one," she added proudly, for a moment trying to imagine how it might feel living with someone who appeared regularly on television and was something of a celebrity. He probably wouldn't want to stay with her if that came to pass. There'd be other, infinitely more attractive people he'd choose to spend his time with.

"An audition? What's it for?"

"He's up for a television series and quite confident he'll get it."

Easing her chair back from the desk, Margaret lit a cigarette and crossed her heavy legs. "Funny," she said finally, "I can just picture him, can't you? Switch on the set and there's Simon. There's something about him, isn't there?"

"I suppose there is," Sarah replied, for the first time finding Margaret ugly, and wondering why.

"Not just that he's good looking," she went on. "Something *about* him." Approvingly, she said, "Fancy you, Sarah, fixing up with someone like that. Oh, I didn't," she quickly amended, "intend that the way it sounded."

"Of course not," Sarah said doubtfully.

"Come to dinner tonight," Margaret invited. "Ian's off to a lecture and I'll be on my own. Come!"

"Yes, all right."

"Good!" Margaret smiled. "We'll have a lovely long natter." She was dying to know if the two of them were having an actual affair.

"It's very kind of you," Sarah said, coloring, then went on to the staff room to put away her things.

She's bringing me luck, isn't she? he thought, heading along the A-426 towards the M-1. *Me and Sarah, we're going to have good times, all right. And with this part on the telly, there'll be pots of money. I'll buy her something to wear, something bloody gorgeous. Good old Sarah, fussing and worrying. Drive carefully now. Didn't I know it'd be right, us together? Bloody perfect.* He touched his bracelet, the gold warm to his fingers. Maybe they'd get a flat in London. Christ! It was going to be bloody marvelous!

Twelve

AFTER TWO GLASSES OF SHERRY, SEVERAL OF WINE WITH DINNER, AND a liqueur Margaret pressed on her, Sarah felt sufficiently self-assured to approach the nub of her most immediate problem and asked, "What does one do, actually, Margaret, about not having babies?" She kept her eyes safely away from Margaret's during the asking of this question, taking her time lighting a cigarette, and therefore missed Margaret's several quick changes of expression.

"You mean to say you *don't know?*" Margaret looked appalled, and felt privately something very like jealousy at being given this privileged bit of knowledge. Somehow the idea of Sarah's receiving the sexual attentions of anyone, but particularly that handsome young man, struck Margaret as most unfair.

"All I know about most things," she said candidly, "is what I've read in books."

"I'm sorry," Margaret said, making a supreme effort to rearrange both her features and her thinking. She was being so bitchy and hostile in her thoughts of Sarah it made her feel guilty. "Of course you couldn't know. But it's positively unbelievable!" she burst out, not sure if she meant Sarah's failure to know even the most rudimentary aspects of birth control, or Sarah's sexual prowess. "A woman of your age, in the year nineteen seventy not knowing ... My God, Sarah! If you'd wanted to know, why didn't you ask John? Or me? You're not pregnant, I hope, are you?"

Flushing, she said, "I didn't feel I could cope with asking John."

"Well, you're going to have to, my dear. You go right round to the surgery tomorrow evening and ask him to give you birth control pills."

"But he'll want to examine me," she protested.

"Certainly he will." Studying Sarah's expression, she said, "You don't mean to tell me you've never had an internal examination?"

Sarah's failure to reply was its own answer. Leaning over to give her a pat on the knee, Margaret shook her head, with a smile saying, "You're going to have to learn the facts of life in a bit of a hurry,

aren't you? I have the feeling you've gone ahead and involved yourself without knowing the first thing about any of it. Didn't your
uncle tell you *anything?*"

"It embarrassed him. He did give me a book to read, but it didn't
make a great deal of sense. Illustrations of rather drunken-looking
bees staggering through the air from one flower to the next."

Margaret laughed and, after a moment, Sarah laughed with her.

"Of course," Sarah went on, "I've read about diaphragms and pills,
that sort of thing. But they never do say how one deals with a
diaphragm. Dutch caps, aren't they called? I've always had an image
of a row of smiling girls in costumes, standing before massive beds of
tulips, all of them wearing those white headpieces that look rather
like large paper constructions. It all," she said a little drunkenly,
"sounds so ... bizarre."

"Bizarre or not, you're going to have to do it. It's not the pleasan-
test thing in the world, but we've all got to put up with it. And
John's a good sight gentler than most. It only takes a few minutes.
Then he'll tell you how to use the pills, give you a prescription and
Bob's your uncle. It's done. You certainly," she said with disdain,
"can't expect your young man to look after you. Men always have
some excuse or another. They're in too much of a hurry, or they
don't care for the feel of it. Always something. It's up to a woman to
look after herself. You don't want to find yourself left with a child,
do you?"

"No," Sarah answered, wounded by Margaret's assumption that
she'd find herself "left." "Did you want children, Margaret?"

"We had one," she said, looking down at her broad, mannish
hands. Her feeling of superiority was at once eliminated by Sarah's
asking this question. "Born hopelessly retarded. It died, thank God.
After that"—she sighed and looked up—"we gave up trying. I didn't
take to the idea of going through that again."

"How sad!" Sarah commiserated. "It must be awful to go through
all those months and then have something like that happen."

"All the more reason to look to one's self and see to it you're properly protected."

"I suppose so," Sarah agreed, attempting to see Margaret as a mother, with her short, thick brown hair shot with gray, her large capable
body and thick neck and big hands. As Sarah studied her, she had a
sudden desire to go at Margaret's face with a bit of make-up, and had
to stop herself from laughing aloud at discovering she was thinking

like Simon. She sat back with her tiny glass of Drambuie, marveling at how readily he'd infiltrated not only her life but her thinking.

"Will the two of you get married?" Margaret asked, recrossing her legs as she lit a fresh cigarette.

"I don't know. I can't imagine why he'd want to marry someone like me."

"Why do you talk about yourself that way?" Margaret demanded crossly. It was one thing for her to think of Sarah in precisely that fashion, but another for Sarah to do it.

"Well, why would he? One must be realistic," Sarah said with a show of unsuspected composure.

"You seem to think he's doing you some sort of favor, my girl, when the truth is, it's more likely the reverse. Think on it, Sarah. You've given him a decent place to live. I'll wager you cook for him and do his laundry. All sorts of perks, not to mention someone to sleep with. You're hardly the type who'd go carrying on with other men to make him jealous. He'd be a damned fool not to marry you."

Suppressing her indignation at Margaret's gross assumptions, Sarah quietly said, "Actually, he does much of the cooking, and all his own laundry. I don't believe either of us thinks in quite those terms."

"Naturally not," Margaret forged on. "You've gone ahead thinking how lucky you are that someone like Simon's paying attention to you. Well, it works both ways, my girl. And you remember that! You're a kind woman, and thoughtful. You don't suppose these twenty-year-olds running about in mini-skirts would offer him what you are, do you? Never! They're all out for a good time and no responsibilities. But you, you're stable. And really quite presentable now that you've had your mouth seen to. He could do a far sight worse, I promise you. Look at you! Lovely and slim. I'd give anything to be as slim. Good skin and lovely color eyes. You could make more of yourself, you know, Sarah."

"Simon's fond of saying that," she said, sobered. Had Margaret always spoken this way to her? Thinking back, it seemed as if she had. Why, she wondered, had she tolerated it?

"Perhaps you'd do well to listen to him then," Margaret continued. "Granted you've got a lot to offer, but if you don't make some effort to keep yourself up to the mark, he might just decide to go off after someone with a bit more sparkle. Men are so bloody *stupid*! You've got to play them like children—which is exactly what they are. I've never in my life met a man who didn't need tending to like a child.

Spoiled little boys, all of them. It's the fault of the mothers, of course. Filling their heads with the notion that they've got the right to expect everything, demand everything. And here we women are, all properly in our places, ready to see to their meals and their clean shirts and socks, to *do* for them and have their bloody children. Oh, I don't know!" she said irritably. "Why do we need them, that's what I'd like to know? Sex. That's all it is. There's not a single thing Ian does that I can't do a damned sight better, faster, and more effi- ciently. But because he's a man, he's the one in charge. Not because he's any better qualified or abler, just that he's a man. And it simply wouldn't *do* to have a woman doing a man's job."

"I had no idea you felt that way."

"I'm not in the habit of making it known that I think I'm superior to my husband. I'd wind up without a job or a husband, and it's too late for starting all over again."

"Would you? Start all over again, that is. If you could?"

"Probably not," Margaret said, looking defeated and tired, and, all at once, old. "It gets to be a habit in the end. I started out with such dreams," she said wistfully, "dreams of how it all would be. I'd marry a doctor, we'd have a lovely house in London and two or three chil- dren. I'd stay young and pretty forever. He'd be handsome, attentive and successful. Instead, I married an administrator. I've grown old and fat, and instead of a lovely house in London, we've got a two-room flat in a residence for bloody old people. And it's all come down to a habit—living next to someone, with all the coded ways you have of making yourselves understood to each other. The pre- dictable answers to predictable questions. Someone to go off on hol- iday with. It's better than being alone. And I do care for him, after all. We've been through it all together. We'd neither of us be able to do for long without the other." Winding down, she said, "I suppose I'm trying to tell you not to take anything for granted, Sarah. That was my mistake really, assuming it'd all work out like a fairy story. Still, it's all right. And you're not as young as I was, with your head off in the clouds."

Sarah went home telling herself that she and Simon were different; they'd never evolve as Margaret and Ian had; they wouldn't make the same mistakes everyone else made. Some of what Margaret said did make sense. It was important that she protect herself. Not for any of Margaret's reasons, but because she was determined they wouldn't be forced into marriage by an unwanted pregnancy. If they did someday choose to marry, it would be because they wanted it, and not for any other reason.

The following evening, she went round to the surgery and suffered the painful indignity of being internally examined by a man she'd known most of her adult life and whom she could not relegate, no matter how hard she tried, to the removed status of doctor. This man she'd known was presented not only with a spread-open ignominious viewing of her most private anatomy but he also performed an interior inspection that sent tears to her eyes. This man, with a preoccupied air, palpated her breasts, pressed his cold stethoscope here and there on her back and chest, pressed his knuckles into her abdomen and generally handled her, she thought, like someone about to buy a brood mare, checking its fetlocks and withers, ascertaining its worthiness. She came away with a prescription for the pills and the feeling that, regardless of how gentle and apologetic he'd been, she'd none the less been violated in a most significant and demoralizing fashion. And it was all for Simon. Because she wanted to keep him.

"Where *were* you last night?" he wanted to know. "I tried ringing for bloody hours."

"I had dinner with Margaret. I'm sorry. I forgot you'd said you'd ring."

"Yeah. Well, guess what?"

"You got the part!"

"Not exactly. I didn't get the one old Teller was after for me, but I did get a part."

"Simon, how wonderful! Tell me all about it!"

"A fortnight's work. But a good part. Hell!" He laughed joyfully. "I've *finally* got a *part*! Come to London, Sarah! Hop in the old car and come down! We'll go out and celebrate!"

"Oh, I couldn't."

"*Why* couldn't you?"

"I've never driven in London. I'd get lost. My sense of direction is dreadful."

"Tell you what then. Drive on over to Coventry, hop on the fast train and I'll collect you at Euston."

"You're going too fast for me," she protested, trying to keep up with him.

"Come on, luv!"

Giddily, she gave in. "I'll ring you from Coventry and let you know what train I'll be on. What's the number?"

He told her the number, added, "Hurry up, luv!" then rang off.

She threw some things into a small bag then ran out to the car and started for Coventry. A weekend in London. It really was so exciting. And he'd got a part. She couldn't wait to hear about it, to see him. It seemed as if she'd been elevated to a place where life contained endless surprises and limitless potential. She and Simon would never be predictable, would never be like any other couple.

He was waiting on the platform and came running to embrace her, swinging her around, exultantly crowing, "I bloody *did* it! Didn't I know you'd bring me luck?"

He hurried her through the barrier and into the station.

"Where are we going?" she asked, his contagious excitement making her heart beat too fast, making everything around her appear to be moving very slowly in contrast to their flight towards the taxi rank.

"Old Teller's loaned us his flat for the weekend. He's gone off to Paris, lucky sod."

"That was kind of him."

"Kind, hell! He'll make … I'll be paying for it, won't I?"

Thinking he was referring to Teller's commission, she agreed.

The flat was in Chelsea near the Embankment, small but beautifully decorated, with highly polished antiques and, in the bedroom, a bed she thought was positively magnificent. It had scrolled head and footboards in glossy mahogany and was piled high with lace-trimmed white pillows, and covered by a very pretty duvet.

"Get changed and we'll go out!" he told her, setting her suitcase down on the bed and opening it to see what she'd brought along. "Wear this!" He pulled out the cashmere. "And these." He extracted the pair of gray flannel trousers he'd coerced her into buying after Christmas but that she'd yet to wear, having never in her life worn trousers.

Dutifully, she removed herself some distance from the unshaded windows and began getting undressed while he lit a cigarette and paced restlessly back and forth with barely contained energy.

"I'll do your make-up when you've changed," he said, coming over to stand very close to her. "I wish you'd leave off the bloody brassiere. I know." He raised his hand palm-outwards. "You'd rather die. But it'd be bloody erotic to see your nipples under the cashmere. Here," he said, setting his cigarette down in the ashtray. "Give us a quick cuddle, then. I was bloody angry with you for not being there last night when I wanted to talk with you." He kissed her shoulder, sliding his hand down her bare arm. "I wanted to tell you all about it," he said softly, licking her earlobe. "Still, you're here now, aren't you? It didn't feel right without you sharing. Let's get shot of this for a minute," he said, unhooking her brassiere. "I want a proper feel of you."

He was displaying such enthusiasm for her and for her body that she wanted everything to stop so they'd be frozen together forever in this moment: his hands fastened to her breasts, his mouth brushing back and forth against hers. Suddenly wrapping his arms around her hard and pressing his lips into the silkiness of her hair, he whispered, "*Christ!*" and caught her up in another display of suddenly urgent and spontaneous need. She went with, it, anticipating it would be very much like every other time when she made herself soften to accommodate him and felt pleasure only in the knowledge that she was making him happy. She derived very little satisfaction from his presence inside her and wondered why there was such a song and dance about it in novels. She'd yet to feel the kind of stirring, thrilling madness described, and suspected the truth was that because men so enjoyed being inside women they went about trying to convince women it ought to be equally pleasurable for them. If the women didn't find that to be the case, then there was something wrong with them. In reality, her greatest pleasure always came as a direct result of his putting his hands or his mouth to her.

His trousers dropped, he lifted the lower half of her into his lap and, looking ecstatic, thrust himself fully into her. She winced, then relaxed, starting to think of her position in all this, how the two of them must appear, but was startled out of all thought by his applying himself to her satisfaction with an avid interest he hadn't previously displayed. He fondled her breasts and then, inspired, applied his fingertips to her, exerting a pressure that made her contract around him and sent her into a kind of frenzy that at last led her into his rhythm and had her whispering, "Don't stop! Please don't stop!"

No longer caring that they were on the floor or that they undoubtedly looked like demented contortionists, she was able for the first time to fix on that elusive rhythm, and allowed him and it to lead her into a quietly gratifying spasm. It hadn't the directness or the explosiveness of those times when he put his hands or mouth to her, but somehow it seemed more meaningful.

When they were dressing, he stood smiling in front of her saying, "That was the first time it was really good for you that way, wasn't it?"

"It's always good," she hedged, disliking talking about the sexual antics they got up to.

"But this time was the best, wasn't it?"

"Yes."

"Don't be shy of talking about it, luv," he said caringly. "For me, talking about it's almost as good as doing it. I could feel you go off, you know. It's like you're kissing me inside."

"Tell me about your part. I'm anxious to hear all about it."

He stared at her for a moment, then laughed. "It's bloody fantastic! I've got dozens of lines. I'm right the way through the whole first episode."

"That's wonderful." She pulled on the cashmere jumper, temporarily distracted by the gentle ongoing contractions inside. It felt as if he was still inside her—an exquisite sensation. "Really!" She turned back to him. "I am so happy for you. When do you start?"

"A fortnight's time."

"And where's it to be done?"

"Here's the part I'm not too keen on," he said. "They're filming in Spain."

"Spain?" Her smile vanished. "For how long did you say?"

"A fortnight or so."

"I see." Her voice dropped and she reached for her bag to get her cigarettes, thinking she went up one moment and came down the next. Was this the way it would always be?

"I know, luv." He touched her arm.

"Sorry?"

"I said, I *know*. I don't fancy going off and leaving you on your tod, but it's my big chance, isn't it?"

"Of course it is. And you're going to be super. I know you are. What sort of part is it?" she asked, feigning enthusiasm, thinking of how empty the days would seem without him,

"If you didn't have that sodding job at the residence, you could come along, couldn't you?"

"Oh, you wouldn't want me tagging along," she argued, pleased that he'd suggested it.

"Sarah luv"—he took her cigarette, puffed at it, then gave it back to her—"I'm really started now. I know it. There'll be more parts after this one, times I'll have to be away. Teller's already raving about finding me a flat. So, I was thinking we'd work something out, eh? Like you'd come down on weekends or I'd come to you. What I'm saying is you're not to worry. It's not bloody likely I'll be getting parts one after the other. Times, I expect, I'll be home weeks on bloody end waiting for Teller to ring up."

"Of course," she said, sensing his absences in advance, knowing how they'd feel. The aimlessness, the loss of direction. "You needn't worry about me, either. I do have my job, as you say, and a lot to keep me busy."

As they were leaving the flat, he reached for her hand and she smiled brightly, saying, "I've decided to sell the house after all, and find a smaller place. It'll give us something to work on when you're home. And something for me to do while you're gone."

"Smashing!" He gave her one of his proud-teacher smiles along with a quick kiss on the mouth. "I hoped you'd see the sense of it."

"You were quite right. I decided," she lied, "on the train, coming down."

"Too bad you forgot to bring the make-up. Never mind! Tomorrow, we're going to buy you a gorgeous new frock, get you properly rigged out. I'm bloody happy you're here."

He squeezed her hand and she squeezed back, feeling very shaky inside. How could she hope to hold his attention when he'd be surrounded by beautiful young actors and actresses? She didn't even know which sex offered more of a threat. She felt deficient, yet was determined to do whatever was necessary to keep him wanting to come back to her.

As they were going out of the front door, she turned to look at him. "It was the best it's been actually. I love you … very much." She wanted him to respond with a like declaration but his eye had been caught by a taxi letting a fare out up the road and he simply said, "Good, luv," and patted her on the arm before running off down the steps, waving his arms and whistling shrilly to catch the cabbie's attention.

"I love you," she said into the air where he'd been.

Thirteen

THEY FOUND THE COTTAGE A WEEK BEFORE SIMON WAS DUE TO LEAVE for Spain.

The estate agent discreetly removed himself to a corner of the lounge to have a cigarette while the two of them deliberated the pros and cons of the place. Upstairs, it had two bedrooms of pleasant proportions, a small box room, a bathroom and loo. And downstairs were a good-sized living room, dining room, kitchen, and pantry.

"This is it, isn't it?" Simon said as they walked through.

"I do like it," she agreed, experiencing a positive flow of feeling for the thick-plastered walls and hand-hewn timbers, the wide hearth of the lounge fireplace and the many diamond-paned leaded windows throughout.

"'Course the kitchen'll need gutting," he said, surveying the primitive fixtures. "And this door'll have to be replaced." He took out his penknife and chipped away at the rear kitchen door, showing how the wood crumbled to his touch. "Woodworm," he stated, and turned to view the room from this new vantage point. "It's sunny though, and there's nothing nearby, no houses either side."

After standing together in thoughtful silence for several long minutes, Simon went to talk to the estate agent. "Tell us the bad news then, mate."

"Ah, yes. Well, the roof's not the best," he said, glancing at Sarah. "And there's a bit of a problem with the plumbing. Old piping, that sort of thing. The electrical system's a shocker." He smiled, revealing tobacco-stained teeth. "Sorry about that. No pun intended. The wiring needs replacing altogether," he went on. "There's a touch of woodworm here and there, but, otherwise, it's quite a sound place. Really quite sound. I'm sure you and your mother would be more than comfortable here."

Sarah stood very still, watching as Simon visibly tensed and color rushed into his face. She was afraid Simon would say or do something out of his obvious anger and, to prevent that happening, she stepped forward, with a smile saying, "We'll be back to you. Thank you very much for your time."

Not sure what had gone wrong, the agent led them out, then locked up, got in his car and drove off.

"That fucking *nit!*" Simon exploded.

"It doesn't matter," she said quietly, belatedly reacting to the insult and wondering if all the people who saw her and Simon together thought, as the agent had, that she was old enough to be Simon's mother.

"Me and my mother!" he shouted, his eyes following the agent's car down the road. "I should've given him one!"

"It doesn't matter!" she repeated.

He whirled around, prepared to say something more, but saw the hurt in her eyes and went silent. He opened the car door for her, then went round and climbed into the driver's seat. They sat for some time in silence, studying the exterior of the cottage.

At length, his temper back under control, he said, "Well, luv, what d'you think?"

"I have a proposition to put to you," she said, measuring out her words with care. "I'd like to use my money to buy this cottage. And I thought you could share, if you'd want to, in the cost of the improvements. I think that would be fair."

"That's not fair!" he argued. "The place is for both of us, isn't it? And it can't be, can it, if it's your lolly buying it?"

"I was thinking that when you get a little ahead, you could start putting aside some money towards your half. You see?"

"No!"

"I'll use the money from the sale of the other house to buy this one. But we'll have the papers drawn up in both our names. When you're earning regularly, you can begin paying me towards your half. For now, we could share the cost of the repairs. You said you've got close to three thousand. The costs will run at least five or six if we're to do the central heating and the kitchen, not to mention the plumbing and the wiring, the roof and what have you. I would like to put some of the profit from the old house aside for holidays or some emergency." As she was speaking, she couldn't help thinking he wouldn't want to go into this with her. He wouldn't want to continue living with a woman the world thought was his mother.

"Dead cautious, aren't you?" he said. "You don't trust me."

"But I do. I trust you absolutely. This just seems the most sensible way to do it."

"It wouldn't be right. The only way I'll go along is if the place goes into your name. Otherwise, it's just not bloody fair."

"To you, you mean?"

"Nah." He smiled and patted her knee. "Not fair to you, is it? Let's go back and put in an offer."

"I do love it," she said again, looking at the cottage, "Are you quite sure you want to go ahead with this? I'll understand if you change your mind."

"You think I care what that nit said?" he asked. "You think it's going to put me off you if some bloody clown who needs his eyes tested blurts out the first bloody thing that comes to mind?"

"I don't know," she said huskily.

"Well, I'm not that easily put off, hear?"

"You mustn't think I don't trust you, Simon. Aside from Uncle Arthur, you're the only person I've ever trusted completely."

"Yeah," he said softly. "I know that."

"You feel my saying that's a demand, don't you? Am I doing that?" she asked anxiously. "Am I being horribly typical and making demands?"

"Nah. I'm just disappointed," he admitted. "I want to be the one to put my money down and buy you the bloody place. But I don't have it. And the one thing I don't fancy is it looking like I'm living off you."

"But we both know that isn't the case."

"One day," he promised, "I'll buy you mink and bloody diamonds. Then we'll see if it looks like I'm living off you."

"You don't have to do that. You already contribute more than your share. Please don't feel that way."

"First off," he went on, "we're going to buy you a new bloody coat. I hate that grotty thing you've got on! We'll do that right after we've been to the estate agents."

He was ashamed of her, she thought, and wished she could hide somewhere.

"And soon's I'm getting up there, I'm going to get you a bloody mink. Mark my words." His features softening, he reached for her hand. "It's what I think that counts, isn't it?" he said. "And I think you're fine."

She closed her eyes and hid her face against his shoulder.

▽

The old house was sold within a week, for twenty-three thousand four hundred, to a young couple with three children. Sarah's offer of eleven thousand six hundred on the cottage was accepted by the solicitor handling the estate of which the cottage was a part.

In the midst of all this, Simon had to leave. Hiding her nervousness, she drove him to Birmingham airport, kissed him good-bye, then stood waving at the blind row of the plane's windows as it took off. Telling herself nothing could possibly happen to him, and that the plane was not going to crash, she went home to continue sorting through everything in the house. She refused to be sentimental and filled the dustbins with rubbish. Finally, she went down to the bottom of the garden to make a small ceremony of burning the old photograph album.

The little boy from next door hung on the fence watching, asking, "Are you burning your diary?" which made her laugh, reducing the moment to its proper proportions.

"Just some trash." She smiled at him, then turned to gaze thoughtfully at the fire, watching it burn.

▽

She invited Margaret to go with her to see the cottage one evening, anxious to share her enthusiasm for the place.

"Small, isn't it?" Margaret said, walking with her through the rooms. "But it does have charm, I'll grant you that." At the sight of the kitchen, she exclaimed, "Good God!"

"A horror, isn't it? We're having it completely done up."

"How long has it been since anyone lived here?" she asked, peering into the musty pantry.

"Several years. An elderly man had it last. He died here, apparently."

"It *smells* like it!" Margaret laughed.

She was a hateful woman, positively hateful. Had she always been this way? Sarah wondered. "Come and let me show you the bedroom," she said, trying to bury the idea of Margaret's hatefulness. Surely she was mistaken.

"Did you go round to the surgery after all?" Margaret asked as they were going up the stairs.

"Ages ago."

"Oh." Margaret waited for Sarah to elaborate. When that failed to happen, she said, "How old is this place anyway?"

"A hundred-odd years."

"What will you do for wardrobe space?"

She shouldn't have invited her here, Sarah thought. The woman's presence and her comments were eating away at Sarah's pleasure in the place. "We're going to knock through the box room walls on either side," she explained. "It's rather lucky this room's in the middle. We'll simply close off this door to the hall, open through from each bedroom and have quite big built-in wardrobes."

"Simon's idea, I take it?"

"He has very good ideas," Sarah defended him. "He's going to build bookcases in the lounge and dining room, and he's promised to make window boxes for the front. We both adore this cottage. I've never had a place that belonged completely to me. Nor has Simon."

"Are you buying it, then?"

"We're buying it together," she lied.

"Well, just so long as you're not giving away anything you shouldn't," Margaret said suspiciously.

"Simon would never take advantage of me."

"Oh, they all will, men, given half a chance. I'm not saying he's better or worse than any of them, mind. I'm simply warning you to be careful. You're on cloud nine just now and not thinking as clearly as you should."

"Cloud nine," Sarah scoffed lightly. "I'm nothing of the sort."

Margaret gave her a knowing smile that irritated Sarah. She gave the impression of knowing better than Sarah herself the condition Sarah was in, and intimated she knew dark things about Simon that Sarah had yet to discover.

"Don't misunderstand," Margaret said as they returned downstairs, their footsteps echoing in the emptiness. "It's good to see you so happy. It's just that in the state you're in, it's all too easy to make mistakes you'll regret later on. And the biggest mistake of all is letting some man get the better of you, take advantage and enjoy himself at your expense. That's an awfully good-looking coat. Is it new?"

"I'm thinking *very* clearly," Sarah said emphatically, looking down at herself, remembering to say, "thank you."

"It is new, then, is it?"

"Yes, actually. Simon bought it for me."

"Well." Margaret sighed, taking a second and last look at the lounge. "Once the work's done, I expect it'll be quite nice."

Quite nice. "I'll buy you a drink," Sarah offered, to Margaret's surprise. "There's a lovely little pub on the road back."

"Have you started drinking, Sarah?"

"We had drinks together when I came to dinner, Margaret. Don't you remember?"

"Oh, that's right, isn't it? I'd forgotten."

She needed a drink, and she was damned if she'd allow Margaret or anyone to destroy her pleasure in Simon, or in the cottage—in anything. But as she drove towards the pub, she felt saddened. Margaret, she now saw, was not a friend. Which meant she had no friends at all, except for Simon.

At the start of the flight, he thought about Sarah and about the cottage, the life they were constructing. He liked the idea of having things to come back to. It could just as easily have been a lad, but he was happy it was Sarah. It did chafe him a bit that he hadn't the lolly to put up to buy the bloody cottage and say to her, Come live with me. But once it did start coming in, he'd see her all right in other ways, get her rigged out in decent gear and buy her that bloody mink so no watery-eyed, weak-kneed wimp could go insulting her.

His thoughts gradually shifted over to considerations of what it would be like working on location for an entire fortnight, surrounded by honest-to-God professionals, and getting paid top bloody lolly on top of it, all for larking about all rigged out in costume. He'd already got his lines down, knew them backwards; he'd had the costume fittings in London, had gone down twice and was getting paid for that, too. Bloody fantastic! Old Teller was eager as hell to keep the ball rolling and was on the blower night and bloody day, touting his new winner. And giving Simon little sermons about taking it seriously, playing the good bloody game.

He couldn't help wondering if his having packed it in and left London when he had wasn't somehow responsible for changing his luck. That, and Sarah, of course. Well, whatever the reason, it'd changed, hadn't it, and here he was off to a damned good part in a series. There was bound to be more after this. It stood to reason, didn't it? he thought, accepting his meal from the air hostess, eating without tasting. The whole bloody lot was paid for, air tickets, hotel, meals, the lot. The dead peculiar thing of it, though, was how strange he felt being without Sarah. He hadn't expected that. He thought of how she worried about him, like the way she got nervous when he started driving too fast, so he'd slow down and watch how, little by little, she relaxed. He'd never thought he'd actually get such a good feeling looking out for someone, but it made him feel good about himself when he did things for Sarah—even something little like easing back on his driving and taking it slow so's not to get her nerved up. Inside, she was just a scared little kid sometimes, he thought, and she needed looking after, didn't she?

He chatted up the make-up girl and the wardrobe woman; he larked about with the extras, and stood to one side finally watching them shoot the scenes leading up to his. Suddenly scared. The crew was dead serious; everyone was. And everything Teller had been trying to tell him for years all at once made sense. He couldn't afford any more fooling about. He had to take this seriously, because he wanted to keep on with it, and if he messed up he wouldn't get any more parts, so he'd never be able to get Sarah that mink or take care of her the way he wanted. Right then, he wanted to be so bloody good that his name would come popping up every time they needed somebody for a quirky part, like this one. With his teeth painted brown and his suit of tattered rags, he was playing a cocky peasant, one of the locals in the village where the hero had his mill. And he got to get killed, too, at the end—a part with some meat to it.

It was easy, he reflected on the evening of that first day's work as he washed off the dust and make-up. Dead bloody easy. This crew were a trickier lot than the advert blokes had been. Still, he knew he'd done a damned good job. The director had said so, hadn't he? "Nice bit of work, Fitzgerald. Keep it up."

There was a gorgeous lad serving drinks in the bar, a kid with lovely tawny skin and that good Latin look.

While Simon was having his drink and a cigarette, the kid kept glancing over. Simon glanced back. He didn't half fancy sitting somewhere quiet-like and looking at the lad. He had the face of a bloody angel and moved like liquid, gliding about with his tray, never smiling. Maybe seventeen, eighteen, with big dark eyes and soft-looking lips.

"Hello there, Simon." Joanna, the props girl, came sliding on to the stool beside his. "Buy us a drink?"

"Sure, luv." He smiled and bought her a drink, his eyes keeping track of the young waiter.

"Everyone's going to a super restaurant for dinner," she said, drawing his attention back to her. "Are you coming?"

"Wasn't invited, luv." He gave her a smile.

"Of course you are. All the cast's coming. There aren't any formal invitations or anything like that. It's simply *understood*."

"Oh!" He nodded. Dead plain, dead earnest, she was the type who'd never be more than the best props girl in the business but who secretly yearned to be a star turn. Roedean and the London Academy, doubtless. Or maybe RADA. But she didn't have the looks nor the ego. His eyes drifted back to the young Spaniard, watching as the boy deftly served drinks from his tray to a table of four. No smile. A bit of a bow and he was off back to his post at the end of the bar.

"Are you coming, Simon?" Joanna asked, halfway off her stool.

"Oh, right! Super!" He went with her, knowing the lad's eyes were on him.

On the third night, when he got back to the hotel, he tried to ring Sarah but there was no reply. She was probably over at the cottage, he decided, picturing her with a scarf tied on over her hair and the Hoover, of all unlikely bloody things, in the lounge. Or standing gazing out of one of the windows. She was always doing that, stopping to stare out with a kind of distance and longing to her eyes, as if she were trapped on her side of the glass. Poor old Sarah. But it made sense, if you thought about it, likely she didn't even know she did it. *I spent seven bloody years locked up in some room,* he thought, *I'd be looking at the outside, too, wouldn't I? Probably be a right nutter.*

"I'll try again later," he told the hotel operator and went down to the bar for a drink before dinner. They were all going off again to some hotel for dinner, some place with dancing. He didn't know how they bloody did it, drinking till all hours, then out there for the cameras by six-thirty a.m. It was bloody hard work standing about waiting for your scenes to come up.

He sat down at the bar, then casually looked around. A different lad was waiting tables tonight. Disappointed, Simon nursed his drink. Joanna came to sit next to him, letting her thigh graze his while she gossiped about the day's business and then, a bit possessively—making it look like they were having it off together—she took hold of his hand when they went to join up with the others. He felt sorry for her, so he let her for a while. Then he lit a cigarette to free his hand and get shot of her. It felt all wrong not having Sarah with him. He had several seconds of extreme anxiety imagining her sprawled on the road, caught in the glare of headlamps, her Morris a crush of ruined metal. Christ! He had to work at it to shake off the image and the fear. She was all right, he told himself. She was just off seeing to the cottage or having a meal with her friend, the sergeant. Whatever happened to the lad? he wondered. Night off, more than likely.

They piled into several cars and set off. He got lumbered with bloody Joanna, her fat arse settled across his lap.

He reached Sarah the next night and felt comforted at once by the soft, husky sound of her voice. He was smiling as he asked how she was and how things were going.

"You didn't ring, Simon. I've been terribly worried, imagining all sorts of things. Please promise me you'll always call the minute you arrive, from now on, so I know you're all right."

"I tried but you weren't in. But okay, luv. From now on, the minute I set foot on the ground, I'll ring you. Now, tell me what's happening."

"There's a lot of paperwork, but they're getting it done quite quickly. I expect they'll be finished by Friday. How are you? What's it like there? Is it warm?"

"Bloody hot! It's hard work, Sarah. I didn't reckon on it being as hard as it is. Up at five every day, out there by six-thirty. The others stay out half the bloody night drinking 'n dancing. I don't know how they do it. I've given up. I could barely think straight this morning. So I'm giving it the go-by. Had my meal on my tod tonight, then I came up here to ring you."

"It's going to be ages, I'm afraid, before the work can get started on the cottage, Simon. Everyone's booked up for months. I do have some people organized to see to the chimney and the roof, and the

kitchen. But I thought I'd wait until you get home before doing anything about the new furniture. Your taste is really so much better
than mine."

She talked about his coming home and he felt suddenly better, less
tired. "I miss you, luv. I'll try to ring again in a day or two. And I'm
dead sorry you were worried."

He rang off to pace the length of his room restlessly for several
minutes, then collected his cigarettes and room key and went down
to the bar for a nightcap. He felt a stab of gratification on seeing the
lad back at his post at the end of the bar. The lad looked over and
actually smiled.

Very nice, Simon thought, sitting at the table instead of the bar so
that the lad could serve him. Very bloody nice indeed. He ordered
Scotch, then sat back to watch the lad go and get it. Slim hips and
a rounded arse like a girl's, wide shoulders accentuated by the
bolero-type jacket of the uniform. Their hands touched as Simon
paid for the drink and, again, they exchanged smiles. The lad, he
learned, spoke almost no English. But never mind, he thought,
glancing over from time to time. Never mind.

While Sarah and Grace were bathing Mr. Sinclair the next day,
Hugh MacCreech suffered a massive coronary attack and died. She
had thought she'd gained some perspective on her affection for these
elderly people, but this man had been special to her, and his death,
his simply going away in just a matter of minutes, shook her. As she
and Grace attended to the body prior to its removal, she was overcome by sorrow and a somehow deeper sense of loss than ever before.
Everyone she had loved was on limited time, including Simon. She
was older than he. Rather than further distressing her, this fact was a
comfort. More than likely, she'd die first, which meant she wouldn't
have to live without him.

Her thoughts circular and muddled, she found herself physically
slowed by the death. Her previous hurried flight through the days
now seemed egocentric, even vain. If she was to continue her job at
Crossroads, which she very much wanted to do, she was going to
have to remember not to get so caught up in the lives of the residents. She could continue to care for them—it would have been
impossible for her not to—but she'd have to refrain from the sort of

familial involvement she'd previously encouraged.

For the remainder of that day, she pressed her usual light kisses and affectionate gestures on the residents, taking the time, as always, to listen to their complaints, realizing as she did that she'd given up her place in the lounge and was therefore obliged to attend caringly to those who hadn't her options. She was still young, after all, and nowhere near infirmity or death. So it was vital she make some effort to ease the passage of those all around her who were. She was reminded that, with Simon or without him, she still had a life of her own. But because of Simon, her future now had some scope.

They met on the beach, the safest place in view of the risk the lad ran in meeting up with one of the guests. They found a hidden spot and sat on the sand.

Later, Simon was disgusted to realize the lad expected to be paid. Furious with himself for being taken in, for having actually *bought* someone's affections, he threw some pesos at him and stalked off back to the hotel, vowing, Never again! He took a long, very hot shower hoping to Christ the lad hadn't given him a dose of something or other, and fell into bed at last, to smoke a cigarette in the dark, feeling aged and even tainted by his hour on the beach. He was getting too bloody old for this rot, he told himself, suddenly missing Sarah deeply and painfully, wishing it weren't too late to ring her again. Very near tears, his throat thick, he smoked down the cigarette, crushed it out and rolled over to sleep in the air-conditioned cool of the room. He dreamed of Sarah lying mangled and bloody in the road, caught in the light of a broken headlamp, her eyes open, forever unblinking, while rain fell steadily into them. In the dream, he was in the rear of a passing car, fighting off a lad who kept grabbing at him, preventing him from jumping out to run back to Sarah.

He had been home less than two months when another part came through, a small supporting role in a film to be shot in England and North Africa. During the time the company was filming in England, Simon managed to get home only once, to spend a discordant afternoon with Sarah, unable to unwind because of his preoccupation with time schedules and his role in the film. He talked obsessively about Michael Caine and the other stars, but primarily about Caine. "He can make it, I bloody can, and that's a fact!" he said numerous times.

Distractedly, he admired the half-completed kitchen and Sarah's paintwork in the upstairs bedrooms. They made love badly and too quickly, had an awkward tea afterwards, and then he was rushing off, apologizing. "I'm sorry, luv. Once this is out of the way maybe we'll go on holiday, take a fortnight somewhere and relax."

"I do understand," she said with a sad smile, and waved him off before going back inside to get on with papering the upstairs hall- way. She'd tried her hand at it to discover it wasn't at all difficult, and most satisfying. She planned to go on to the kitchen and dining room, telling herself it was best to keep busy, to acclimatize herself to Simon's absences. The more successful he became, the less time they were bound to have together. But she felt far lonelier than she'd ever been; her time alone seemed less valuable for his failure to be there. And she no longer felt comfortable with Margaret, so there was no one to talk with. Simon went off apologizing, and she was left to fill her free hours with wet strips of wallpaper.

▽

The following week Teller rang.

"Are you never home?" he asked with a laugh. "I've been trying to reach you for days, but you're simply never there."

"Has something happened to Simon?"

"No, no. Not at all. I merely thought it was high time the two of us met and got to know one another. After all, we do have Simon in common. I'm on my way up to Stratford and I hoped you might come out to dinner."

"Oh! When?"

"This evening."

It was too soon, she thought. She needed more time to prepare for this. "I see," she said, stalling.

"Will you be free?

"Well, actually.

"Oh. hell! They're buzzing me. Seven-thirty?"

"All right, but …"

"Looking forward! This evening, then!" he said and was gone.

She was extremely nervous. It was one thing to have talked to the man on the telephone for months, but quite another to come face to face with him. Teller represented the other half of Simon's life, the half about which she knew almost nothing. Meeting him was bound to bring revelations she wasn't sure she cared to know.

She hadn't anything suitable to wear. In the grip of acute tension, she drove into town to look through the shops, searching for an outfit. Nothing seemed right. Trousers or a dress? Something simple, or dressy? She stopped in the middle of trying on a wildly expensive black trousers suit, telling herself she was behaving like a fool. She replaced the suit on the hanger, put on her own clothes and went home. What she wore wasn't going to make a great deal of difference.

She got out the blue cashmere and the gray flannel trousers, then bathed and put on a bit of make-up, and was ready with ice in a bowl and a drinks tray when the doorbell sounded.

She opened the door to him saying, "I'm terribly nervous, I'm afraid. And the cottage is nowhere near ready to be seen, but do come in. Hello."

"So am I, actually," he admitted endearingly, with a smile.

He was a shortish man, wonderfully handsome, and nowhere near as old as Simon had led her to believe. She'd expected someone in his fifties, and Lionel Teller was forty at most. He had silver-gray hair and a beautiful speaking voice; his manner was most self-effacing.

"Will you have a drink?" she asked.

"Have you Perrier by any chance?"

"I do. Please do sit down." She gave him some Perrier, poured herself an extra large Scotch and went to sit down.

After looking around the room, he turned to face her. "You're not at all as I'd thought you'd be," he said candidly.

"Nor are you," she replied with equal candor. "I was anticipating ..."

"Oh, *do* tell me," he said eagerly, smiling. "Then I'll tell you what *I* was anticipating."

"Well, someone more ... I'm not sure. From speaking to you on the telephone, I thought you'd be—taller, bigger."

"And I thought you'd be much smaller, the overly pretty, clinging type."

They laughed and she offered him a cigarette from the box on the table. He declined but reached into his jacket pocket for a silver

Dunhill to light hers.

"You're also younger than he led me to believe," she said, after a moment, warming to him.

"You're older, I'm afraid. I really did have this dreary mental pic-ture of a sweet, slightly daft young thing of twenty or so, with shock-ing taste but a very kind nature."

"Good lord!" She laughed again, relaxing, noticing he had a love-ly smile and very white teeth, the two front ones slightly overlapped.

"Indeed!" he agreed. "Cheers!" He took a swallow of the Perrier then carefully set the glass down, sitting back comfortably, crossing his legs. "How long has it actually been?" he asked, looking around again. "The place is charming, positively charming."

"Thank you. Would you care to see the rest of the house?"

"I'd adore it!"

They got up and she showed him the dining room and kitchen, then led the way upstairs, asking, "How long has what been?"

"You and Simon. I'm simply mad for it," he said, looking into each of the bedrooms. "Simply mad!"

"Thank you. Not very long," she answered, thinking it seemed as if she and Simon had been together for years, but in reality it had only been a matter of months.

"I've known him going on for seven years," he said, with no hint of superiority. "I suppose that makes us—you and I—family, in a sense."

"I suppose it does," she concurred, leading the way back down-stairs. She watched him settle himself gracefully on the sofa, asking, "Why is it that Simon's suddenly starting to do so well?"

"It's hardly sudden," Lionel replied, his eyes on hers as he circled the rim of his glass with one manicured finger.

"I do know he spent six years in London trying, but it does seem odd that he's so in demand all at once."

He studied her for a moment, liking her. She was rewardingly unaf-fected and unpretentious. And her eyes, he thought, were exquisite both in color and directness. "At the beginning," he said, "he was too much of what one might call an idealist. One could even say he was rather rebellious. I sent him out on scores of auditions, you know. Scores of them. They liked him well enough but there was a certain something about him, a nuance perhaps, they didn't care for. They could see in him what I saw—the talent and the tremendous energy—but I think they felt he was mocking them. Getting that

Cadbury's advert was a damned lucky break. It was his photograph that sold him. He does photograph wonderfully well. But I don't mind admitting I was frightened he'd botch it the way he'd botched every other thing I'd sent him on up to that point."

"How did he botch it?" she asked.

"A lack of seriousness, I think. That certainly put people off. He'd fool about, making a joke of things. Well, we all know the business is nothing more than a grand joke, really, but the trick is to let them believe one's taking it quite as seriously as they are."

"He calls it a game," she contributed, intrigued by this emerging new view of Simon.

"That's *exactly* what he thinks of it. Yet, underneath, he's so keen. I had no idea what it would take to get him to stop waltzing about and start playing by the rules—not that he'll *ever* knuckle under and play by anyone's rules, of course—but at least the penny seems to have dropped. And I can't help feeling it's you who's made all the difference."

"Me? Why?"

"Because there's simply no other logical explanation. I was there when he came down to Cornwall to do the advert. He started out with his usual antics, and my heart was literally in my mouth. But suddenly he sobered and got to work and did a thoroughly professional job of it. Just as I'd known he could. It was as if he'd decided it was worth the price, that the price wasn't beyond his capacity to pay after all."

"I don't truthfully see that I could have had anything to do with that," she said. "We scarcely knew each other at that point."

"Ah, but he spoke of you," he said importantly. "I recall it very clearly." What he'd said, Lionel remembered, was that he'd met this woman who was such a bloody mess in every conceivable way that he had to get to know her to find out why she was the way she was. What he'd said was, "I like her. I don't have the foggiest why, but she's different, isn't she, all shy and stringy, tight like an old woman. But I know she's not *really* like that."

"What did he say?" she asked.

"He said you were a bloody mess, but that he liked you."

"That's only part of it, isn't it?" she said with a slow smile. "I expect the truth runs more like this: He'd met this peculiar woman who went to bed at eight at night and who had an odd way of speaking because of a harelip and who was frightened of absolutely everything."

He looked hurt, disappointed. "Is that how you think of yourself?"

"It's how I am ... *was*. You really mustn't credit me with too much, Mr. Teller. I am far more in Simon's debt than ever he could be in mine."

"Lionel," he corrected. "And I think you're wrong. What an odd woman you are! How one looks isn't important in the last analysis. Oh, assuredly, looks do matter. But not to Simon and not to me, really. I grant you he'd see the challenge. He's always loved that aspect of things, wanting to make people over to show up the best qualities. But if anything, I think you were more of a challenging *personality* to him. And," he added, "a physical one, if you'll forgive my saying so."

She wondered suddenly if this small, elegant man sitting opposite didn't see her, as the agent had, as being old enough to be Simon's mother. And she wondered if Simon had actually gone into the details of the surrender of her virginity. Color slowly seeped into her face and she looked down at her hands. "Did he actually tell you that?" she asked in a low voice.

"Oh, never!" he said, distressed. "We're simply talking of 'assumptions' here, you understand. Simon's really very discreet, you know."

"Is he? I'm not sure I know *what* he's capable of."

"I've upset you," he said unhappily. "How dreadful of me!"

"Do I look to you old enough to be his mother?" she asked, throwing her head back to confront his eyes.

"*His mother?* Good God no!" he said, then asked, "You're not that old, surely?"

"No. But I am older than he is. Almost three years older."

"Does that matter?" he asked.

"Doesn't it?"

"I can't see how," he said honestly.

She shivered, saying, "This is sounding rather like a post mortem."

"It's inevitable," he said, regaining his calm. "After all, we're two strangers. Aside from Simon, what have we to talk about? *Did* you have a harelip?" he asked bluntly. "Simon's never mentioned it."

She nodded. "I had it corrected not very long ago." Her hand rose automatically to her mouth. "I feel quite odd," she said, returning her hand to her lap. "We've been inside each other's homes; we've been inside each other's lives, in a way. I think we do have a lot to talk about, now that I consider it. Are you lonely, Lionel?" she asked surprisingly. "I am. When he's away, I'm very much at odds with myself. I have my job, and work to do on this house, but there's always a kind of emptiness. He fills such a lot of space."

"He does, doesn't he?" he agreed softly, so that she didn't hear.

"I'm sorry?"

He looked up at her blankly.

"I have a hearing problem. I missed what you said."

"Oh, do you? How dreadful for you. I was agreeing with you"—he raised his voice—"about his taking up space. He does."

"Yes."

There was silence. Then, with sudden strong sincerity, he said, "I hope we'll be friends, Sarah. We do, after all, have so much in common. And I find you wonderfully easy to be with." Unlike most women, he silently added, grateful.

For a few moments, she had an intimation of herself and this man ten or fifteen years hence, sitting in exactly the same places, having a similar conversation. The image was quite comforting.

"I'd like that," she said.

"Well, shall we go to dinner?" he asked with old-world charm, an affectionate smile.

"Yes." She returned his smile. "I'll just get my bag."

Fourteen

His work in the film kept Simon away six weeks. He made a point of telephoning immediately upon his arrival in North Africa, which made them both feel better. And while he was gone, Teller rang up once or twice a week to chat and to tell Sarah the latest gossip. She looked forward to his calls, becoming more and more fond of him. After a call from Lionel, she usually felt cheerier, even more ambitious about the bulk of work remaining to be done on the cottage.

By the time Simon came home, the rewiring and plumbing had been done, the kitchen was completed, and the entire house had been repainted; all that remained were the bookshelves, the window boxes, and the wardrobes Simon had promised to do.

For his first few days home, he was still keyed-up and couldn't apply himself to the task of measuring and then going out for timber, or even considering starting work on any of the projects. She went off to Crossroads in the mornings and returned home in the evenings to find him, each time, on the telephone with Teller.

One evening he stayed on half an hour longer while she went ahead getting a meal ready. Then he sat down to eat with her, bubbling over at the prospects Lionel had outlined in the course of this latest call. She wondered if Lionel had ever mentioned their meeting.

"I'm up for bloody *everything!*" he exclaimed, eating quickly. "It's really happening, Sarah."

"It seems," she said slowly, "to be making you frightfully nervous."

"Yeah, I know. I'm going to have to do something to work off some of my steam."

"Why not start on the wardrobes?" she suggested, watching him lay down his knife and fork. She was scarcely halfway through her food. "We do need them badly."

"Yeah," he agreed, watching her eat. "I'll get going on it tomorrow."

He said nothing further about Lionel, so she had to assume Lionel hadn't told him. She wished he had.

The following evening when she arrived home, it was to the sound of hammering upstairs. She hung away her things and went to get their meal started before going up to see that he'd already knocked through one of the walls and was nailing boards into place around the opening.

"You've done such a lot," she said, pleased. "It's going to be super, don't you think?"

"Dead easy," he said, hammering the last of the nails before turning to give her a quick kiss on the mouth. "I figured I'd better hop to it. Teller rang this morning."

"You've got another part," she guessed.

"Don't even have to audition this time. And it's a full supporting role."

"Another film?"

"Telly. BBC. It's a ninety-minute play, modern. I'll be able to come home weekends. I've got a week's rehearsal, a week's shooting."

"That's wonderful!" She smiled, relieved. "I could come down at the weekends if you don't feel up to driving back."

She was putting herself out for him, he knew, and wasn't sure how to discourage her. Teller had plans of his own. This staying with old Teller was getting out of hand, he thought. He'd have to get a flat. "We'll work something out," he hedged.

Sensing something amiss, she returned downstairs.

As they were eating, he said, "I've been thinking about getting a flat in London. I think it's the answer, really. I've about had it with kipping at Teller's digs. I've got no time to myself, have I?"

The chop suddenly like so much gravel in her mouth, it occurred to her that Simon had to be sleeping with Lionel those nights he stayed in the city. There was only the one bed in the flat. Why hadn't she realized it sooner? Her stomach was aching all at once, and her hands were very cold. She wasn't sure how she felt about this. Had Teller been inelegant, she didn't think she could have borne it. Somehow, his being so very charming and sensitive seemed to elevate Simon's relationship with him.

"Do you sleep with him, Simon?" she asked, staring down at her place.

"Yeah, actually," he answered, glad to have it out in the open. "It doesn't mean anything, though. It's just that he's been good to me, hasn't he?"

"Of course," she said thickly. "He's been very good to you." Did they both, she wondered, talk about her and laugh? Simon's glib dismissal of the relationship made her feel badly for herself, and unexpectedly, for Lionel too. Perhaps Simon spoke of her to Lionel in this same fashion. Perhaps she and Lionel were both being used by Simon.

"Ah, look, luv," he said, seeing her eyes glazing. "It's nothing, is it? If the time ever comes when I don't give you a straight answer, then you'll have something to worry about. I want to be straight with you so we haven't got secrets between us. Teller doesn't *mean* anything. He's a nice enough old thing and he's been bloody good to me. A couple nights' kip with him is nothing, bloody nothing."

"He's not the only one, though, is he?" she pursued it.

"A couple here and there. I told you ages ago, Sarah. It's just a bit of fun for an hour or two. But it's you I come back to, isn't it, you I live with. The most I've got to give anybody, I'm giving to you."

"I do believe that," she said, still unable to look at him.

"Then don't bother yourself thinking about the other. I mean, you could be having it off and I wouldn't be bothered."

"I *hate* it when you say that!" she cried, dropping her knife and fork. "Please stop giving me your permission to have other men! I don't *want* them! I'm sorry if my not wanting anyone else constitutes a 'demand,' but I can't help that. It doesn't make my having to share you with God knows how many others any easier. I'm trying not to let it bother me. I do try very hard. But I *love* you. I can't bear it that I'm not enough for you. It makes me feel so inadequate, as if I'm lacking something vital, something terribly important that would keep you with me."

"You're fine for me as you are," he argued. "Don't let's do this, luv," he pleaded. "There's nothing I'm taking away from you to give any-body else. Not a thing, I swear it. Just don't keep *thinking* about it! You go making it bigger than it is. Sometimes, I wish you'd had other men, then you'd know how bloody little it is. It's got nothing to do with feelings or caring, Sarah. It's just a bloody itch you've got to scratch now and then."

"You reduce me when you say that. You put me into the category of another cumbersome chore you've got to attend to: scratching Sarah's itch."

"You're not a *chore*! And when I've got the feeling, I love having you. I'm bloody sorry I don't happen to feel it when you do, but there you are. That's life, isn't it?"

"Is it?" she asked plaintively.

"Look," he said patiently, "if you'd wanted a clerk in some bloody civil service job, you'd have had one. But you didn't want that, did you? You wanted me. Now you've got me, you've got to take the sweet along with the bitter. At least it isn't the same boring palaver month in, month out, is it?"

"It's anything but boring," she agreed, seeing the irony.

"Right then! So don't think about the other. But don't go trapping me into talking about it, either, letting me think we can be free with each other when we're not, 'cause that's bloody unfair. I want to think you and me can talk about bloody anything that comes up. It's important; it's what makes it different from a night's kip with some bleeding ponce. Okay?"

"Did Lionel tell you that we've met?"

"'Course he's bloody told me. What did you think?"

"Why didn't you say anything?"

"It hasn't to do with me, has it?" he said. "It has to do with you and him."

"Doesn't it matter to you?"

He faltered. "Well, yeah, it matters. I mean, it'd matter if the two of you weren't friends, like. But you are, aren't you? So it hasn't to do with me."

"Are you saying that if we disliked each other, then it would have to do with you?"

"Something like that, yeah."

"That doesn't make sense, Simon."

"Sure it does. I mean, you're friends, right? So there's no bother. And I did say, didn't I, that I wanted to find us a flat?"

"Yes, you did say that."

"Right! So that ought to show you I'm not after keeping old Teller on the bloody string. I want a place so when you come down weekends we can be together."

"All right," she said, giving up in complete bewilderment. "I'm sorry," she added, not knowing why.

"Forget it," he said feelingly. "No harm's done, is there?"

She couldn't answer; she didn't know how.

▽

He left for his four days' work in London and rang the first evening to remind her to be sure to watch him that night in his episode of the series. "I'll ring you back later so you can tell me how bloody marvelous I am." He laughed. "Have to run, luv. Ring you later."

She'd thought he'd done splendidly at simply being himself in the Cadbury's advert, and she settled in front of the television set, curious to see how he'd be playing an actual role. His being an actor, for all the evidence of his career's reality, seemed something of a fantasy both of them actively perpetuated. It was difficult to believe it was real, perhaps because she'd yet to see any proof, or to hear anything about it beyond Lionel's continued enthusiasm.

From the outset she was so involved in the plot, and the characters, and the locale—the BBC at its superb best—that when Simon initially appeared on the screen it took her several moments to recognize him. It wasn't just his being in costume with his teeth made to look brown and broken, but his characterization and the bursting energy he brought to the part of an earnest, ignorant young peasant who begged the hero for a job in his mill. His Cornish accent was perfect; the blend of hope and despair he brought to the role was so compelling, she watched completely entranced. He really was gifted, even inspired, and she was awed.

When he rang up asking, "Did you watch? What did you think?" she said, "I saw it," then gave an exhilarated laugh. "Simon, you're wonderful! I'm so impressed. I simply can't tell you."

"Yeah, I wasn't bad, was I?" She could almost hear him grinning.

"I think," she predicted with an atypical lack of caution, "you're going to be very famous, darling. It was *so* good."

"Darling, eh? What's this, then?"

She laughed, embarrassed. "Shouldn't I have said that?"

"Yeah." He laughed. "I like it. How'd you like the way I died, then?"

"You were brilliant. I wish you were here. I'd go on for at least another hour telling you how good you are."

"Not to worry. You can tell me this weekend. I want you to come down. I think I've found us a flat in South Kensington. Well, Fulham really, near World's End. It's going to need some fixing up, but I reckon it's a fair deal for the price. Come Friday night. And listen, luv! Buy yourself something smashing to wear, will you? We'll go out."

"Yes, all right."

After throwing the top and bottom bolts on the kitchen door, she stopped to look out at the stand of trees a hundred-odd yards to the rear of the property. Her heart was racing; she felt excited. He really was an actor—a stunningly good one.

Upstairs, she went into Simon's room, opening the wardrobe to see his clothes hanging there. On impulse, she gathered an armful of his clothes and pressed her face into them, breathing him in. There were times when he made little, if any sense, to her. And his motives were often incomprehensible. But standing there with her face buried in his clothes, all she could think and feel was how painfully much she loved him. And perhaps he was right—perhaps nothing else did matter.

The flat was a wreck. "But it's going at a good price," he told her as they picked their way through the rooms. "A few more years and anything at all in London's going to be worth a bloody fortune. Once we've got it fixed up, it'll be smashing."

"Well, it is quite big," she said, horrified by the condition of the place. Plaster was crumbling from the walls, leaving gaping holes. Water stains, brown at the edges, covered the ceilings. The loo was a rusted stinking mess. There was no kitchen, and no wardrobe space.

"I thought we'd make this the lounge, see," he said, "and make the lounge the bedroom. Makes sense, doesn't it, to have the lounge on the street side. We'll close off the door here and open a door the other end. Make this second bedroom into a kitchen and cut off part of it to make the bathroom bigger."

"It's going to cost a fortune," she said, hating the place.

"Nah, not if we do a lot of it ourselves."

"But *when?* We only seem to have the weekends together now as it is. And I've got my job. It could take years to put this flat into any sort of order. One certainly couldn't live here in its present condition."

"I've been thinking about all that," he said, lighting a cigarette and flicking his match into the disused fireplace. "There's brick underneath here, you know," he said, placing his hand flat on the wall above the scarred mantelpiece. "We stripped all this muck off, it'd look smashing, a brick wall."

"It needs such a lot of work."

"I want to buy the place. I reckon we can rent the other two flats and let the place pay for itself."

"You want to buy the *building?*"

"That's right. And it's freehold, to boot."

"Are the other flats in this bad condition?"

"They're all right, really. They *could* do with a bit of painting and plastering. People're bloody desperate for flats hereabouts. If we get those done up first, we could rent them and have income coming in to cover the mortgage and help pay for the work that needs doing up here."

"If the others aren't in quite such bad condition, why decide on this one for us?"

"It's the top floor. We'd have no one above us. I don't fancy having tenants stomping away over my head. Look, Sarah, we'll get married. You could come down here and help me work on the flats, and maybe we'll get started on some kids."

It was so unexpected she could only stare at him for several moments. Then she asked, "What about my job?"

"Chuck it! You'll be busy enough what with working here."

"And the cottage? What about it?"

"We'll keep it, for weekends or whatever."

"Simon, I don't want to give up my job, or the cottage. We've only been in it a few months. I would like very much to get married. I mean to say, I do want to marry you. But I don't like London all that much. I really don't want to live here. And what would I do with myself once the flats were put to order? I'd go mad! I couldn't bear just sitting about every day waiting for you to come home."

"I want us to work this out," he said stubbornly. "I'd like us to get a few things settled."

"I'd like that, too. It's just that I couldn't give up everything I have to … to … This is frightening!"

"That's nice, isn't it? I ask you to get married and all you are is frightened. Flattering as hell, that is."

"You've got a career here," she argued. "You're starting to become successful. I rarely see you as it is. It would be simply dreadful being here in the city, not seeing you."

"Take six months off from working, then. Have a word with your friend, the sergeant."

"Simon, I've got to think about this. I'd love to be able to make decisions the way you do, but I can't." Instinctively, she moved towards the smeared, grimy window and stood looking out.

"What's so bloody wonderful about that stinking job anyway?" he demanded. Bloody women! he thought. They never would do what you bloody wanted them to.

In a subdued voice, she said, "Nothing would change all that much if we got married, would it? We really needn't do it unless you're sure it's what you want. I'm quite content to go on as we are."

"Right then! We'll forget it!" He was so furious with her he felt like turning on his heel, going off and leaving her there.

"Don't be angry. You're asking me to give up everything familiar—my job, my home, my way of life—to come here and live in this *rubble*, to help you turn it into something livable. And what you're offering me in return is your name and the responsibility of looking after any children we might have. Of course, that's not the way you see it. But then, why should you? I can almost hear what you're thinking: *Sarah's so bloody difficult.* And ungrateful. Perhaps that's true. But since we met, all I've done is make changes. First on the house, then on the cottage. Not to mention all the changes I've had to make in myself. Now, you're proposing still more changes and I can't help wondering how I'm supposed to benefit. Yes, I love you. I just don't know if that's enough. Do you see?"

"No, I don't bloody *see*! You *needed* changing! And whatever you've done, it's been because you decided to do it, not because I ever forced you."

"That's true ," she agreed, her voice going lower as his rose higher. "I admit that."

"What the bloody hell do you *want?*"

"Things to go on as they are, I suppose. I'm getting tired of all the work, all the change, all your rationales for behavior I don't, half the time, understand."

"And what you're *getting*," he raged on, disregarding her answer, "is to be with me here. That's what I'm trying to work out, damn it! You want to go changing things, that's your bloody problem, mate! I thought you'd *want* to work on this with me. We'd be *together* for a bloody change instead of just a weekend here and there, or maybe a fortnight together when I've got one free."

She stood away from the window, every muscle in her body gone tight, asking, "What do we do now?"

"*I'd like to* hit *you!*" he shouted. "You *nit! You bloody nit! Stupid,* that's what you are! You'd like to stay your life tucked away, looking out some bloody window at the fucking world passing by. I'm trying to get you *out* of all that, don't you see? Do you see? No, you bloody *don't!*"

"All I see," she said very slowly, sensing they were approaching a parting of the ways, "is that you're asking me to start work on yet another set of rooms when I've scarcely had time to enjoy the place I've just finished. You're treating me like some sort of exotic, unskilled laborer. To be perfectly honest, I dislike this house intensely. If you buy it, I won't help you with it. In fact, I'd be happier if you'd go on looking and find something more suitable. Actually, I think I'd better go now." She took another step away from the window, nearly undone by his anger. "I know you'd like me to picture this as it could be, but I'll be *damned* if I'll oversee any more shoddy workmen who spend more time on tea-breaks than they do on the job they're being paid to do." She'd never before had to fight, not anyone about anything, and the effort was making itself felt in her lungs, in her chaotic heartbeat, in the perspiration running down her sides under the coat. "I simply will *not* do it! My time, my life is just as important as yours and I will not waste any of it trying to turn this *indescribable mess* into something livable." She took several more steps, paused, then went out, gingerly making her way down the stairs, and along the foul-smelling hallway and out into the fresh air. The voice in her head was telling her: *It's over, ended. You've put an end to it. He'll send for his things and you'll never see him again. You've been a complete fool, and this is how it ends.* All she wanted, at that moment, was to find a telephone and talk to Lionel. He'd be able to help; he'd be willing to discuss matters.

Simon stood staring at the open doorway, then swore loudly and turned to look again at the room. All right, it was a bloody shambles and no two ways about it. But Christ! She'd actually walked out. Where the hell did she think she was going? *Sarah*, of all the bloody unlikely women, had *walked out* on him. Where the *hell* did she think she was going?

He turned and ran, taking the steps down two at a time. Arriving on the pavement, he looked this way, then that and saw her turning the corner into the Fulham Road, moving at a good clip. He just couldn't believe she'd walked out that way and that she intended, from the look of it, to keep right on going. He took off after her, pounding along the pavement with no idea what he wanted to say to her; he only wanted to catch her, to stop her. She couldn't just leave, just go away from him that way. She moved fast, he thought, speeding up to overtake her. Then, for several seconds, he was overcome by a dizzying sense of *déjà vu*. This had all happened before: he would put out his hand to touch her. She'd stop and turn. Her face would be dead white and awful. She wouldn't say anything.

He threw out his hand, grabbing hold of her sleeve. She gave a little cry of surprise, then stopped and turned. Her face was ashen, her lips bloodless.

"I won't buy the bloody place! All right? We'll forget it!"

"You'll blame me," she said through numb-feeling lips. "But I'm not wrong! I'm not!"

"I won't blame you," he promised, sighing, his voice back to its normal register. "I won't bloody blame you. The place *is* a stinking mess. We'll look for something else."

"I thought ..." She had to stop and take a breath, stricken by the idea that she might actually begin weeping in the middle of a busy street. "I thought you were letting me go. I felt as if I were *dying!*" Her voice broke on a high, jagged note.

"Come on." he said, putting his arm around her. "A bit of a blowup, that's all."

"But you were so angry," she said against his jacket.

"Yeah, I was. It doesn't mean anything, though. So were you, for that matter."

"I don't want to do any more of it, Simon, living so unsettled with workmen constantly coming and going, never finishing when they say they will, everything disordered. Couldn't we pool our money and get a decent flat?"

She was no bloody dishrag, was she? he thought, filled with new admiration for her. "Listen, are we getting married or not?"

"You're serious? It's what you really want?"

"Nah. I'm always going on, aren't I, asking things I don't mean?" He smoothed her hair. "We're getting married. That way, I reckon, the next time we start rowing you won't think we're having the big split just 'cause we don't happen to agree. Let's go in here and have a coffee." He steered her into a Kardomah coffee bar and over to a table in the corner where they both, at once, lit cigarettes somewhat shakily.

"Get good 'n mad, don't you, when you feel like it?" he said.

"I've never done anything like that before. It's left me feeling quite ill."

"You liked me, did you, in that show?"

"What has that to do with this?"

"Nothing. I just fancied a change of subject. Two coffees, luv," he told the waitress. "And a round of those. What're those, cheese?"

"Cheese and tomato."

"Right, bring us a couple of rounds." The girl went off and he turned to watch Sarah unbuttoning her coat. She was wearing a new beige woolen dress and some makeup. "You look nice," he said quietly. "You're coming along a treat, these days."

"I feel like hell, like absolute bloody hell. I *loathe* arguing."

"It's healthy though, clears the air."

"It may be all of that, but I hate it. Our getting married isn't going to change anything, Simon."

"Probably not. But I'd like to all the same."

"It's ridiculous," she said, "but so would I." With a confused little smile, she took hold of his hand. "What's to become of us? We're hopelessly mismatched."

"It'll keep 'em all on their toes, won't it?"

"Will you agree to our buying a flat together? I feel so tired after racing about nonstop since last Christmas. And you haven't another part lined up, yet, have you?"

"Teller's bound to come up with something. He's got more irons in the fire than a bloody blacksmith. Has me up for films, the West End, telly, adverts, radio, the bloody lot."

"And so he should. You're good. He thinks so and so do I."

"You think so, eh?"

"I think so." Her voice dropping, her hand hard around his, she whispered, "I love you, Simon. Nothing has ever been better, or worse. I wish to God you were of a mind to take me somewhere and make love."

Turning his head slightly away, he said, "I wish I were, too."

"If I could just tell you how it feels, never knowing if this time will be the time you want me. It's so awful, wanting you; it's like some sort of frightful disease. I don't know what to do about wanting you. It's like *pain*," she whispered, sensing how uncomfortable she was making him. "Nothing seems to want to ease it. I wake up when you're away and feel as if I'll die if you don't touch me. I know it makes you uncomfortable when I talk about it, and I do try not to. I've been very good about it, haven't I? Will you admit that?"

"I admit it."

"Oh, God!" She closed her eyes for a moment, clinging to his hand. "I hate the irony of this, *hate* it! I'll stop in a moment, I promise. Do you ever"—she opened her eyes to look at him beseechingly—"*ever* think of me when we're apart, and want me?"

"We'll have a kid," he said placatingly. "Maybe a couple. It'll help."

"I feel as if I'm *begging*. It's so shameful, feeling as I've got to beg you to want me." She wondered, suddenly, if Lionel felt this same way. If he did, they had more in common than she'd thought.

"Here's our coffee, luv," he said brightly, alerting her to the waitress.

She released his hand as a plate of sandwiches and a cup of coffee were set down in front of her. She didn't dare look up for fear of finding the waitress's eyes on her, or worse, on Simon. She picked up the cup with both hands, then set it down again to light another cigarette. "I'm sorry," she said hoarsely. "I know it's most unfair of me." She turned to see he hadn't touched his food.

"It's just as unfair of me to go volunteering you into another sodding lot of improvements. Let's say we're even and call it quits. I've got to ring up the estate agent on that place and tell him it's no go. Fancy having a look at some others?"

"Fine, that would be fine. Simon?" She took hold of his hand again, searching his eyes. "*Do* you love me? Really, do you?"

"Yeah," he said softly, running his thumb over her eyebrows. "I do, really. Eat up, luv. I'll go ring up and be right back."

He went to ask the waitress for the nearest call-box, then went out, disappearing past the café window. Sarah lifted her cup and tasted the coffee. Strong, bitter. She dropped in a cube of sugar and sat stirring mindlessly, feeling demoralized by her outburst and wishing she'd had the courage to leave her longings undeclared. It was a burden she was placing upon him; bad enough that she had to carry it herself without loading him down with it, too. And one child, or even six, wouldn't alter her need to have him offer her physical reaffirmation. Nothing would alter that. She'd simply have to learn to cope in silence. Again she thought of Lionel. And again she sensed that he shared her feelings. How odd! she thought.

"Bloke's expecting us in half an hour," he said, returning to devour his sandwich quickly and, with a wry face, drink down the coffee. "Bloody bitter that! Aren't you eating, luv?"

"You have it." She slid the plate towards him. "I'm really not hungry."

"Still upset?"

"It was wrong of me to burden you that way with a problem that's entirely mine."

"Nah, luv," he disagreed. "That's where you're wrong, see. When you tell me how you feel, that's when I love you the most, 'cause I know you're being straight with me. And that's never easy. So, I figure, if you're straight with me even when it's bloody hard for you, then I can be the same way with you. And that makes it all real between us, see?"

"That makes sense."

"It's all forgotten now, isn't it?" He smiled around a mouthful of sandwich.

"Oh, Simon." She smiled, touching his cheek. "You really are far cleverer than I. You make such sense of things sometimes."

"Right impressive that bit of a show was you put on," he said. "C'mon." He dropped some money on the table. "Let's go find us a decent flat."

They agreed on a flat in Sussex Gardens in Bayswater, on the ground floor of a three-story terraced block of converted flats. It had two bedrooms, a spacious lounge and a kitchen, and was in need only of fresh paint and paper. The price was three times that of the building near World's End.

Simon's only comment was, "We're going to have to make do without furniture for a time, but we'll manage." And, looking very proud, he wrote a check for the deposit.

The following month, Teller landed him four days' work in another television show.

Simon said, "If we're going to do it, luv, we might as well get it done now before I've got to go off."

So with Lionel and Beaconstead as witnesses, she and Simon got married at the Kenilworth Registry Office, then they all went out to lunch.

Later that same afternoon, Simon and Teller left for London. Before he went, Teller took Sarah aside to hold both her hands in his for a moment, in an undertone saying, "Bless you, darling. And be happy."

She looked into his eyes, seeing there only the depths of his sincerity, and felt both warmed and defeated. Whatever Simon's relationship was with this man, and however Simon chose to minimize it in words, there was caring and concern involved, and she couldn't dismiss the caring or the man.

"I do wish you were living in town," he said. "I'd enjoy seeing you more often."

She said, "Thank you," and kissed his cool cheek, then watched her new husband and his sometime lover drive away.

She changed out of her wedding dress—a pale blue silk Simon had chosen with great care—and went to put on the kettle. All that had changed was her name and the fact that the properties were to be listed now in both their names.

That same night she stopped taking her birth control pills even though she strongly doubted they'd ever succeed in making a child; they seldom spent an entire night together in the same bed.

Fifteen

To all outward appearances, they might never have been married at all. But now when she was home alone, she wore a pair of Simon's old jeans and an ancient golfing cardigan of Uncle Arthur's over one of Simon's shirts. The act of wearing his clothes seemed confirmation of their commitment to each other, as was the money he insisted on giving her whenever he received payment for a part he'd played, and the gifts he brought her from his trips abroad: gold earrings from Morocco, a lace shirt from Spain, high-heeled sandals from Italy, ebony worry beads from Greece. As his earning power increased, so did his generosity and his absences. She learned to accept both his offerings and his departures graciously—he taught her.

He was happier, more golden than ever. She began to have night-mares.

In the worst of her nightmares, her teeth turned brown and, one by one, loosened and dropped out of her mouth. Or her hair came away from her scalp in handfuls, revealing a rapidly spreading, shiny bald patch. The roof of her mouth reopened like the dome of the London Planetarium and her ability to make herself understood leaked away through the vast opening like so much air. Her hands turned into crippled arthritic claws that sought, beneath Simon's horror-strick-en gaze, to caress him. Her belly swelled, her breasts turned huge and painful; she found herself spread upon a massive stainless steel exam-ining table being delivered of an enormous, hideously misshapen creature that snarled and screamed and then shriveled to nothing and vanished.

She dreamed she was at the dentist's surgery; she was having a laughing conversation with the dentist and his assistant when she suddenly realized she was hours late and that Simon was standing outside the London flat without a key, waiting for her to come and let him in. The dentist and his assistant sought to detain her, hope-ful of prolonging the pleasant conversation, but she ran out in search of a telephone in order to ring the next-door neighbors and ask them to go out and let Simon wait in their flat until she could get there. But none of the telephones had dials, and disembodied voices told her, "We only receive calls, we don't make them." She then ran outside to find her car gone, and tried stopping people but the cars kept swinging past her, cutting wide paths around where she stood in the road, frantically waving her arms and pleading for someone to stop. No one would. When she felt herself beginning to scream, she dragged herself awake.

To Simon's distress, he periodically had that same dream of Sarah sprawled on the road in the rain while he was held captive by the arms of some lad in the back of a passing car. Fortunately, he didn't dream it often, and usually only when he'd been on location for a week or two and was starting to feel the pull towards her, the need to have reality returned to him in the form of Sarah's quietly pragmatic reasoning, her tremulous embraces, and her enthusiasm for him rather than for his accomplishments. When, from time to time, he found himself involved with some lad or other, the involvement, no matter how brief or inconsequential, was always tainted with the faint flavor of guilt. He couldn't help wishing he were able to give what he was giving to the man of the moment to Sarah. Yet, when they were together, he was, at best, no more than fifty per cent actively drawn to making love with her. The rest of the time both of them had to be content simply being together. Sarah was growing increasingly attractive and better put-together, and he did occasionally wonder if she wasn't perhaps availing herself of the attentions of other men. But when he was home, when he saw her, spoke with her, and touched her, and she responded with increased appetite for him, he knew he'd simply been woolgathering, perhaps even indulging in wishful thinking. Part of him wished she'd use up a bit of her sexual energy on some anonymous other man. But the rest of him grew instantly, heatedly outraged at the idea. Sarah was his: his creation, his real success. Nevertheless, he suffered at picturing her long naked thighs opening to some other man, at this other man's hands on her sweet, heavy breasts or narrow waist. It put him into a paroxysm of desperation that without fail sent him to the telephone to ring her up and hear her voice, thereby reassuring himself.

▽

At Crossroads, Sarah performed her job as always, deriving consistent pleasure and even comfort from her daily contact with the residents. But Margaret seemed to be growing increasingly short-tempered and irritable, not only with Sarah but with everyone. It came to a head one late afternoon as Sarah was bringing in Mrs. Elgon's tea tray. She arrived in time to see and hear Margaret shrieking at the cringing elderly woman who had, apparently, once again lost her Biro. This time, it seemed, the pen had managed to get pushed down under the bedclothes and had left a large blue indelible stain on the sheet.

"*You'll have no more pens!*" Margaret ranted. "You're *impossible!*"

"*Margaret!*" Sarah said quietly, shocked by the woman's insensitivity and loss of control.

Margaret glanced over, her face white with rage, then looked back at Mrs. Elgon. "You people," she exclaimed "are simply *careless!* You don't care how much work you make for the rest of us!" She waved the offending Biro in Mrs. Elgon's face as Sarah set down the tea tray. Sarah straightened, prepared to defend the old woman who sat huddled in her bed, weeping.

"Margaret," she began again, "don't you think … ?"

"I'll see *you* in my office straight away!" Margaret ordered, and stormed out.

Sarah sat down on the side of the bed taking hold of Mrs. Elgon's cold cadaverous hand, automatically stroking it.

"That woman shouldn't have the sort of job she does," Mrs. Elgon wept. "She's most unkind. Really most unkind! It's only a bit of a mark from the Biro. And if she takes it away, how shall I write to my children?"

"You'll have your Biro," Sarah said, reaching for a tissue to dry the woman's face.

"It's not as if I soil the bed like some of the others," Mrs. Elgon defended herself. "I don't do *that*."

"I know," Sarah said, feeling a little ill, and wondering what was wrong with Margaret. It took her half an hour to get Mrs. Elgon calmed down and started on her tea. Then Sarah went downstairs to the office.

Margaret glared at her, saying, "How dare you keep me waiting half an hour when I told you to come down at once?"

"Mrs. Elgon was in quite a state."

"You'd best sit down!" Margaret commanded.

"Is something wrong, Margaret? It isn't like you …"

"We're going to have to let you go," Margaret cut in.

"Let me go?"

"It simply will not do to have you undercutting my authority with the residents!"

"Oh, but surely you …"

"Under the circumstances," Margaret went on, "it would be best if you left at once. Your cards and money will be sent along."

"Does Ian know about this?" Sarah asked.

"*Ian* has nothing to *do* with the hiring and firing of the *staff!*" she near-shouted. "Please collect your things and leave at once! We can't have you here disrupting everything!"

"Margaret," Sarah said softly, "you're not serious, are you? I really don't want to leave. And if I do, you'll be terribly short-handed."

Margaret lit a cigarette and stood up. She stared at Sarah for a moment with hate-filled eyes, loathing everything about her from her made-up face to the shrimp-colored matching jumper and skirt she knew had come from Jaeger's. "You do more harm than good," she said. "Your influence on the residents is counterproductive to our aims here."

She hates me, Sarah thought. Why? And what did she mean by counterproductive? Sarah wanted to argue the matter but suddenly felt sick at the stomach and ran out of the office, down the hall to one of the lavatories.

Afterwards, she rinsed her mouth with cold water and then went back to the staff room to collect her string carrier and handbag. As she was pulling on her coat, Grace and Doreen appeared in the doorway.

"She's a right bitch," Grace said, while Doreen stood looking frozen with shock. "She's got no call to go givin' you the sack. It's her should be gettin' it, not you." It was, for Grace, a very long speech.

"It's 'cause she's jealous, isn't it?" Doreen contributed. "She's all the time goin' on about your clothes and your Simon an' how he's just after your money 'n all."

"I don't want to leave," Sarah said helplessly, her stomach knotting painfully.

Grace nodded sympathetically. Doreen looked down at her feet. Sarah buttoned her coat, then picked up her things, afraid to say anything further for fear of crying. Grace and Doreen stepped back into the kitchen and, in awkward silence, Sarah moved to go. Grace extended her hand and Sarah placed hers in it, warmed by the bony strength of the woman's grip. "Don't think back on this," Grace said gruffly. "She's due for her comeuppance. I'll miss you, I will. You've never said no to hard work 'n you deserve better than this."

Doreen enfolded her in an embarrassed embrace, then broke away, red-faced, to resume gazing at her shoes. Close to tears, Sarah left the building and started towards her car as nausea again overtook her. She vomited on one of the frozen flower beds, then wiped her mouth with a tissue and climbed into the car to drive to John's surgery.

The nurse said, "If you'd care to wait, I'm sure he'll see you at the end. I'll just pop in and tell him you're here."

Sarah thanked her and sat down in a corner of the crowded waiting room. She stared at a tattered copy of *Queen*, wondering why she'd come here. Because, she told herself, she wanted John to make sense of what had happened at Crossroads. As staff doctor there, he was bound to have some idea why Margaret had behaved as she had.

Finally, the room was empty and the nurse beckoned Sarah inside.

John smiled, asking, "What seems to be the trouble?"

For a moment she couldn't answer. Then she said, "Margaret's let me go."

"Sit down, Sarah. Let you go? She's *sacked* you?" He looked amazed.

Sarah nodded. "She was shouting at Mrs. Elgon and it was entirely wrong. Perhaps it wasn't my place to interfere ... and I didn't really. But she was simply livid." She stopped, feeling the nausea again.

"You're a frightful color," he said. "Are you feeling all right?"

"Actually, no." She swallowed, then moistened her lips.

"When did this start?" he asked.

"She's been becoming increasingly more irascible ..."

"Margaret's menopausal," he said, then smiled. "I meant how long have you been suffering from the nausea."

"Menopausal? Is that it, do you suppose? Would that be why she's been so difficult?"

"That and frustration, I expect, at not having more of a say in matters than she does. Has it just started?"

"She upsets me, and upsets invariably go directly to my stomach."

"Have you missed any periods?"

"That's odd," she said as if to herself. "I haven't. But I've been spotting. I assumed ... I'm not sure what I assumed."

"I think we should have a look."

While she was undressing behind the screen, the nurse busied herself beside the examining table, and John washed his hands at the basin in the corner of the room, saying, "Ian's not been well, I'm afraid. And Margaret's been carrying most of the load herself. Unfortunately, she hasn't the ease or the affability to make a go of it without letting everyone know precisely how heavy that load is. She wants approval but she's succeeded only in creating more and more unpleasantness. The board of governors is well aware of the situation."

"Are they?" she asked from behind the screen, folding her clothes and placing them on the little shelf.

"Oh, definitely," he said.

"But what will she and Ian do?" she asked. "I know they haven't any money to speak of and the job's very important to her. The residents never minded her all that much ... before."

"The families are complaining bitterly," he said as she came out from behind the screen and sat on the edge of the examining table. "Even the volunteers are refusing to work with her. Slide down here a bit more. That's fine. It's only a matter of time before they're replaced. I know this is uncomfortable but do try to relax. Otherwise, it'll be even more uncomfortable."

She gazed at the ceiling. "I had no idea there'd been complaints. I mean to say, I thought that I'd offended her somehow ... by implying criticism, I suppose."

"Ah!" he said. "Just as I suspected." He went on with the examination for another minute or two then withdrew his hand and smiled at her. "I'd say between three and four months."

"Are you sure? I mean, can you tell that way? Aren't there supposed to be tests?"

He helped her to a sitting position then lowered the gown to examine her breasts. "Your cervix has thinned out, and there's definite growth in the uterus. Tender here?"

"A bit."

"I can't say I care for this spotting. Has it been heavy?"

"Medium. Between three and four months?"

"Closer to four, I'd say. I expect the spotting's thrown you off."

"I hadn't the faintest idea," she said, stunned.

"I'll give you a prescription for some tablets to ease the nausea."

"Thank you."

He patted her knee, saying, "Get dressed now and we'll have a chat in the office."

Woodenly, she got down from the table and returned behind the screen to dress. She was trembling as she wiped the jelly-like lubricant from the tops of her thighs with a tissue.

"How is Simon these days?" John asked as she slid back into the chair in front of his desk. "What's he been up to?" While he talked, he quickly wrote out several prescription slips.

"He's just back from making a film in Paris."

"I didn't know he spoke French."

"He doesn't." She laughed, forgetting herself. "I helped him learn all his lines phonetically. As he was playing an Englishman, it was really all right." She gave a small shake of her head. "He's going to be doing the second lead in a new musical in the West End next September. He's been taking all sorts of lessons—singing and dancing." She went quiet for a moment, remembering how the previous weekend he'd danced across her bed in an explosion of exuberance, singing at the top of his lungs so that the man in the flat next door had started banging on the wall. "Silly sod doesn't appreciate good music," Simon had declared.

"It comes as no real surprise to me," John was saying. "Simon's always had a certain something. No," he went on, "you're the surprise, Sarah. Obviously the two of you are very happy."

She answered, "Yes," thinking that people talked such a lot about happiness, as if it were something one needed constantly to remind oneself of and had to work terribly hard for. But they did have it; they'd had it all along and had simply been putting the wrong name to it.

He slid the several slips across the desk to her, explaining, "This one's for multi-vitamins. This one's for the nausea. And this one will, I hope, see to the spotting. But if it continues, you're to come back. Don't let it go on longer than another fortnight."

She put the prescriptions into her bag, then asked, "How are you getting on, John?"

"Oh, I'm settling in as well as can be expected. It takes some doing getting used to living on one's own. It's been a year since Elizabeth left, you know."

"Yes," she agreed, looking at her wristwatch. "If I hurry, I could just make the eight-twenty from Coventry."

"You'd better get on your way then," he said, smiling again as he got up to see her to the door. "Congratulations. And to Simon, too. Don't forget to come straight round if the spotting doesn't clear up, or if it gets worse."

"No, I'll remember."

She drove home to throw a nightdress and her toothbrush into a small bag, then tore back out to the car and drove like a madwoman over the foggy back roads in order to make the train.

Throughout the ninety-minute train trip she found herself alternating between a surging euphoria and a mounting depression. How she reacted to this pregnancy was going to depend on Simon. He'd been talking from the beginning about the children he wanted. Now they were going to have one. And since she no longer had to concern herself with her job at Crossroads, a baby would certainly keep her busy enough. Her thoughts in this direction were temporarily suspended as she reviewed what had happened earlier at the residence. She wanted to weep. But then she thought again about the baby. She'd wait and see how Simon took it. He was bound to be excited and she'd allow his excitement to carry her past the grinding disappointment and near-despair that swept over her every time she thought of how cruelly Margaret had dismissed her.

She took a taxi from Euston and let herself into the flat. Both the television and the radio were going. Puzzled, she went down the hall towards her bedroom where the lights were on. She came to a stop in the doorway, her hand automatically seeking support on the doorframe. She wanted to turn away and run but couldn't move, and was unaware of the low whining sound that had begun in her throat and caused the heads of both men to jerk up, their eyes, round and startled, fixing on her.

This was it, she thought. This was how it happened, how she finally had to witness first-hand the unknown side of Simon's life. Why in the name of God did she have to see?

The second man got to his feet with what she thought was exceptional grace. The recording part of her brain continued to run on with unaffected detachment as the tall, slim young man turned his back and reached for his clothes, exclaiming, "Oh, God help us! We're going to have one of those dreary little domestic scenes where the wife carries on and hubbie explains."

She made herself turn and, with legs of lead, move down the hall to the front door, leaving it open as she escaped from the flat. She headed towards Bayswater Road to find a taxi, wanting only to go home and, in privacy, think about what she'd seen. She sat in the back of the taxi with her hand over her mouth, fused to an image of that young man kneeling on the floor as Simon's hand lovingly stroked his long glossy hair.

The train wasn't due for twenty minutes and she suddenly wanted to speak to Lionel, to hear his voice and tell him what had happened. He'd understand; he was the only person she knew who possibly could.

There had been times after their initial meeting when she'd wanted to hate Lionel Teller, and had willfully tried to use him as the focus for whatever dissatisfaction she'd felt with Simon. But every time she'd managed to work herself up to the point of active resentment, Lionel would ring up and, in his melodious voice, say, "Darling! How are you? Why do you never come visit?" And whatever negative feelings she'd had about him dissolved. It was impossible to dislike someone who so consistently displayed overt fondness and enthusiasm for her. And besides, she enjoyed him. He was witty, intelligent, and sympathetic without ever being rancorous. When she was in town, he insisted on taking her to lunch or dinner and played raconteur, telling her inside stories about the business, harmless bits of gossip and news. Then he'd give her a kiss on the cheek, see her into a taxi and prepay the fare before going on his way with a jaunty air.

She looked forward to his calls and visits. She could discuss with him things she could speak of to no one else. They always talked of Simon in the abstract, as if at the outset they'd tacitly agreed that his introduction into their conversation might weaken or even damage the friendship they'd created. So, while it was Simon who'd brought them together, it was Simon who might potentially separate them.

There had been times when she'd longed to take hold of Lionel's slim, manicured hand and beg him to let go of Simon's life and, therefore, of hers; beg him to retreat into the professional distance and allow her and Simon the freedom to deal with each other and their problems as they arose, instead of always being there in the background as the obvious focal point for whatever discontent she might feel. But these moments invariably passed and she'd come to cherish this man who had evolved, finally, into her dearest and most valued friend.

She ran to the bank of telephones, dialed Lionel's number and stood with pennies at the ready, desperate for the sound of his hello. But the ringing went on and on, and as it did, the last shreds of her strength and purpose seeped away. She returned the receiver to its cradle feeling numb again. Why wasn't he there when she needed him so badly?

Moving within a cloud of impenetrable, deadly calm, she went to have a cup of tea and a cigarette in the station tea-room, thinking about how her rightful place had been usurped by that young man of twenty-two or -three. A young man, arrogantly handsome, with long black hair and a beautiful body. She reran the scene so that instead of doing what she had—which now seemed to her cowardly and utterly ineffective—she removed her clothes and both men commenced making love to her. The sheer ludicrousness of this fantasy undid her. She drank the too-strong tea, lit another cigarette, then went back into the body of the rather deserted station to present her ticket at the barrier. She walked very slowly down the platform to a smoking compartment where she sat beside the window, crossed her impossibly heavy legs and, with some effort, turned to look at the deserted adjacent platform. She felt nothing more than a deep aching need to get home and go to sleep; she was too exhausted even to cry.

Simon's only clear thought was that she was going to kill herself. He had no doubt that if he didn't find and stop her, he'd never see her alive again. He ignored the bitchy remarks of the lad who seemed bent on a caustic effort to prove himself superior to the silly woman who'd just intruded upon them and then lumbered off as if in a trance. Simon dressed in a frenzy, literally shoved the lad out of the flat, ran back to snatch up his keys and money, locked up and dashed out to the car, heading for Euston Station. It was the likeliest place he thought she'd go.

Cursing at the traffic, recklessly cutting in and out, he tried to remember if the trains still went on the hour and half-hour. He left the car illegally, haphazardly parked outside the station and tore inside to stop a porter and ask the train times.

"Coventry? You've missed it. It left ten minutes ago. But you've got plenty of time. The next one goes at twenty past."

He ran breathlessly through the station to the barrier to check the platform, more frightened with each moment at failing to spot her. She might have made the earlier train, he decided, and he flew back to the car just as he was about to be given a ticket. He unlocked the door and climbed in—apologizing all the while—and headed for, the North Circular Road praying she'd been on that earlier train. If she'd gone anywhere else, he'd never find her.

Why couldn't she have rung up like always to let him know she was coming? She *never* came down without letting him know. And if she couldn't reach him, she usually left a message with Teller. Why hadn't she done that this time?

He was technically still supposed to be running in the new Aston Martin, but he put his foot to the floor and shot up the M-1 at a hundred and twenty, chain-smoking and sweating heavily. He felt sick with guilt that did battle against his strong sense of self-justification. After all, it wasn't as if he hadn't always been truthful with her; she'd known from the beginning. But why the hell hadn't she picked up the bloody blower to let him know she was coming? None of this would've happened, would it, if she'd just done that. She had to have had some reason for wanting to surprise him, he decided. And this made him feel even worse, because not only had she caught him going at it with the lad, but catching him had also put paid to her surprise, whatever it'd been. He prayed she wouldn't do anything stupid. All he wanted was a chance to talk it through.

He thought on, admitting that no matter how justified he believed he was, it was seeing that upset her. If his sometime daydreams of her and another man shook him badly, then what she'd seen had to have been bloody awful for her. That was the bad part, he knew, the part that might prompt her to do almost bloody anything. Because had their positions been reversed, he'd have wanted to die. So she had to feel the same way.

She sat gazing sightlessly out the window, picturing herself going to the flat above the surgery to surprise John. She'd invite herself inside and then, with pathological determination, she'd undress while he stood watching in bemused, but aroused silence. She'd bare her breasts first, and then, slowly, the rest of herself, before moving into his arms. And with cold premeditation she'd avenge herself on Simon by taking John into her. In the process, she'd soil the child inside her. She grimaced at the improbable yet profoundly upsetting image of another man's semen spurting over the lump of coagulating tissues that was going to be hers and Simon's baby.

Perhaps she'd go into that charming little pub near the cottage and solicit some tweedy stranger. They'd climb into the back of his car where, with overwhelming self-possession, she'd remove her underpants and then close her legs around the eagerly thrusting haunches of this faceless stranger.

The images gave her no satisfaction. She had the presence of mind to know she'd do damage only to herself. She had no power to hurt Simon because, from the start, he'd given her his blanket permission to do whatever she chose with whomever she desired. Unless he was there as an unwitting observer—as she had been—the act would have no impact on anyone but her. And, in reality, she was incapable of going after another man in an attempted retaliation for the hurt Simon had given her. He'd brought that young man into their flat and made love to him on *her* bed, in *her* room, surrounded by things *she'd* chosen. He'd fouled the place. Grief-stricken, she thought he might at least have done it in his own room with the door closed. Why her room, and with the door open?

Her chest felt crowded with unshed tears, and waves of pain that seemed to ebb for moments then come flowing back to beat against her ribs with very real pain. The entire day had been a nightmare. She'd lost her job and the last of her illusions.

She tripped climbing down on to the platform from the train and a tall, thin teenage boy took hold of her arm to help her up, asking, "You all right then, luv?"

She nodded dumbly, dusting off her coat, and limped along the platform to the stairs. Like the child who'd gone back to the window again and again for three days and nights, looking down at the mews, wanting her mother to come into sight, she now longed for the sight and comfort of the cottage. She wanted to lock herself inside, to lie down in the dark and sleep forever. She and the child inside her would go to sleep and not wake up again.

He got stopped. And while precious minutes ticked away, he underwent the breathalyzer test, passed it and accepted the caution and the fine, as well as the information that he'd lost points off his license. In all, it cost him half an hour. He got back into the car and continued up the M-1 at a sedate seventy, his shoulders and thighs hurting from the restraint he exercised in not jamming the accelerator back to the floor.

By the time he turned off on to the A-426, he was crying out of fear and sheer exasperation.

As she undressed, she saw she'd badly scraped both knees and her right elbow in the fall, and her left knee didn't seem to want to stop bleeding. She went to start the water going in the bath and while it was running—sending steam over the sunny yellow-patterned tiles Simon had selected—she investigated the contents of the medicine chest. There were the painkillers she'd been given after the surgery. Would they still be potent after all this time? she wondered. She set them to one side as she continued her search, discovering sleeping pills from the same era. She couldn't remember ever having taken any. She set these aside, too. She emptied the contents of the vials, along with a full bottle of Disprin, into a small enamel basin kept in the bathroom for purposes she'd long since forgotten. Then, naked, she carried the basin of tablets down to the kitchen while she plugged in the kettle and stood shivering in the cold, her arms wrapped around herself, as she stood on one foot, then the other, waiting for the kettle to come to the boil.

She used some of the water for a cup of tea and poured the rest over the tablets, then set to work with a spoon, stirring and crushing, making a thickish white paste. The tea in one hand, the basin in the other, she limped upstairs to the bathroom where she set both down carefully on the rim of the tub. Surveying the scene, she decided she wanted her cigarettes and went to get them and an ashtray. Satisfied, she locked the door before climbing into the very hot water and easing herself down. Her knees and elbow stung in protest.

She had a sip of tea, then a puff of the cigarette, then held the basin, poking her finger into the mixture to test the consistency which was very smooth. She took a large swallow of the mixture followed by a sip of the tea, then reached for her cigarette and lay back, the basin resting on her chest. From time to time she took another swallow of both the white mixture and the tea.

In all, she felt quite serene. As Margaret was fond of saying, decisions were good for the soul. She remembered Margaret, while in her cups one evening, saying that women were hopeless at making decisions. "They're forever throwing out the negative possibilities and worrying over the outcome instead of taking pleasure in making the decision itself. Men do it all the time, effortlessly. Big decisions and little ones. But women can't even make up their minds on a piece of furniture without consulting their bloody husbands!"

Well, she'd made a decision. And Margaret was absolutely right: it was really a splendid feeling. Now that she'd decided, she had all the time in the world. She'd finish her tea and cigarette and then the remainder of her basin of cream of tablet soup. She smiled at her whimsy. She stared at the ceiling, ignoring the stinging in her knee and the odd dull ache low in her back. She considered the aspects of death: darkness, silence, peace. Life was a grim joke, really, and she wouldn't give it any further consideration.

Sixteen

He WAS ALMOST SICK WITH RELIEF AT SEEING HER CAR PARKED BESIDE the cottage. He parked behind it and got out to find that the front door was not only locked but bolted from the inside. He ran to the rear. The kitchen door was also bolted. Frightened again, he went around the house testing the ground-floor windows, finally returning to the rear to wrap his jacket around his arm before putting it through the pantry window. He released the catch, opened the window, and climbed inside to stand catching his breath.

She heard him come running up the stairs and sat upright in sudden panic. This wasn't at all the way she'd planned it. He wasn't supposed to be here. He pounded at the door, shouting, "*Sarah! Open this door!*" She lifted the basin to her mouth and began trying to swallow the last of the chalky liquid as fast as she could. She gagged, tears came to her eyes, but she kept on. Then she stopped. If she didn't answer, he'd undoubtedly break in the door.

"Do go away!" she called out. "I don't want to see you!"

He stopped pounding. She drank down more of the pill mixture. She had almost finished it when he began pounding again, shouting, "Stop being stupid and open the bloody door! I want to *talk to you!*"

"Go to hell!" she cried, then got down the last of the pills. She pulled the stopper and climbed out of the tub just as he threw himself against the door and burst in demanding, "What in bloody hell d'you think you're doing in here?"

To her complete disgust and frustration, she realized she was going to vomit and ran to the basin as her mouth opened and what seemed to be gallons of fluid spewed out.

Watching, he again demanded to know, "What've you been up to?" He gazed at her naked, dripping buttocks and thighs as she held on to the sides of the basin and kept retching. He moved to turn on the cold water, then stood with his hand on her spine. She heaved and heaved until, too weakened and humiliated to move, she remained with her head bent, tears dripping down her nose and chin, her stomach contracting painfully. She wanted to hate him but how could she possibly hate someone who could stand by and watch her being sick and seek instinctively to comfort her? His hand remained on her spine and, despite everything, she wanted it there.

After a few moments, he ran a glass of water and held it in front of her. "Drink it," he said tonelessly. "Come on! Drink it!"

She took the glass, rinsed her mouth, then emptied the water into the basin and carefully set the glass down.

"Talk to me!" he pleaded. "Shout at me! Do *something*!"

She shook her head, wiping her eyes with the back of her hand.

"If only you'd rung up," he said, more defeated by her silence than he'd have been by screaming recriminations. "None of this would've happened, would it, if you'd rung up!"

"I wanted to surprise you," she said, then began to cry, staring at the lumpy white residue left around the perimeter of the basin.

"You did, at that."

How could he try to be funny at a time like this? she wondered. Yet she was able herself to see something like black humor in the situation. Here she was unable even to kill herself properly, bent naked over the basin without a shred of dignity. She straightened and threw herself against him, winding her arms around his neck as she sobbed.

"I'm sorry, luv," he said, startled to find himself responding strongly to her nakedness and her larger-than-ever vulnerability. "Christ! I really am sorry." He didn't know if he was apologizing for what had happened or for becoming aroused. She was shivering. The back of her hair was wet, her skin felt damp and cold under his hands. "We'd better get you dry and into your nightdress," he said, reaching for the towel and trying one-handedly to drape it around her.

"I wanted to surprise you!" she said again, aware of what was happening to him. She stepped away, catching the towel as it slipped from her shoulders, and stood holding it, trying to understand why, of all times, he was aroused by her now. "I also," she said, faltering, "wanted to tell you Margaret gave me the sack today."

"Ah, luv." He sighed sympathetically, looking at her breasts, at her cold-shriveled nipples. Then he was looking into the air where she'd been. It was the second time she'd walked out on him. "Bloody hell!" he exclaimed, following her to the bedroom. With anger and resignation in her movements, she threw back the duvet, switched on the electric underblanket, then lay down pulling the duvet around her. She was shivering so hard her teeth were chattering audibly as she curled into herself and closed her eyes tightly.

His sudden lust gone, he sat on the floor beside the bed, leaning back against the night table as he lit a cigarette.

"Look, Sarah," he said quietly, studying his hands. "I never trusted the sergeant. I told you she was dead dodgy, didn't I? We'll find you something else, some other job." He drew on the cigarette, then went on. "I guess it was bound to happen, wasn't it? But it's not as if you didn't know about me and the lads, not as if I ever lied to you. I'm bloody sorry about everything, that's all." He stared at the open wardrobe door. "The silly part of it is I haven't done that much of it lately." He looked over at her but she still had her eyes closed. "I haven't got the energy. And you *know* it doesn't *mean* anything. It's just sex, isn't it, just scratching the old bloody itch." This time when he looked over, her eyes were open. "That's all, it is, really. He was just a cheeky lad I took a fancy to in the local on my way home. I never saw him before and I'll likely never see him again. It hasn't anything to do with *us*, luv."

"*Of course it has to do with us!*" she erupted in a cracked voice. "It has *everything* to do with us! Why can't I be enough for you? Why do you have to go picking up boys and bringing them home? And if you *had* to do it, couldn't you have at least taken him into your own damned room and closed the damned *door?*"

"I know," he said shamefacedly. "I know. I didn't feel right about that from the start, being in your room."

"Then *why* did you *allow* it to *happen?*"

"Dunno," he said truthfully. "I don't bloody *know* why."

She realized that something was happening, something low in her belly. That dull pain was growing stronger in her back, and there was an increasing pressure in her groin. Perhaps the fall, combined with everything else … Caught all at once in a spasm of rage, she sat up, pulling the duvet around her like an enormous shawl, crying, "Go to hell! Fuck you! I wish to God I'd never set eyes on you!" She put her head down on her bent knees, weeping loudly. The pressure was intensifying but seemed to be momentarily eased in this position. She admitted to herself that none of it was true: she could no more have resisted him than fly to the moon. And she didn't know why she was carrying on at him when all that really mattered was that he'd come after her and was here with her now.

He'd never heard her swear. It was jarring, awful, like seeing someone beautiful take a terrible spill on the pavement and go sprawling.

He put out his cigarette and sat up on his knees, leaning on the side of the bed. "I'm sorry," he repeated. "I don't know what else to say or do."

"Don't *do* anything!" she said harshly, lifting her head to glare at him. "It's all been done. We're a pair of complete, perfect fools—you playing about with your boys, and me living in an absolute dream world. It's all a deplorable farce. I haven't even the wits to kill myself properly. And you haven't the wits to keep your squalid little dalliances private."

"Ah, Sarah." He sighed, placing his hand over her foot. "Please, don't let's do this, luv. I don't like your talking about us that way."

"Margaret didn't want me there. Not because she was jealous—that's too laughable—but because I made such a show of caring for that hopeless lot of discards. And because, by rights, I should have been a discard, too. God, it hurts!" she said wonderingly, the pressure building to the point where she couldn't ignore it.

"I know, luv," he said, wanting to console her. "I'm dead sorry. But it isn't the end of the world."

"I'd better ring John," she thought aloud, turning inwards to the pain.

"What?" Thoroughly at sea, he watched her shrug off the duvet and swing her legs over the side of the bed to sit for several moments as if gathering her strength. "Why are you going on about ringing John?"

"Where's my nightdress?" she asked, looking around.

He found it on the floor on the far side of the bed, picked it up and walked back holding it out to her, asking, "What are you going on about, Sarah?"

She didn't answer. The pain rippled down her belly, somehow cementing her spine as it gained in intensity. She stood up clutching the nightdress to her breasts and turned her head very slowly to look at him. Her face was filled with a kind of innocent surprise that made her look very young. "I think I'm losing the baby," she said, then went to take a step and, as if pulled by an invisible cord tied around her midsection, she jerked backwards before falling heavily to the floor.

▽

She lay in a confused place of semi-realities, trying to separate the

real from the remembered. Every so often she came back with a violent start, prepared to strain against heavy straps that weren't there.
They were alone, she saw, just she and Simon in this small, pale
green room. Pain crept about at the edge of her consciousness.

He leaned over her, still stunned by the horror of having seen the
dark blood puddling under her. "You'll be all right, luv," he said,
deeply anxious she should know that he cared.

Her eyes seemed to take ages to come into focus on him. Thickly,
she said, "They tied me down, you know, Simon. Straps on my wrists
... ankles. Masks ... I couldn't see their faces ... I just knew they'd
kill me. Uncle Arthur ... He said I couldn't possibly remember
because I was only eighteen months old. But I remembered ... all of
it. All of it. I'd have wanted it for you ... something I could give
you."

"It doesn't matter," he said.

She closed her eyes.

He sank back into the chair, covered his face with his hands and
cried noisily.

For weeks, Simon went about with a stunned expression, as if he'd
been struck a blow somewhere on his body and, while he could feel
the pain, he hadn't yet been able to locate the site of the injury. He
persuaded Sarah to return to London to be with him while she recu-
perated, and she agreed willingly enough, but they no longer seemed
able to talk to each other. He was very afraid she'd leave him once
she was completely recovered. His fear made him fidgety and rest-
less; he couldn't sit or lie still for more than a few minutes at a time.
He went to his singing and dancing classes but couldn't concentrate.
It was the end of March and rehearsals for the musical wouldn't be
starting until mid-July. If he didn't do something soon, he thought
he might go off his nut. He rang Lionel every morning to ask if there
was anything in the offing and Lionel patiently replied, "I'll let you
know the instant something comes up, old dear."

Sarah spent a fortnight in bed, drinking tea and reading novels one
after the other. Lionel brought her half a dozen new ones each time
he stopped by, and Simon never returned from a trip outdoors without two or three more. She accepted the books, said thank you, and
added them to the stack on the bedside table. Diligently, she worked

her way through every one of them.

When it was time to leave her bed, she put on her clothes, moved her books to the lounge and established herself on the sofa where she continued to drink tea and read. Novels no longer held her interest. They seemed to have no bearing on reality as she'd come to know it, and the majority of the characters seemed two-dimensional and shallow. So she switched to mysteries and thrillers, able to involve herself in the solving of murders and the successful completion of dangerous missions. She and Simon were treating each other, she thought, like cell-mates in a prison—with courtesy and respectful distance. She wondered how long they could continue in this fashion before one or the other of them threw in the towel and called it quits.

Finally, one morning Lionel rang Simon to report an offer of a small film role. "But you're not to take it," he said.

"I'm not? Why?"

"Would you actually go flying off?" Lionel asked. "What about Sarah?"

"I'm not doing either of us any bloody good hanging about here, am I?"

"How could you be so bloody *stupid?*" Lionel demanded.

"I didn't know she was coming."

"That's rather simple-minded of you, Simon. I really don't know why she stays with you. Any other woman would have left."

"Sarah's not *like* other bloody *women!*"

"Precisely! I don't suppose it's occurred to you that I feel fairly much as I'm sure she does just now."

"What's that supposed to mean?"

"You're so damned indiscriminate," Lionel said, his tone subdued. "It makes the people who sincerely care about you feel … diminished, to say the least."

Simon wanted to argue but he suddenly heard an echo of himself telling Sarah how unimportant his relationship with Teller was, and felt ashamed. Teller was important, and so was Sarah. "I don't know what to do," he admitted miserably.

"Why don't you take her off somewhere?" Lionel suggested. "Mend your fences now before it's too late."

"A holiday?"

"Do you love her, Simon?"

"'Course I bloody love her!" he exclaimed.

"Then you'll want to do the right thing, won't you?"

"'Course I want to do the right bloody thing!"

"Don't shriek at me, there's a good lad. I'm trying to help."

"Sorry. I suppose after I've got Sarah all straightened round, you'd like me to take *you* off on bloody holiday, to mend *your* bloody fence."

"That would be lovely," Lionel said with a laugh. "But unnecessary. Have you got enough money?"

"Yeah, I've got enough," he answered. "Ta."

"Good! Take her somewhere plush and put things right between you."

"I don't know that she'll go with me," Simon said quietly. "I'd like her to, mind. But I'm scared I'll say something wrong."

"Would you like me to have a word with her?"

Eagerly, gratefully, Simon said, "Yeah, I would at that."

▽

What distressed her most, she decided, was the loss of her job at Crossroads. Perhaps, she thought, she should have grieved over the loss of the baby, but the baby had never been real to her the way the residents had. It hadn't had features or a voice or even any form. Every last one of the residents was real and still in possession of her caring and concern. What would become of them with Margaret browbeating and abusing them? They'd die in self-defense, she thought. She sat with a Dick Francis paperback in her lap, gazing into space, feeling more devastated with each passing hour.

When Simon announced he had to go out for a few hours, she gestured that she'd heard, then got up and went to the bedroom to undress and climb into bed. She lay with the curtains drawn wishing she'd said no to coming to London. She felt weak and purposeless and old. At the rate they were going, it was bound to be only a matter of days before Simon announced he'd had enough and was leaving.

She fell into a heavy sleep and dreamed she was at Crossroads. The place seemed oddly deserted and as she walked along the corridors her footsteps sounded hollow. She looked into one room after another, becoming more grief-stricken with each moment as each room revealed its share of dead old people. Every bed contained someone she knew: Mrs. Elgon, Miss Morgan, Mr. MacCreech. All were dead. Bereft, she made her way down to the kitchen where Grace and Doreen stood by the stainless steel draining board, staring at the floor. In a corner of the kitchen, Margaret sat at the small table, holding a knife and fork, gazing hungrily at a plate that held an old, wrinkled hand arranged on a bed of leaf lettuce.

She awoke to the ringing of the telephone and she reached for it hoping it would be Simon. She wanted to ask him to come back. She badly wanted to talk to him.

It was Lionel. "Darling," he said, "are you hideously depressed? You sound as if you are. Shall I come round?"

"Please!"

"I'll be there directly."

She got up and went into the bathroom to wash her face and brush her hair. Then she got back into bed. She didn't have the energy to make a pretense of well-being for Lionel. He was a friend, after all; he'd understand.

Without preamble, Lionel said, "Simon's most upset about all of this. I've given him a good talking-to, and now I've come to give you one. You look simply dreadful. Is there something I can get you? You're not in pain, are you?"

"I'd love some tea, if you wouldn't mind."

"You could do with more than tea, my darling. I'll fix you a little something to eat while I'm about it, shall I?" He went off to the kitchen leaving behind the lemony scent of his cologne. Within minutes, he was back with scrambled eggs and toast for her, and tea for them both.

"I've been thinking," he said, setting the tray across her lap before pouring the tea. "And I've decided that the two of you simply must get off somewhere and sort things out."

She stared at the food without appetite, then reached for a cigarette. He jumped up and removed it from her fingers, saying, "You really must eat! Cold eggs are positively foul!" He wrinkled his elegant nose, then took a sip of tea. "He's most dependent on you, Sarah. Had you realized that?"

Her fork poised in mid-air, she looked over at him. "I'm the dependent one." She shook her head slowly. "You've got it reversed."

"You're quite wrong, darling. Quite wrong. I hate to claim seniority in this matter, but I do have it after all, and the only times I've known Simon to range so out of control were before he met you and during these past weeks. I simply cannot imagine what would hap-pen to him were you not around. It's really quite frightening to con-template."

She smiled and put her fork down. "You're being dramatic, Lionel. You do rather enjoy overstating cases."

"I'm not dabbling in the dramatic at all," he insisted. "Simon's a lovely-looking, talented, oversized *child*. Not," he quickly added, "that I'm saying he thinks of you as a mother! Nothing like that, you understand. But he is essentially a simple, uncomplicated being. You're not well just now, so he hasn't got you as an outlet for his energies. If you don't *start*, I'll have to feed you! You're refusing to *hear* me!"

"Frankly, I haven't the faintest idea what you're talking about."

"Eat!"

"Oh, all right!" She picked up the knife and fork. "My God! You're more of a mother than *I* could *ever* be!"

"You've become horribly thin," he observed. "You've got a little stepladder running down your chest."

She laughed around a mouthful of toast.

"Well it's most unattractive," he said defensively. "You've got quite big breasts, after all, and it looks odd, all that bone showing through."

"You can't see through this nightdress, can you?" she asked, look-ing down at herself, undisturbed by the possibility that he could see through it. He was too truthful and too much of a friend for her ever to be offended by anything he might say.

His eyes moved over her, his expression both thoughtful and appraising, before he answered, "Naturally I can't see through it. But I can see enough of you to know you've lost far too much weight. You do have exquisite skin," he said. "Exquisite. Now, where was I? Ah, yes. A job or two's bound to come in before rehearsals start in July and he's got to be up to snuff. Were he to go on location in his present state, he wouldn't be worth tuppence hapenny to anyone. He needs you and your life together running smoothly so he can calm down sufficiently to put in a decent performance. Just," he added, "as he has to have me put in an appearance on location to reassure him."

She looked up at him in surprise.

"Not quite what you thought, is it?" he said with a hint of a smile.

"To be truthful, not at all."

"Isn't it amazing how one can know someone years and still never *really* know him?"

"Amazing," she agreed, trying not to taste the eggs as she ate them. "How old are you, Lionel?"

"Forty-three. And you?"

"Almost thirty-five."

"That's as I thought," he said. "Simon's heading for the big leagues, you know, darling."

"Yes, I know that."

"I do not believe he can do it without us."

"Oh now, Lionel, I'm not sure I care to feel quite so directly responsible. I don't even know if I accept your evaluation of the situation. Would you mind taking this? I can't eat any more."

He looked disapproving as he removed the tray. He poured them both fresh cups of tea, then returned her her cigarette and got out his Dunhill to light it for her. Again he studied her, admiring the flawless beauty of her skin. Her eyes seemed even larger and more darkly blue contrasted to her pallor. He was relieved, though, that she hadn't lost her sense of humor.

"May I ask you a very personal question, Lionel?"

"Fire away!"

"Are you bisexual, like Simon, or purely homosexual?"

"Oh, completely the latter," he answered quickly.

"Is it that you wish you were a woman?"

Delighted by this, he laughed. "Not at all. I enjoy being a man."

"Then what is it? Why?"

"It's a matter of preference, darling. Women have never held any great fascination for me. Oh, I adore them; I adore *you*. But I could no more make love to a woman than walk on water. Unlike heterosexuals, I don't find women sexually challenging, or even especially mysterious. And it's mystery, and the intrigue of the challenge that attracts people to one another."

"I suppose so. But where does that leave Simon, then?"

"Oh, I think he's a classic example of the people of the future: completely androgynous. I've no doubt that's the direction we're all headed. Half a dozen times in as many months I've looked at what I thought was a perfectly beautiful young man only to discover I was ogling a perfectly beautiful young woman."

"Hmmn. Androgynous." She thought about that for a minute or two. "I'm very fond of you, Lionel," she said, at length. "Next to

Simon, you're my closest and dearest friend. But your theory's all wrong. Simon's no more the idealized prototype of some future perfect species than you or I. None of us is the way we'd like to be. Simon and I, we're two people crippled in small, subtle ways. It's not that he's dependent on me, or I upon him, but rather that *together* we manage to make one effective *unit*. Do you see? Neither of us is stronger than the other, or more able, but together we seem to become strong. The reality is that we need each other simply to live because neither of us is all that good at living on his own."

"I've never been a threat to your relationship," he said worriedly.

"I quite agree. If anything, you've enhanced it. Simon loves you. I've always known that. And so do I. You've been a good friend to both of us."

"Will you consider going off on holiday with him?" he asked.

"I don't know. One moment I feel as if there's such a tremendous chasm between us now that we'll never be able to put ourselves back to where we were. I've lost whatever innocence I had, and probably all my illusions. But then I sit here with you and talk, and think of Simon and me as a unit and all I want is to keep all of it intact forever."

"Go off with him and put things right," he said softly. "If you have to have a reason, do it for me."

"I'm sorry, I didn't hear. What did you say?"

"For God's sake, Sarah! You're the only two people I know who've managed to make a marriage that seems to work. And I *enjoy* you so. If it ends, I'll lose both of you and I'm getting too old to make new beginnings. I'm happy to keep what I've already got. You're the only woman I've ever known who's *even begun* to tolerate something she doesn't really understand. Not that I do. Make peace and sort things out between you." He slid back his cuff to look at his watch. "Hell! I've got an appointment. I do adore you," he said, smiling as he got to his feet. "I would even if Simon wasn't involved." He gave her a kiss on the forehead. "I'll put the latch on on my way out. And *eat*, damn it! I won't have you rotting away in here like some frightful third-rate Marguerite Gautier!"

She caught hold of his hand. "I love you, you insulting beast. And thank you."

▽

Simon came in and lay on the bed, reaching out to place a plastic rose between her breasts.

She picked up the flower and looked at it, then smiled at him.

"Run out of books?" he asked.

"No. I've just decided I've had enough of reading."

"You look better."

"Lionel came round."

"Here, give us a kiss!"

It wasn't the usual little peck on the lips, but a full-blown, heady application of his mouth to hers that made her breathing quicken and her insides draw together expectantly. He rested with his head on her shoulder and slipped his hand inside her nightdress, asking, "What did old Teller have to say then?"

"He made me a meal, actually."

"Lionel? He's a bloody rotten cook. What'd he give you?" He sat up and watched his hand caress her breast.

"Scrambled eggs and toast. Not awfully good."

"And the two of you talked about me, right?"

"That's right. We did."

"I knew it. Listen! I booked us a holiday."

"Where?"

"The south of France."

"France? Simon, how lovely!"

"Yeah. Sarah, look. There's this lad I know who works in a residence over in West Kensington. I told him about you and he was dead keen, says they're bloody desperate for someone like you. There's not much in the way of money, but he was pretty certain you could have a job. So I said maybe you'd ring him and go round when we got back."

"I don't know," she said doubtfully. "It wouldn't be the same."

"Yeah, it would. All you'd need is one look at that lot of old codgers and you'd be for it."

"You didn't commit me, did you?"

"Nah! I wouldn't do that. I just told him you'd ring."

"All right. I suppose I could do that."

He withdrew his hand from inside her nightdress and she turned towards him, threading her fingers through his hair.

"You up to a meal out?" he asked, touching the faint scars on her lip.

She nodded.

"And it's on for France?"
"Yes."

▽

It was her first experience of flying and she found it terrifying. He found it terrifying to witness her fear. She gripped the arms of her seat in frozen panic, her face completely drained of blood. She kept her eyes closed and didn't speak or move until they'd landed. As they were clearing customs, she said, "From now on, every time you have to fly somewhere, I'll be living in dread until I've heard you've arrived safely. Please, could we rent a car or take a train home? I couldn't face another flight."

"I'll take care of it," he promised.

She thanked him, starting to regain some of her color.

He handled her like someone made of porcelain crazed with fine cracks. He was afraid she might, if touched or addressed too sharply, be shattered irreparably. She did actually feel very much that way, yet, perversely, she wanted more than anything else to have him squeeze the breath out of her lungs in an overpowering embrace.

They explored the countryside and strolled the beach each day for a week, trying to find some way to talk about all that had happened. He felt guilty. She simply felt hurt, and relieved at realizing she didn't blame him. At dinner that Saturday night, she reached across the table and took hold of his hand. "I want you to know," she said, "that I don't blame you for anything. You *have* always been truthful with me. I think for a time I was pretending we were other than we actually are. And that's my fault, not yours."

"I'd just like us to forget it and get on with things."

She gazed penetratingly into his eyes, softly asking, "Could you possibly understand how it makes me feel, living day after day, knowing I'm not enough for you? It's such a slap in the face. Oh, I tell myself constantly that I'm wrong to feel that way, that you give me the most and best of what you've got to give anyone. And on a purely objective level, I do believe that. But, Simon, I've had nothing in my life, no experiences to prepare me for someone like you. You need men from time to time, and somehow I'm to accept that and live with it. I'd so like to be the sort of person who could take it in her stride and not feel minimized. But I've tried, and so far, I'm not doing all that well. I'm not entirely happy with the way we live, but I couldn't bear to live without you. You mean so much to me. Won't you help me reconcile this?"

"Are you saying you want to call it quits?" He looked frightened.

"No. No, I don't. Do you?"

"I'm not the one who's unhappy, luv. I like the life we've got. It suits me down to the ground. But if it's going to make you wretched, then ..." He shrugged, lost for a solution.

"I have to change the way I feel," she said. "I suppose other women would think I'm a complete ass. After all, you are good to me, and wonderfully generous. It's just that I didn't plan on needing the sexual part of it as much as I do." She gave him a watery, self-deprecating smile. "It's really rather funny, if you think about it. I used not to be able to imagine making love, having a man want to put himself inside of me. But in the last three years, it seems I've thought of little else. Would you rather be in London full-time, accepting all those invitations to Mirabelle and Prunier's, the parties Lionel's always ringing up to invite us to?"

"Nah, I don't care for all that. You know I don't. When I'm not working, I want to be home with you. And when I am working, I want to do the bloody job, then come home, study up on my lines, have a meal with you and go to sleep. Larking about, that's all part of the old game, isn't it? D'you think you'd want to try again, Sarah? With another baby, I mean."

"Perhaps the answer would be for me to come down to London. We could use the cottage for weekends, or the odd week here and there. I haven't met any of your London friends except for Lionel."

"You could do," he said, showing very little enthusiasm.

"Has it anything to do with your being on your own so much? If I were with you more, would it make a difference?"

"I don't know, luv. Let's find out. Come stay with me, and if I've got to go abroad for a part before July, you'll come with me." He gave her one of his most engaging smiles, then said, "Let's go walk on the beach and talk outdoors. I can't talk properly in here with all the clatter and people nattering. Come on!"

Leaving their half-eaten meals, they got up and went out. The air was cool and scented, with a slight breeze. He took hold of her hand and led her down across the lawn towards the beach. He breathed deeply, saying, "Beats hell out of bloody England, doesn't it, luv? Gorgeous bloody country this is."

She turned for a moment to look back at the lights of the hotel.

"Do you realize," she said, facing forward again, "that we'll be together here longer than we've ever been anywhere? Perhaps it does have to do with being apart so much. Do you think?"

"Could be. Here, give us your shoes." He stopped with his hand outstretched while she slipped off her shoes and gave them to him. He kicked off the espadrilles he'd bought in town the day before and jammed them into his back pockets.

The sand was cool and damp. They walked along in silence for a time, then he said, "Let's sit down here." Once seated, he draped his arm across her shoulders, soberly saying, "Let's make it work, Sarah. Let's beat the bloody system and come out the far end happy. I want us to be together. We'll get it sorted out. The thing is, see, I love you. I don't fancy going back to living on my tod any more than you do. I know none of it's easy, but you and me, we're all right."

"No one but you ever thought I was worth so much as a glance," she said. "I had no idea what fun was until you came along. I don't think I have the right to expect the impossible, not when—as you say—we have so much. What," she asked, broaching the subject for the first time, "did you think when I fainted that way?"

"I don't mind telling you I was dead scared. I thought you'd gone ahead and died on me. Christ, but it gave me a turn! I was so bloody scared I nearly passed out myself. All that *blood*! It was like you were real and I should've known it all along, but I didn't really know it until I thought you were maybe going to die."

"I was so damned angry when I couldn't keep those pills down." She laughed, remembering the cream of tablet soup.

"Christ!" He grinned at her in the dark. "You should've seen yourself when I came bursting in! Bloody incredible, it was. You're good when you've got a full head of steam up."

They laughed, then fell silent.

"Simon?"

"What, luv?"

"It isn't because I'm too old, is it? I mean …"

"I know what you mean and you're not too bloody old. Look, do me a favor and get shot of this habit of looking to yourself for the faults, 'cause it's me, always has been me. And if I'm not blaming myself, then why should you blame yourself?"

"It does feel as if it's my fault somehow."

"That's bloody rot, that is! It's nobody's fault, all right? It's just the way bloody luck would have it. And we're never again going to talk this way. We're going to stick it out together if it's the last bloody thing I ever do."

"Will you make love to me?" she asked with such longing in her voice that it made him ache inside.

"Is it okay?"

"John said it would be."

"All right, then. Let's go on back to the hotel."

"No. Here," she whispered. "There's no one about."

"Maybe we should get out a bit, do some partying, have us some fun."

"Make love to me," she said softly, turning to him.

"I know some people you'd like to meet," he continued, touching her face with his fingertips the way a blind man might.

"*Make love to me!*" she pleaded, trying to get at the zipper of her dress. It was so dark she couldn't clearly make out his features, could see him only as a solid shape at her side. She got the zipper undone and freed her arms, pushing the dress down to uncover her breasts. "I've left everything off," she whispered, "the way you're always after me to. Simon?" If he didn't respond to her now, she didn't know what she'd do. All the talking in the world about love could never mean as much as his actively demonstrating it.

The clouds slid past the crescent of moon so that they were all at once visible to each other and he looked at her as she knelt half-naked in front of him, feeling a spiraling misery at knowing he was, for the first time, going to have to pretend. For the sake of their future together, he would have to step past his sexual indifference and perform.

"I'll help you, darling," she crooned, urging him down on his back. Unaccustomed to playing the aggressor, her movements clumsy, she got his trousers open then bent her head to his lap, willing him, with her hands and mouth, to respond. Something in her wanted to upbraid her for this pitiful, begging display, but she ignored it. He was responding. She straddled his lap, guiding him into her, then came forward to coax his mouth with hers as she lifted and fell slowly, feeling terribly alone and manipulative. Her desire was quickly turning to shame, and her movements slowed. She wanted to stop now and didn't know how.

Sensing how she felt, he steadied her, his hands curving over her shoulders, then her breasts. He kissed the tender part of her shoulder where it rose into her neck, thinking that it was always Sarah who paid. It seemed she had to pay because she dealt in a different kind of currency of caring. Nothing came easily; everything required payment in some form or another. Poor old Sarah, he thought, pressing his lips into her babyfine hair, his hands now on her hips. It wasn't right, was it, that he should ride for free while she always paid full fare. It wasn't right at all. So he took control, slipping his hands up under her dress and over her buttocks, directing her. He could feel she was poised to go in either direction—into him, or away from him. "I want you with me," he murmured against her ear, then kissed her, carrying her deftly to the edge. What he loved best about her, he thought, was her gentle lack of expectation. Everything he did, no matter how small, was a gift he gave her. There weren't too many people in the world who could make a person feel important that way.

It was different, she thought, very aware of their two bodies and what his flesh seemed to be telling her. Something had changed. It showed in the way he was holding back on his own pleasure and concentrating on hers. Perhaps she finally had managed to become real to him.

He kept her hovering on the edge and still her hands remained gentle on him. Dear old Sarah. "You're lovely, you are," he whispered, and threw her over the edge, still holding back in order to prolong her pleasure until he could no longer resist the inner pull and had to let go.

Afterwards, he felt a rare selflessness in understanding that it had cost him very little to do this. He leaned on the sand at her side, contentedly caressing her breasts and belly until they heard voices approaching, and they leapt apart, frantically grabbing for their clothes.

They stood at the water's edge, holding hands. At length, she said, "I'll never do that to you ever again. I needed you. But it was wrong of me."

"Don't go saying things like that."

"I dislike the idea that I'd force you into something you didn't want to do. I know you didn't want to."

"See, that's where you're wrong. I *did* want to. I love bringing you off. That's the best part of it."

"It was wonderful," she said, leaning against him. "At the beginning, I couldn't really enjoy it. Now it seems to require so little. You inside me, and everything happens. I have to tell you," her voice deepened and dropped. "John recommends against our trying for another child. In fact, he suggested sterilization."

"Why? And why didn't he tell me that?" he asked angrily.

"I asked him not to. I needed to know how things would go between us."

"And if things hadn't gone well, what would you have done?"

"I'm not sure."

"Don't you think I *care*? I watched all your stinking blood ... I thought you were *bleeding* to *death!* Did you think I didn't care?"

Her hand was very cool on his cheek. "I've always known that you care, Simon. But I've had to learn how to deal with the way you choose to show your caring. I'm sorry about the baby. I know you wanted children."

"I don't care about bloody babies, you twit! I care about *you!*"

"I know," she said softly. "It's getting a bit cool. Perhaps we should start back."

He took her hand again and they walked along the beach towards the hotel. He lit a cigarette and offered her a puff, asking, "Will you come down and be with me in London, then?"

"Yes."

"We'll have to start having people around."

"We could have a party, if you like." She smiled, then said, "Simon, I've just decided. Let's do be happy together."

"Oh, let's do!" he said in what he called his upper-crust accent. "Let's do!" He stopped and put his arms around her, suddenly holding her very hard. "Yeah, let's really," he said fervently. "We're bitchy and foolish with each other sometimes, but it's like that, isn't it, being married and apart such a lot. You want to go saving things up, like. But we're good together and it feels right, the two of us. I love you and you've got no cause to go doubting me."

"I've never seriously doubted you," she said. "No matter what's been happening, in the back of my mind I've wondered why we were making such a fuss when we'd already settled everything." It was going to be all right, she thought. They could survive anything. And who was to know or care if they were fools? "I love *you.*" She laughed, then kissed him. Suddenly filled with a sense of warmth and well-being, she freed herself from his arms and ran off down the beach.

"I bloody love you, too!" he shouted. He stood a moment, experiencing an unreasonable blind panic at losing sight of her in the darkness. "Sarah!" he called out. "Sarah?" He waited a moment longer, then took off at a run after her.

▽ ⚉

About the Author

Charlotte Vale Allen was born in Toronto Canada and lived for three years in England before moving to the United States in 1966. After working as a singer and cabaret/review performer, she began writing full-time with the publication of her first novel LOVE LIFE in 1976. The mother of an adult daughter, she has lived in Connecticut since 1970.

Get in Touch

If you would like to comment on this book, or you would like to be added to the author's mailing list in order to receive notification of forthcoming books, please write to:

Charlotte Vale Allen
c/o Island Nation Press LLC
144 Rowayton Woods Drive
Norwalk, CT 06854

Visit the author's website at:
http://www.charlottevaleallen.com